WIT
LITTLE
LIES

THE WITCHES OF HOLLOW COVE
BOOK TWELVE

KIM RICHARDSON

FABLEPRINT

FablePrint

Witchy Little Lies, The Witches of Hollow Cove, Book Twelve

[1. Supernatural—Fiction. 2. Demonology—Fiction. 3. Magic—Fiction].

BOOKS BY KIM RICHARDSON

THE WITCHES OF HOLLOW COVE
Shadow Witch
Midnight Spells
Charmed Nights
Magical Mojo
Practical Hexes
Wicked Ways
Witching Whispers
Mystic Madness
Rebel Magic
Cosmic Jinx
Brewing Crazy

THE DARK FILES
Spells & Ashes
Charms & Demons
Hexes & Flames
Curses & Blood

SHADOW AND LIGHT
Dark Hunt
Dark Bound
Dark Rise
Dark Gift
Dark Curse
Dark Angel
Dark Strike

WITCHY LITTLE LIES

THE WITCHES OF HOLLOW COVE
BOOK TWELVE

KIM RICHARDSON

CHAPTER
1

I woke up in a fret. Today was June 15. It was also Marcus's birthday, and I still had nothing planned for him. Not that I stopped throwing ideas around in my head. I didn't. Just nothing stuck, like throwing dry spaghetti at the wall. Nothing was good enough for my wereape.

Forget about cooking him a nice dinner. We all knew I was a disaster waiting to happen in the kitchen. I never did learn, and I had no time for that now. I wanted to do something special for him, to show him how much I loved him. Yes, I used the L-word, which is not a bad word. Because I did, and there was no shame in showing my affection. I just hadn't figured out *how* I was going to do that.

But I had a brain, questionable at times but functional. And I was going to use it.

I'd woken up a few hours earlier, wanting to surprise him with some hot, acrobatic morning sex, but the chief had already left for work. So I'd let myself fall back to bed in a frustrated mess. Not surprising. He always headed out to work before 7:00 a.m., way too early for anything to function correctly, in my opinion. But I wasn't Hollow Cove's chief with an entire office of people working under him. As a Merlin, I still had responsibilities when it came to our town, but I didn't have employees. I could barely take care of myself, yet I did have three aunts who needed looking after from time to time.

Marcus and I were engaged and living together, and I couldn't have been happier. When I came here a little over a year ago, my life had been a disaster on top of a hot mess going up shit creek without a paddle. I'd been broke, dumped, and miserable. Now I was as happy as Kim Kardashian at a Spanx sale.

I had a job I loved, a man I adored, and my own home—a miniature, lovely version of Davenport House, which I'd named, consequently, Davenport Cottage.

Though lesser in size, it made up for it with the farmhouse look I loved. Like the big house, the cottage had white wood siding, a glorious wraparound porch, and a black metal roof. Furnished with elegant Oriental rugs over white oak floors, gleaming white walls ended in high ceilings with oak beams, and a kitchen I could cook in—one day, I promise. House had given me this gift of a smaller version of himself so Marcus and I could begin our lives and have the privacy we needed. The bonus? It was just a few feet away from the big house and my aunts.

Thinking of my aunts, I swung my legs out of bed and headed to the bathroom. If anyone could help me with Marcus's birthday plans, it was them. They usually had some great ideas, if not over the top and odd at times, especially when it came to Ruth. But with their help, I had no doubt we'd come up with something perfect for the chief.

After I'd relieved myself, I pulled down on the handle. There was no sudden loud gulp of water slurping down into the drain. Nothing. The toilet didn't flush.

"Weird." I moved over to the vanity, grabbed the faucet, and turned. No water dripped from the tap. "Okay, that's even weirder." I exhaled. "House? Can you turn on the water, please? Need to wash my hands and brush my teeth. And a shower would be nice."

I waited for the familiar pulse of magic from House—yes, I still referred to him as a butler—and the floor to tremble as though we were hit by a small earthquake with a few lights flickering on and off. But nothing happened. "House? Hello?" I pressed my palms on the cold marble vanity top, waiting for the water to start pouring out of the faucet. But it was as dry as the Sahara Desert.

"What is going on?" I let out a frustrated breath as I headed back into my bedroom, grabbed my glass of water I'd put on the night table before going to bed last night, and used that to brush my teeth and wash my hands.

After I was done, I pulled on a pair of jeans and a T-shirt and headed to the kitchen. Nothing like a good cup of coffee in the morning to wash away all my troubles and give me the caffeine kick I needed to focus on Marcus's big day. Standing before the coffee machine, I flicked the switch. The on button didn't turn red, which usually happened when the device was functioning.

"Okay. This is *not* how I wanted to start my morning." I moved over to the wall and flicked the switch for the pendant lights over the kitchen island. Nothing. No life sparked from the bulbs.

There's no power? How can there be no power? This is a magical *house. We don't need electricity from the city's power lines. The house* is *power.*

"House? Why isn't there any power?" I pressed my hands to my hips and tapped my bare foot impatiently on the hardwood floors, but House never answered. In fact, the cottage felt... silent and empty, as though the magical entity that was House had packed his bags and left.

Adrenaline surged, and I sent out my witchy senses, searching for the familiar pricks of magical energy. But I got nothing. It felt like an ordinary house, a human house.

Uh-oh. Had something happened to House? We Davenport witches had our share of enemies and then some. Maybe someone had sabotaged House? Put a curse or a hex on him? Even maybe killed him? If that were even possible? My thoughts went to the Dark wizards. They had burned House down once, and I always felt we hadn't seen the last of them. Could this be them? Their revenge?

My heart jumped. I suppressed the fear that was threatening to take over this morning. There had to be a logical explanation as to why I felt no magic here. And the only ones who would know were my aunts.

I rushed out of Davenport cottage, all thoughts of Marcus's birthday forgotten, and hurried about forty feet across the lawn to push open Davenport House's back door.

The first thing that hit me was the voices. I didn't recognize the varied mix of cadence, tones, and speech. Definitely *not* my aunts. Once I waltzed through the kitchen, I found the cause of the commotion.

A dozen women, witches by the scent of pine needles and earth, with the added lingering scent of sulfur and vinegar—White and Dark witches—were gathered in the living room. Some sat on the couch, while others stood in tiny groups, conversing, all seemingly very happy to be here and engaged. I recognized a few, namely Martha, our local beauty salon owner and stylist witch, who held an orange, cylindrical object that was way too thick to be a wand and kept jabbing it at Dolores. My aunt's fingers twitched, looking like she was about to hex Martha's hair on fire. And rightfully so, because if my eyes didn't deceive me, that object Martha was swinging at my aunt was a vibrator.

But that's not why my mouth flapped open.

Hanging at the top of the living room wall was a pink banner that read EMBRACE YOUR INNER VAGINA!

"Hot damn." This was a waking nightmare.

"Oh, hi, Tessa, darling," said Beverly as she sashayed over to me, her green eyes glistening. "Isn't it marvelous?" She shook her head, sending locks of her perfectly styled, blonde hair brushing over her shoulders. She had that glamourous old Hollywood actress vibe, with a snug red dress accentuating all her curves. She tapped her red shoe on the floor as she smiled at me.

"Uh…" What the hell did I say to that? "What's going on? What is this?" I spotted Ruth standing in the archway between the living room and the foyer. Her petite frame shifted from foot to foot like she was winding herself up and would bolt at any second. The bun that usually sat on the top of her white, cloudlike hair hung on her shoulders in messy strands as though she'd fought with the brush this morning. The lines at the corners of her blue eyes deepened with her scowl. I understood the feeling. I didn't want to be here either.

"This is our annual meeting." Beverly flashed me her flawless smile accompanied by her perfect teeth. "Last year, we were at Lucille's place." She pressed a hand on her cocked hip, stuck out her chest, and said, "*I'm* hosting it here this year."

My eyes found a folding table topped with more vibrators and other sex toys, as though my aunt had bought whatever was on display at the local sex shop. Where did she get all this? Last I checked, Hollow Cove didn't have a sex shop. The closest thing to a sex shop was at one of the local witch stores, Hocusses and Pocusses, where you could buy yourself some love potions, Viagra-type tonics, and lubricants that glimmered and produced a magical mist, depending on your arousal level. Nothing remotely close to this exhibition. Because that's exactly what it looked like—a freaking sex exhibition.

"What *is* it exactly?" I couldn't believe I had asked the question, but the words flew out of my oral cavity before I could stop them.

"It's about embracing your vagina," answered Beverly, her eyes gleaming. "Welcoming that inner power means not letting our energy be wasted on things that don't cultivate our strengths, reinforce our values, and let us evolve. To reclaim your truth and step into your vagina power."

"My vagina power?"

"It's the most powerful tool any woman has."

"Okay."

"And all those wonderful feelings and sensations—"

I raised my hands. "It's a little early for me to talk about my lady V." In fact, there was *never* a proper or appropriate time to talk about it. Ever. Especially not with a group of strange witches. Where was Ronin, my half-vampire friend? He would *love* this.

Beverly let out a disappointed sigh. "We usually serve hors d'oeuvres and appetizers. Lucille will never let this go. How Beverly Davenport couldn't even match her meeting from last year." My aunt's eyes zeroed in on a pretty, voluptuous, red-haired witch who no doubt was this Lucille in question and clearly my aunt's nemesis. "Argh. She's just loving it. Ruth was supposed to cook bite-size cheesecakes in the shapes of really cute male privates."

I snorted. "Bet Ruth *loved* that." When I looked over at Ruth again, a smaller, shorter witch was trying to get her to hold on to what I could only describe as some sort of plastic vagina model you'd sometimes see at the gynecologist's office. Ruth's face was screwed up like she was about to spit in that witch's face or cry. She looked like she was in hell. Her cheeks were flushed, and I'd never seen her so uncomfortable before. My Aunt Ruthy didn't deserve to be assaulted by some plastic lady garden.

"But the oven isn't working." Beverly slammed her red heels on the floor. Her body taut. "You couldn't have picked a worse time, Davenport House," she hissed under her breath. "I'll remember this. Don't you forget it."

I raised my brows, leaned closer, and lowered my voice. "Yeah. About that. What's going on? I have no power or water over at the cottage." Some of my tension eased a little at her reaction. She wouldn't be so angry if it was a curse or an attack.

Beverly met my eyes. "Davenport House... is on *strike*."

I shook my head, not sure whether to laugh or not. "What? Did you just say *on strike*?" This had to be a joke. But she wasn't laughing.

"Davenport House is angry with us. *Frustrated*." Dolores's five-foot-ten frame appeared as she joined us, the long gray skirt that matched her gray hair flowing around her. Thick brows met in the middle, and her scowl was something fierce.

"Really? Why?" The only time I'd seen House angry was when Marcus had thrown a fit in the entryway, damaging the walls and the floor. And House, well, it had tossed him out on his ass. I couldn't imagine my aunts doing anything that would warrant this kind of response from the magical building. Who knew? Maybe they did.

Dolores looked past the dining area, through the kitchen, her eyes settling on the basement door. She yanked her long gray braid behind her back. "Because it *believes* we've been neglecting it."

I cast my gaze around the room to the polished wood floors without a scratch, which was unusual, considering the number of heels that had gone through there. The white walls and trim gleamed in the light. The paint looked new, as it always did. Just like the paint on the exterior siding, which always looked magically fresh. I wasn't seeing any signs of neglect. House was always in pristine shape, no doubt the benefits of being a magical house.

Beverly rolled her eyes, and a downcast expression tarnished her lovely face. "We haven't been bringing over any *meat* for a while."

I narrowed my eyes. "Meat?" Why did I have a feeling she didn't mean ground beef?

Beverly let out a sigh. "Cheating husbands, wayward boyfriends, abusive partners. You know, that kind of thing. The house is upset because we haven't thrown it a bone in a while, so to speak."

"Ah. Right." I'd nearly forgotten that our lovely, magical home liked to eat men, or rather, lobotomize them. It'd never really been clear what went on when my aunts brought over one of their intended victims and tossed him in the basement. I knew House took something from these men. Their minds? Possibly, or a part. They always came out looking dazed and confused. But that was all I knew on the subject.

"Just picked the wrong day to throw a little fit," growled Beverly and then plastered a smile on her face that was Oscar-worthy at a group of witches who were watching us.

"What's the point of having this ridiculous gathering here if you can't even offer proper refreshments," pointed out Dolores, eyeing the vibrator table with a determined stare, like she wanted to blast them up in one of her fire spells.

Beverly's face turned sour. "You're just angry and jealous because people like me. If you waxed that upper lip, maybe you'd make friends."

Oh dear.

Dolores's scowl could scare away a pack of wolves. She thrust out a hand and pointed in the direction of the gathering. "Some things are not meant to be on display," said my tall aunt. "They're meant to be private."

11

Beverly grinned and pushed out her chest. "I'm always on display."

"Like an Amsterdam window whore," snapped Dolores.

Ouch. But when I looked at Beverly, she had the biggest smile, as though her sister had just paid her the highest of compliments.

I laughed. I couldn't help it. I knew coming here was a good idea. I might not have had any more ideas for Marcus's birthday, but the interaction between these two could always lift a girl's spirit.

Beverly caught me staring. "It's okay, Tessa. Dolores is just mad because she could never fit her sasquatch body in those red window rooms."

This was much better than the vajayjay party in the living room.

Dolores's face went two shades darker. "Just accept it. This sex-instructional gathering is a failure, Beverly."

Beverly's head whipped back around. Her green eyes sparkled as she said, "Beverly Davenport never fails where the word sex is involved. Never." Beverly's beautiful face spread into a knowing smile. "And never in the bedroom."

The funny thing is, I totally believed her. I looked up at Dolores. "How long will House's strike last?"

Dolores put a hand on her hip. "Depends. The last time it lasted a month."

"A month?" I practically shouted, and when heads turned my way, I quickly lowered my voice. "I can't wait a month. It's Marcus's birthday today."

"Is it? Bet you've got all kinds of naughty things planned for him," said Beverly, raising her brows suggestively. "You want to borrow my rainbow handcuffs?"

Ew. "Thanks. But I think I'll pass."

Beverly shrugged. "Your loss. They're fantastic." She wiggled her body like she was getting shivers just thinking about them. "Sends my feminine urges into overdrive."

Double ew.

And with that, my aunt paraded to the living room to join her group, swinging her hips.

"Where's Dildo?"

I spun around at the sound of an unfamiliar voice, nearly choking on my own spit, to find a petite woman, who seemed to have fought with her closet this morning and ended up piling layers of clothes over her small frame without a thought. "I'm sorry?"

"Where's Dildo?" repeated the woman, who showed me she was a White witch by the scent of wildflowers and summer meadows.

"She means Hildo." Ruth stood at my side, a cat with silky black fur clutched in her arms. Her animal familiar. His yellow eyes narrowed

13

on the witch, his ears flat against his head. "I'm not giving him up, Wanda," hissed Ruth, shooting Ginsu knives at the witch with her eyes.

The witch called Wanda propped her hands on her hips. "Now, Ruth. My niece is turning sixteen next week, and she needs a familiar. At your age, you don't need one anymore. You're too old."

Yikes. Not exactly the thing to say to my Auntie Ruthy.

Wanda spread her face into a false smile. "How about you do the right thing and pass him along to a younger witch."

Ruth's face narrowed until her brows partially covered her eyes. "How about I pass you this." Ruth gave the other witch the finger, spun around, and marched into the kitchen.

I snorted. "I don't think I've ever seen Ruth this angry." I watched as an offended Wanda returned to the living room. Ruth and Hildo had bonded like any witch and her familiar. I didn't know who this Wanda thought she was, demanding Ruth to give him up.

"Wanda is a fool." Dolores had a tiny smile. Guess she'd enjoyed that too.

"I can't wait a month for House to give us back power," I told her. And water. And magical protection. "How can we speed up the process? What can we do?"

Dolores eyed me from her tall frame. "Do you know of any cheaters? Lowlifes who use their wives as punching bags?"

"No."

"Then you'll have to wait like the rest of us. The house will eventually magic itself back on. It always does. Just need to be patient."

My birthday-idea balloon was deflating as fast as Wanda's rejection. "This is not how I planned Marcus's birthday." I'd have to figure out something else. Which was probably me looking for some scumbag husbands and boy-friends. That wasn't the hard part. The hard part was getting them back here. And then what? Toss them in the basement to be lobotomized by a magical house? Meh. I'd done worse.

"Tessa." Beverly came back, swaying her hips. "Would you mind going over to Witchy Beans Café and picking up some refreshments? Cordelia, the owner, agreed to help us out with the... *kitchen problem*," she added in a low voice.

"Sure." What else did I have going on? I wasn't about to discuss my "inner vagina" with some strangers.

Beverly hooked her arm in mine as we walked through the living room to the entrance. "Try not to bend the joysticks, darling. Okay? They're party favorites."

"Right." I tried not to imagine the joysticks she was referring to. Too late.

I walked down the front porch steps, spun around to give House my stink eye, made my way over onto the sidewalk, and headed south on Stardust Drive.

The scent of freshly cut grass filled my nose, and a warm summer breeze lifted my spirits — just a little. I rounded Charms Avenue and saw Martha's tall, pink, two-story Victorian. HOT MESS WITCH, BEAUTY SALON written in bold letters flashed just above the front porch. A smile perked my lips. I always thought it was the second most beautiful house in Hollow Cove. Davenport House was first, of course.

A scream split the air.

Adrenaline shot through my veins. First, I froze because that's what a well-trained witch does. Then I whirled around, trying to get a sense of where that scream had come from.

A crowd was moving down the street toward where the scream had originated.

Another scream sounded.

I ran forward and hit Charms Avenue, sprinting past Martha's beauty salon with my heart lodged somewhere in my throat. My thighs burned from the effort of pushing my legs with speed and not doing those squats I promised I would do to improve my physical strength. Sue me.

"Coming through. A *Merlin* coming through." I'd always wanted to say that. I pushed my way through the crowd, trying to catch my breath. They were all staring at something on the patch of grass between Martha's place and the neighboring house.

And when I finally made it to the front, my stomach clenched. Thank the cauldron I hadn't had breakfast yet because it would have come back out to say hello.

Lying on the grass, sprawled on her back, in a puddle of her own blood, was the body of a girl.

Oh, shit.

CHAPTER

2

"You found her like this?" Marcus knelt next to the dead girl, and I say *dead* because of the amount of blood she was lying in, combined with the lifeless expression in her big blue eyes. But there was also the fact that her jugular was torn open. No one could survive that.

After I'd ushered the townspeople away, I'd called Marcus to tell him about the body. Beverly's edible joysticks clearly forgotten.

"Yeah. You know her?" I stared at the girl's face, a strange feeling of familiarity darting through me, but I couldn't pinpoint where I'd seen her before.

Marcus shook his head. "No. She doesn't look familiar. Could be a family friend visiting from out of town."

My eyes traveled over the girl, her red-hooded cloak matching the blood around her and adding more of a morbid touch to the scene. Her chest had been torn to bloody ribbons, and her arms and legs carved like someone had taken a knife to them, slicing her up for fun. It was sick.

I moved around her to get a look at her face and stifled back a gasp. Her face was the worst part. Her tiny features were twisted in pain and suffering as though she died screaming in agony.

"Damn it." I gritted my teeth.

"The slash around her throat is what killed her." Marcus pointed to the girl's neck. An angry, deep gash slid across her neck, and blood spilled from the wound and down her chest.

I clenched my jaw, a fresh feeling of anger rushing through my body. "Who would do that to a girl?"

Marcus let out a sigh and stood, his thick brows furrowed in worry. "The wounds are fresh. She was killed a few minutes ago. A half hour, tops."

"Can't be demons," I said, knowing that demons couldn't be out under the sun. If they were, they'd suffer their true death and combust into flames, leaving only ashes. "And the lacerations look… look like something with claws did it. Too rough to be a dagger or a knife."

Marcus made a sound of agreement in his throat. A storm brewed behind his gray eyes. "This is a vicious killing. Mindless. It looks…"

I glanced at the chief, seeing his anger and worry doubling with his deep frown. "What?"

"Like whoever or whatever did this… enjoyed it."

My stomach churned. "That can't be good." My eyes traveled over his handsome face. His glossy, dark-tousled hair framed his chiseled jaw. The chief wore his signature black leather jacket, dark jeans, and a casual black shirt. He sidled next to me, and I got a good sniff of his natural scent mixed with sweat and some kind of masculine soap that sent my pulse rocketing and making me want to lick him.

I was a very lucky girl. Yet totally inappropriate thoughts of me and the chief in the bedroom popped into my head before I quashed them. "What are you thinking? What could have done this?"

Marcus ran his hand over his jaw. "My guess would be a werewolf or a werecat. One consumed by a sickness or possibly a curse, making them the most dangerous kind of predator."

I raised my brows, fear rising anew. "You think there'll be more attacks? You don't think they'll stop?" Of course, as a wereape, Marcus knew a hell of a lot more on the subject of being consumed by your beast, your animal, and what that meant.

His eyes met mine, and butterflies took flight in my belly. "No. It got a taste for fresh blood. For human flesh. It's never going to stop. Not unless we stop it."

My morning was not starting out to be the happy, rainbows-coming-out-of-my-ass kind of day. "We will. We can't let this crazy were loose in our town. I won't let another girl die." Not on my watch. A wild, hot rage hit my gut, a feeling I got whenever children or animals were killed or in danger. They were innocent. And this thing had prayed on the innocent.

The scuff of shoes on the pavement pulled my attention behind me. A group of curious paranormals, an older retired-looking group, crept closer to the scene.

"Nothing to see here," growled Marcus, using his large, thick frame to hide the girl's mangled body in the grass.

"That's not what I heard," said a short, stout man with gray hair, a navy bow tie, and large, reproachful brown eyes. He pushed a female paranormal out of his way to step closer. "I heard there's a dead girl. What happened to her? Why is there a dead girl in my town?"

Marcus glanced at the tiny shifter lazily, like he posed no threat other than his annoying voice. "We've got everything under control, Gilbert. No need to worry."

"No need to worry?" Gilbert's voice rose a few octaves. "*I'm* the town mayor. It's my business to know everything that happens here—murders being top of the list. And I can see a dead girl in the grass right there."

I could tell Marcus wasn't in the mood to start throwing his theories around to our mayor and his entourage, which would only start a panic. It would also alert those responsible that we were onto them.

"We've got this," I told him. "It's what we do. Why the town employs us."

Gilbert eyed me suspiciously. "You better. You're still on the hook for not advising me that you'd lost your magic while the town continued to pay your salary. Our tax dollars."

A slip of irritation fluttered through me. "I know. No need to rub it in." One of these days, I was going to roast this owl shifter and feed his fried wings to Hildo.

Gilbert made a face, pressed his hands on his hips, and leaned forward. "The annual Oyster Festival is scheduled for tomorrow. Five hundred pounds of oysters have already been ordered. I can't have a dead girl ruining it. I won't reschedule. I've been planning this for six months."

Of course not. "But maybe you should... hold off just for a few days." We still had no idea who was doing this, and the last thing we needed was for the town to feast on oysters, not knowing a killer was in their midst.

Gilbert stared at me like I'd suddenly grown a third eye. "Are you insane? Do you know how much time and money the town's invested in this?" Spit flew from his mouth. "Absolutely not. You're a Merlin." He pointed at me with a grubby finger and then swung it in Marcus's direction. "You're the town chief. Do your jobs!"

The owl shifter reeled on his heels, pushed through the crowd, making one of the females fall, and headed down Charms Avenue.

He'd moved faster than I'd anticipated. I'd envisioned sticking out my foot and tripping him. "I don't think I've ever hated someone as much as I hate Gilbert," I said, thinking about how he'd deducted from my pay when he found out I'd lost my magic. Like *that* wasn't bad enough.

Marcus chuckled. "He's a pain in the ass."

I shook my head. "And our mayor. How the hell did that happen?"

The chief lost his smile as he regarded the dead girl. His worry deepened to actual fury. He was pissed. And when he got all full of rage, he was both frightening and crazy hot.

I blew out a breath once the crowd had moved along. "So, now what? We round up all the shifters with claws big enough to do this and start investigating?"

The chief nodded, his jaw clenched harder, making his facial muscles stiffen. "Someone in this town did this. I would have been notified if

23

an out-of-town shifter or were came through here."

"Really? How?"

"Strangers smell different. I'd know. Any shifter or were would know. They would have notified me."

True. Marcus and the average shifter all had excellent abilities in the scent department. Speaking of smells, I hadn't taken a shower yet, and I was sweating already, stress sweat—the worst kind of perspiration. I gave my armpits a covert sniff. Yup. I was a stinker.

"Did you notice the no hot water or electricity this morning?" I wanted to change the subject, even if it was for just a moment. The dead girl at my feet was doing all kinds of strange things to me, like making me want to punch holes in whoever killed her.

Marcus rolled his eyes over my body, spreading heat from my middle. "Yeah. I took a shower at the office. No big deal."

"You say that because you don't know."

"Don't know what?"

"It might not be a simple fix."

Marcus moved closer until his front rubbed against my breasts. "What are you talking about? Did your aunts do something to the house? Was it Dolores?"

He wasn't wrong about that. I'd always felt Dolores was jealous that House had birthed me a smaller version of itself and not her.

"No. It's House. He's angry at us because we've neglected him." At his frown, I waved my hands. "Nothing we can do about it for now. Except, you might find yourself taking showers at your office for a while. Until House calms down." I didn't want to have to tell him that it could take a month. Cauldron help us if it was longer.

Marcus pulled out his cell phone and began to tap in a rapid fashion. I heard an answering text beep from his phone, and then he pocketed it.

Murmurs reached me. Another crowd of paranormal onlookers huddled near the sidewalk next to a parked car, snapping pictures and filming with their smartphones. I scowled at them. Idiots. Everyone in town would know of the dead girl in a few hours.

Marcus narrowed his eyes at them, and that alone sent them scurrying away. He shuffled out of his leather jacket, me enjoying the view, and placed it on the girl so her face and most of her bloodied chest were hidden.

"They left her here in broad daylight for us to see." I looked up at Marcus. "Why? Why would they do that?" Either because they wanted us to find her, or they just didn't care.

A dark shadow crossed over the chief's face. "I don't know. They're cocky. Could be that they wanted us to find her. Know that they're out there, doing this."

"Like your average psychopath serial killer. They wanted to be talked about. To be famous. What's going to happen to her?"

"Scarlett and Cameron are going to pick her up in my Jeep. We'll take her to the morgue for now until we can identify her and contact her next of kin."

I let out a breath. "Her parents. Oh my god. Her parents are going to flip." Not flip. But be devastated. Completely destroyed. That's how I'd be if my baby girl were killed. Murdered? That's how it felt. Marcus was right. As far as I could tell, it was a brutal, vicious killing with no real motive. Not a single thought was put into it. Just a mindless butchering.

I pulled my eyes away for a second, scanning the grounds for clues or anything that could help us discover who the killer was.

"Wait a second." A weaved basket lay a few feet away from the girl, hidden by tall grasses, which explained why I hadn't seen it when I arrived. I picked it up. "She was carrying food. There's bread and some jams. Cheese too."

My eyes searched the girl again. Under her red-hooded cloak, she wore an old-fashioned, simple linen shift, something you'd see actors wear in medieval plays or movies.

"Is it me, or does she look like Little Red Riding Hood?" She was covered now with Marcus's jacket, but her cloak spilled from under it. And I'd seen her dress, albeit shredded.

Marcus's head hung low, his dark hair covering his face. "Like in the kids' stories?"

"Yeah. I mean… I know I'm still learning a lot about our community, and I know some stories and fairy tales have some truth to them. What about…"

"The little girl and her grandma that get eaten by the Big Bad Wolf?"

"Yup."

Marcus shook his head. "No. That's just a fairy tale. This is just a girl playing dress-up like most girls her age."

I never did, but I wasn't about to disagree with him. Not yet.

I narrowed my eyes, not feeling any better about seeing how the little girl had been torn to shreds. Not eaten, but still.

I couldn't rub off the feeling I was getting from this now. Now that I looked at the scene, the girl in the red-hooded cloak and the basket. Maybe Marcus was right. Maybe he was wrong.

Was this a little girl just playing dress-up? Or was this something else entirely?

The only thing I knew for sure was I was going to find out.

CHAPTER
3

After Scarlett and Cameron had hauled away the girl's body in Marcus's Jeep, I'd headed over to Witchy Beans Café, picked up a tray of joysticks, which were pastries in the shape of penises, stuffed with cream cheese, and sneaked back into Davenport House through the back door.

When I stepped into the kitchen, I found Dolores and Ruth hunkered next to the coffee machine, their heads bowed in what I could only guess was some serious plotting. Hildo lay on top of the fridge, his ears flat on his head, still looking like he was about to scratch one of those witches' eyes out if they tried to grab him. Poor kitty.

My eyes fell back on my aunts, and I laughed. "Are you guys hiding?"

"No. Yes," said Dolores and Ruth at the same time.

I laughed harder. "I don't blame you—"

"Tessa!" Beverly came rushing into the kitchen, her kitten heels tapping the hard floor. Her beautiful face was flushed, accentuating her beauty even more and making her emerald eyes sparkle like jewels. "What took you so long?"

A dead girl. "Something came up. Here." I handed her the platter, which she took, spun around, and marched back to the living room.

When she arrived in the center, she hoisted the platter above her head. "I promised you cheese joysticks, and cheese joysticks you will have!"

The witches cheered and clapped like they'd just been told some hot, muscled firemen strippers were on their way.

"See?" Ruth glared in the direction of the living room. "Sluts." She flicked her fingers in their general direction as though she'd just cursed them.

I bit the inside of my cheek to stop the bubble of laughter that wanted out. Ruth was so damn cute. Even when she was furious, I just wanted to squeeze her cheeks.

"Why *did* it take you so long?" Dolores eyed me suspiciously. "What happened? Spit it out. I can see it all over you. Your aura's all out of balance."

"Yeah. We see it," agreed Ruth, who was still shooting daggers in the direction of the living room, where I could hear the distinctive oohs and aahs. Cauldron only knew what that was about.

I lowered my voice and quickly gave them an account of the dead girl. "Marcus thinks it's a were or shifter that's sick or something." I decided to keep my Little Red Riding Hood theory to myself for now. Just uttering it out loud made me sound insane. I needed to keep some of my crazy just for me.

Dolores nodded. "He's probably right."

"It's happened before?" I couldn't help but notice the touch of familiarity in her voice.

Dolores's jaw tightened. "In Hollow Cove... only three times that I'm aware of."

"Three times too many," said Ruth, her face twisted in concern.

Another cacophony of female shrieks and laughter erupted in the living room.

"Tramps," hissed Ruth, and then she kicked out with her leg in a makeshift karate move, her bare feet slapping the floor on her return.

"Twice, young werewolves were overcome with their beast," said Dolores, her cynical eyes grave. "It was a full moon, and sometimes the bloodthirst is too strong for young weres. They can't control their inner beast."

The thought was scary, but I could understand how that could happen. As a witch, a Shadow witch, with powers in both White and Dark magic, I never shifted into another form, animal or human—except that one time when I'd switched bodies with Ronin. Yeah, that was weird. I could only imagine the inner strength and control it took just to shift back and forth. "And the other time?"

Dolores pressed her lips together in thought. "An old werecat by the name of Bill. He was sick. Senile. Thought he was under attack when he was the one doing the actual attacking."

"Lost his marbles." Ruth made the motion with her fingers around her temple, giving me her wide eyes.

"They took the girl's body to the morgue," I told them. "Marcus thinks it's someone local. First, I'm going to take a shower, and then I'm going to help him look." If I was right, there should be just enough hot water in the hot water tank for a minute-record shower. So even if the cold water didn't work, technically, it shouldn't affect the hot water.

Dolores tapped me on the head like I was a well-behaved Labrador retriever puppy. "It's good you told us. I'll check my list of weres and shifters. We have a good excuse to leave this wretched party, and we can begin canvassing today."

My brows shot up. "You have a list of all the weres and shifters in Hollow Cove?" Why didn't that surprise me?

Dolores pressed a hand to her hip while using the other like a wand as she spoke. "Of course I do. I'm a Merlin." As though that explained everything. "Ruth and I will start with the shifters. You do the werewolves with Marcus."

Why did that sound dirty? "Fine." I wasn't even bothered that Dolores decided to take charge. As the eldest of the Davenport witches, she claimed that throne long ago. Before I was born, probably.

I left my aunts to it, sneaked out the kitchen back door before Beverly asked for more favors, walked a few feet across the backyard, and popped into Davenport Cottage.

I yanked out my phone, and seeing only fifty percent of battery life left, I texted Iris.

Me: *Hey. There's no power at Davenport House. Long story. Better stay with Ronin if you want hot water.*

I'd give her the gruesome details of the girl later. Then, setting my phone on the kitchen counter, I made my way to my bathroom. I needed a shower. I wasn't about to go around town and talk to people without showering first.

Once I peeled off my clothes, I stood in the shower, dreading what was about to happen.

"House. I need hot water. I need hot water because I need a shower. House?" I waited for the familiar sound of answering pipes and a vibration in the floors and walls but got nothing.

"House? Please. I had no idea you were… neglected." Which was totally true. Not sure what I would have done had I known House needed some male scumbags to feel as though he wasn't neglected. "It's Marcus's birthday today. The least you could do is turn on the power. House?"

After standing naked in the shower for another few minutes, I did what any dirty witch would have done in my place. Bracing myself, having already loaded my loofah with body-wash and opened the shampoo bottle, I twisted the hot water knob—

And screamed.

It wasn't hot water that came pouring out. It was ice-cold water.

The pipes moaned as though House was laughing. Yeah. I had a feeling House had done that on purpose. I knew plenty of hot water was left in the tank, but he gave me cold water instead.

Cold water? More like freezing-rain-with-ice-droplets kind of water. I screamed like a banshee the whole time—a full two minutes and thirty-four seconds.

I turned off the ice water, grabbed a towel, stepped out, and… "Ah!"

A pretty fifty-year-old woman with dark hair and my eyes stood in front of the vanity mirror, adjusting her hair.

I pulled the towel around myself, covering all my essential bits. "Mom. I'm naked here. Hello?"

My mother gave me an annoyed expression through the mirror, something she had carried with her over the years like a best friend. "Please. I gave birth to you. I've seen you naked plenty of times."

"Still. You could have knocked."

"I did."

I frowned at her. "And you just pushed in when no one answered?" That was a horrible thought. What if Marcus and I were busy with our sexy time, and my mother walked in on us? I was going to ask House to lock the doors from now on. Right. House wasn't answering.

My mother looked at me like I'd done my eyeliner all wrong. "Why were you taking a cold shower? There's no steam in here. Is this the cold-bath thingy I've been hearing about? It's supposed to boost your metabolism."

I tightened the towel around me. "House is on strike. He's punishing us."

My mother's full mouth fell open. "So your father can't visit you here?"

"Uh. I hadn't thought of that. Probably not." Damn. That was true. I kind of liked having access to my father whenever I wanted, and it was the same for him. The basement door was a portal to the Netherworld that enabled my father to cross over when he wanted. I'd only crossed over to his home world once, but that didn't mean I didn't plan on doing it again.

I really needed to do something about House. But right now, I had bigger problems than hot water.

"Did you need something?" I realized my voice came out a bit rough, but I wasn't in the mood or dressed to be subjected to my mother's invasion.

"I wanted to invite you and Marcus for dinner tonight," answered my mother. "Your father will be there."

I blinked. "You want me and Marcus to come over for dinner?"

My mother narrowed her eyes at me. "Are you deaf? That's what I said."

"Can't."

Color flushed on my mother's cheeks. "Why not? What is more important than having dinner with the woman who gave birth to you?"

My dear mamma. She always tried to guilt her way into getting what she wanted. I thought about lying but found it easier just to tell her the truth. Lying was too much of an effort. You had to remember your lies, and I had a terrible memory.

"Because there's a potential murderer on the loose in Hollow Cove. We found a dead girl near Martha's place. Looks like she was killed by a were or something with big claws and pointy teeth. Werewolf, maybe?"

My mother made a face. "Never trust a werewolf. They can't control their inner beast. I've always said so." My mother's face paled. "What's the girl's name?"

I shrugged. "Don't know. I didn't recognize her. Neither did Marcus. But tonight I'm going canvassing with him. See if we can get a lead on the culprit." I still had that strange feeling of familiarity at the sight of the dead girl. I wanted to pursue that feeling. Follow my own instincts.

"You can still come over to dinner," said my mother. "There are many hours in a day. You can sacrifice a few for your mother and father. Can't you? Or is that too much to ask in your busy schedule?"

Here we go again. "I can't. Maybe when we find the murderer."

"I'll see you at six tonight, then," said my mother as she walked out of my bathroom, like it was all settled, and she hadn't heard a single thing I said.

Irritation hit me as I followed her out, still wet and naked but for the towel around me. "Mom. Did you hear what I said?"

My mother waved dismissively at me as she moved toward the front door. "Yes, yes, yes. A dead girl. I still don't see the point of you missing out on a special dinner. When was the last time you had dinner with your mother and father?"

"I seem to recall a time at Davenport House."

"Never at *my* house. And never with just your parents."

I sighed. "No. That's true." No way would I go over there and have dinner and pretend there wasn't a murderer of kids in our town. She'd be pissed when I didn't show up, but I could handle her moods. I didn't want to disappoint my father, though.

"You don't want to disappoint your father," said my mother, like she had just read that thought across my forehead.

I clamped down my jaw, my annoyance stirring. "Not playing fair."

My mother flashed me one of her victory smiles. "Life's not fair."

I opened my mouth to tell her exactly what I felt at the moment, but the front door swinging open interrupted me.

Marcus walked through the entrance, his gray eyes flicking from me to my mother. "Hello, Amelia."

My mother flashed one of her fabulous smiles that made her look like Beverly for a few seconds. "Marcus. I've just invited you and my daughter to dinner tonight."

"Uh…" Marcus shifted uncomfortably. "Tonight?" he repeated, like he was trying to find the right words to let her down gently. He looked at me, and I just shook my head.

"Yes." My mother walked right up to him. "Six o'clock. And don't be late. Late is rude."

So is what she's doing right now. "Mom." I rushed after her. "I just told you tonight's not a good night for us."

"Wear something nice, will you," said my mother. "No jeans. It wouldn't kill you to dress up once in a while and wear some makeup."

I shook my head. That witch really got under my skin. I let out a frustrated breath and glanced at the chief. I could see the smile on his face as his eyes rolled over me very slowly.

"Nice outfit."

Delicious heat skimmed over my skin at the huskiness in his voice. "Yeah, well, I didn't have time to put on clothes before my *mother* showed up." Perhaps a few rolls in the hay were precisely what I needed at the moment. I stared at his face. "What's wrong. Something's up." And I knew it wasn't my bossy mother.

"Something's happened to the body," said Marcus. His voice was tainted with bewilderment like he couldn't believe what he was telling me.

"What body? The dead girl's?" My mother looked between the two of us. I knew by her face, she was expecting, no, *demanding* that we answer her.

I rolled my eyes and glanced at Marcus, whose face was grimmer than it had been when he'd first arrived. He and my mother had a history. She'd left his best friend to fend for himself a few years back, a move that had gotten him killed. I knew he'd forgiven her, but I could tell he still struggled with it.

My mother was a bit of a narcissist. You just had to learn to ignore her most of the time.

"Have you decided on a date for the wedding?" My mother crossed her arms and had her business face on.

Oh. Hell. No.

I glanced at a shocked Marcus before answering. "Uhh. Not that that's any of your business—"

"Does Katherine know?" asked my mother, completely ignoring me as though deciding the date of my wedding only concerned Marcus. She was acting weird today.

Marcus took a deep breath. "Well... my mother... you know how she is..."

My mother's eyes rounded. "*She* knows, but you neglected to tell *me*? Is this revenge because I forgot to pick you up after school that one time?"

"Try eight times." The thought brought a wash of anger through me. But that was a long time ago. And I couldn't hang on to that anger. It wasn't healthy. And I knew my mother was doing her best, even if it was a tad rude and pushy. "Hang on to your broom, Mother," I said. "We haven't decided yet. So just relax before you give yourself an aneurism."

My mother seemed to relax at the comment. No. Wait. She seemed... thrilled?

"Good." She let out a puff of air. "Then we'll discuss it over dinner and pick a date."

I pulled my attention back to Marcus, holding my towel with one hand. "What were you saying about the body?"

Marcus glanced at the floor before returning his gaze to me like he was trying to make sense of something. "It's gone."

My eyebrows shot to my hairline. "Gone? Someone took it?" I found that extremely surprising and unlikely, seeing that the morgue was in the basement of the Hollow Cove Security Agency, which was Marcus's office. You'd have to be a damn fool to steal a body from there.

"See? You don't have a body. You have no excuse not to come to dinner," declared my mother as she walked past us and strode across the lawn. She turned her head, and I noticed how she frowned at Davenport House. I had a feeling it wasn't because House was on strike

40

but that she hadn't been invited to the "inner vagina" party.

Some days, I wondered if we were actually blood related. We were so different with nothing in common. My mother was a White witch with barely any power, and I was a Shadow witch with the ability to bend ley lines. You couldn't deny the physical resemblance, though, but that was it.

"Do you know who took it?" I asked him.

Marcus ran a hand through his luscious dark locks, making me want to take his hand away and do it myself. "That's the thing. No one took it. I was in the morgue with Scarlett and Cameron. We were standing right next to the body, going over the list of parents with a girl between the ages of seven and ten. And then… then the body just vanished. She was on the table one second and the next… she wasn't."

Oh, fockin' hell.

CHAPTER

4

Have you ever had a body disappear on you? Yeah, me neither. And how does one look for a body that vanished into thin air? No idea.

My progress with magic was improving by leaps and bounds.

I'd hoped to do a revealing spell to see if we could find out more about who killed her. But without a body, we had nothing.

So, I needed to call in the big guns for help, which explained how Iris and Ronin appeared at Davenport Cottage fifteen minutes later.

"So, this girl was dressed up as Little Red Riding Hood and got killed for it?" The half-vampire's face was serious. His mess of brown hair was sticking up at odd angles in a modern style. He whistled and said, "Poor kid was just trying to celebrate Halloween a few months early and got whacked for it." He stuffed his hands in his jeans pockets. His pale skin was a stark contrast to the black leather jacket around his shoulders, but his features were flawless, sculpted, and handsome. Just like all vampires and half-vampires. Irritating as hell.

"Or this is someone's idea of a sick joke," said Iris, curling a lock of silky, black hair behind her ear. "Lots of serial killers like to dress up their victims in their twisted fantasies." Her pixie-like face was drawn tight like she was imagining those victims in her head as her lips pressed into a worried line. "We have to catch this guy."

"Guy?" Ronin shook his head. "Who says a female didn't do this? I mean, it could have been a female were. You said it, Tess. A sick were or shifter did this. Could be male, but it also could be female." His face spread into a smile. "Could be an angry cougar."

Iris smacked him on the arm. "Try to act serious."

"Ronin's right. We can't rule out the females." A buzz came from Marcus's phone. He put it to his ear and squeezed my hand before letting it go and moving into our living room.

Iris caught me staring at his ass and flashed me a smile. "Still going strong, I see," she whispered but didn't need to. Wereapes had incredible hearing. And I knew he'd heard when he angled his body toward us and met my eyes.

"Can't complain." No, I couldn't. I was engaged to the hottest guy in town. The chief of Hollow Cove. How the hell did that happen?

"Still no power, huh?" Ronin looked around the house. "That can't be good."

"Yeah. But I'm sure my aunts will figure something out. Beverly can only last so long without her hair dryer."

Iris choked on a laugh. "So true. Unless she uses a magical hair dryer."

"A magical hair dryer?" I looked at Ronin, but he looked just as clueless as me.

"A magical hair dryer," repeated Iris, beaming, and I had a feeling this was something she had used before. "It's no big deal. Just gusts of wind on repeat. But you don't get the hot air, so it's not as good as a regular hair dryer."

I stared at the Dark witch. Iris was something special, and I was glad she was my friend.

"So, the killer sneaked in and stole the body to cover his or her tracks," said Ronin.

I shook my head. "Marcus said the body disappeared in front of his eyes."

"Like a magic trick," commented the half-vampire, a frown on his handsome face.

I stared at Ronin. "I don't know. It's weird, though. Right? Vanishing like that. Leaving no trace for us." I didn't think I'd ever heard of a body disappearing into thin air. It only happened in the movies.

Iris's dark eyes widened. "Very weird."

Murmurs of dread crawled into my mind. Something was extremely unnerving about this situation. "Weird, yes. But there was still a dead girl. I saw her. And it wasn't a magic trick. Someone or something killed that girl. And they're trying to cover their tracks." But there were still ways to find them. Or so I hoped.

Marcus returned to the kitchen and joined us. His dark hair fell back as he tilted his face to me, his mouth slightly open in concentration. His biceps tightened, and his pec muscles popped under his shirt as he stuffed his cell phone in his pocket. I could watch this show all day… and all night.

Sweet mother of all that is holy, Marcus was beautiful. And mine. Mine. Mine. Mine.

"That was Gilbert," said the chief. His jaw tightened in tension. Something was up.

"Uh-oh," I told him, trying to erase from my mind's eye the show of muscles I just saw.

Marcus met my eyes and said, "There seems to be a bit of a panic in the town square. People heard about the dead girl and now are demanding answers."

"And let me guess: Gilbert wants the killer found, so he can have his Oyster Festival tomorrow. Right?" I was surprised a mob wasn't pounding on Davenport House.

Marcus flashed me one of his panty-dropper smiles. "Right." Damn. He could still put that charm on me. The man had skills.

"I'm upping his rent," declared Ronin. "He annoys me."

"I gotta go." Marcus grabbed my hand and pulled me closer to him. "Do you mind checking out the names on the list I gave you, without me? I don't know how long this is going to take. I'll meet you when it's over."

I looked over at the counter to the piece of paper with the names of all the shifters and weres in Hollow Cove. "Sure. No problem."

He squeezed my hand, and I leaned in, enjoying his nearness and drinking in his scent, which had to be some wereape pheromone cologne. I wanted to bathe in it.

"'Kay. See you later."

I watched the chief's broad back and fine ass exit the front door. Today was his birthday, and I didn't even get him a gift. Worst fiancée ever. With a dead girl on our hands, and the fact that she'd vanished, it didn't look like I was going to get a break anytime soon.

Iris snatched up the paper on the counter. "Where do we start?"

I thought about it. "With the werewolves. We use what we have, an estimated time of death. So we look for those without alibis. Ruth and Dolores are going to canvass the shifters in town. But I was hoping we could go to the lab and search for clues. Maybe try a few revealing spells?"

"How? The body is gone," said Ronin.

"The physical body is gone, but the spirit or the aura is still there," said Iris and handed me the list. "Well, some of it. I think we could conjure up a revealing spell either way. We should try, at the very least. I brought Dana. We should be good." Iris tapped her messenger bag wrapped around her shoulder. Dana was the name she'd given her album of paranormal DNA she'd collected and stored for future curses and hexes.

I nodded. "Okay. We'll go to the lab after we've checked these out. But first, I have to tell Dolores and Ruth about the body's disappearing act. They'll want to know."

Ronin rubbed his hands together. "Excellent. I've always wanted to see the inside of those vagina parties."

I stared at the half-vampire. "How the hell did you know that?"

Ronin's face pulled into a mischievous grin. "Skills, baby. All kinds of skills."

Iris snorted and pushed him toward the front door. "Let's go, Casanova."

Laughing, the three of us left Davenport Cottage, walked a few feet, and then entered Davenport House through the kitchen's back door.

"You're back?" Ruth looked up from the kitchen island, Dolores next to her. A giant ledger was opened between them.

The sounds of whistles and cheers coming from the living room, along with the smell of alcohol, hit me all at once, making my head spin.

Damn. What kind of party was this?

"Later, ladies." Ronin moved past us and strolled into the living room with the strangest smile I'd ever seen. I glanced at Iris to see if she'd be upset, but she had moved to the kitchen island. She was staring at the ledger, seemingly unaffected or uninterested in Ronin's participation in the festivities.

"Where's Marcus?" Dolores pulled her reading glasses from her nose. "I thought the two of you were going to take care of the werewolves."

I bumped my hip against the counter's edge. "A rowdy crowd is gathered at the town square. They heard about the dead girl, and they're demanding answers. Marcus went to smooth things over. Iris and Ronin are going to help me until Marcus settles things."

"Did you know there're one hundred and thirteen shifters in Hollow Cove?" Ruth beamed, twirling a pen in her hand. Her fingertips were marked in blue, and a streak of blue ink smeared her left cheek.

I shook my head. "No, I didn't. That's a lot of ground to cover." I placed the paper with the list of names Marcus had given me, on the counter. "This is Marcus's list of all the were-wolves in town. There're only thirty-seven. A lot less than the shifters. Maybe we should take some of the shifters off your hands and make it even."

"Okay. We can do that." Dolores pointed with her glasses at me. "I've listed them alphabetically by their last names." She tapped the finger from her free hand on the ledger. "We'll take A to P, and you can do Q to Z."

"Oh. I just had a thought," said Ruth.

"Congratulations," snorted Dolores.

Ruth gave her sister her "mad eyes," which was basically the narrowing of her brows and a slight widening of her eyes that only made her look like a cute, angry doll.

"Here," she said to me. "You can write the names on this." Ruth flipped through the papers in her notebook. Each page had either small hand-drawn images or what looked like recipes for potions. I couldn't see a blank page. Finally, her blue eyes looked up at me. "Oops. I don't have a spare page."

I smiled at her. "It's fine." I yanked my phone from my pocket. "It'll be faster if I just take a picture."

Both Dolores and Ruth stared at me as though I'd just told them magic wasn't real as I flipped through the ledger, flicked the pages until I found the first and last names that started with the letter Q, and began to snap pictures.

Chanting pulled my attention to the front of the house. Ronin was on the coffee table, an older woman under each arm as he sang and kicked out his long legs in some weird version of the Rockettes while Beverly clapped and cheered him on.

I shook my head. "I'll never understand that vampire."

Iris looked over at her boyfriend and gave him a thumbs-up.

I'll never understand that Dark witch.

"So it's settled." Dolores grabbed the ledger and stuffed it in her large canvas bag before sliding the strap over her shoulder. "We should get going. We have a lot of ground to cover and not many hours of daylight left. I'd prefer not to meet this… deranged paranormal in the dark. The night seems to bring out more madness."

"And it's a full moon tonight," added Ruth. Her eyes widened. "Really full."

"Your intellect astonishes me," snapped Dolores.

Ruth beamed at her older sister as though she'd just paid her a compliment. "You're welcome."

We all knew the full moon brought out another breed of crazies. I leaned my elbows on the counter. "Listen. Before you go. There's something you should know."

Dolores narrowed her eyes at me like she was trying to pull a mind read. I would have inched away a little if she wasn't my aunt. "What haven't you told us?"

Ah. I quickly told them about the dead girl's body disappearing and waited for their reaction. When they just stared at me with their mouths open, like they'd each swallowed a golf ball, I said, "Have you ever heard of a dead body vanishing into thin air? Have you seen this before?" I was really hoping they had. It would help and perhaps give me more clues as to who was responsible. But I still didn't know why.

Dolores and Ruth exchanged an uneasy sidelong glance between them, the kind that needed no words to communicate, the type of look that only siblings or those who'd lived together for a very long time could understand as though they were communicating telepathically.

I shared a look with Iris before glancing at my aunts. "You have, or you haven't?" I didn't like the sudden silence.

Again, Dolores and Ruth shared a look that I didn't like. Translation: they either had or hadn't, but they agreed it was bad.

Dolores let out a long sigh after a moment. "The only time a person or a body vanishes like that... is because they're a demon. Only demons can mysteriously disappear into thin air, as you say."

I shook my head, knowing that Lilith and her husband, Lucifer, could also magically disappear with the snap of a finger. But they were gods. "No. It was broad daylight. It couldn't be a demon. The body would have combusted into ashes under the sun."

"I know," answered my aunt.

I narrowed my eyes. "So, you believe the little girl was a demon?"

Dolores looked at me for a moment without speaking. "Or a very powerful spell, a transportation spell, took the body away."

I rubbed my temples. "Wait a second. To do a spell of that magnitude, you'd need to be there in the room. Right?" I wasn't that learned yet in all things magical, but I did know that the magical practitioner had to be in the same vicinity if they wanted to perform a spell. Unless I was clueless, and you could conjure up spells from a distance? That didn't sound right.

"Exactly," answered Dolores. "If the body truly disappeared, and it wasn't… say… an invisible spell, you would need to be near it to perform it. You can't make long-distance spells. That's not how magic works."

"Genevieve Grossweiner disappeared once," began Ruth, her eyes round with excitement and her face brightening. "She was a werecow."

"A werecow? Really?" Okay, maybe this wasn't so bad. Though I'd never heard of a werecow before. But this was Hollow Cove, where the unbelievable was believable. "Did you milk her?" I laughed. They didn't. I cleared my throat. "She vanished?"

"Mhm. We found her skeleton buried in her backyard six months later. At the time, her husband made meat pies and sold them half-price from his garage. And then we knew why." Ruth wiped her face and added another long, blue ink streak from her nose to her forehead.

I stared at her. Ruth. No one in the world was like her.

"Or." Dolores's voice was low and severe. "This is a new breed of demon that can walk under the sun."

"A day-walker." Ruth waggled her eyebrows.

Holy leprechaun balls.

The hair on the back of my neck rose at the fear in her voice. I let that information sink in for a bit. Not all demons were bad. Hell, I was part demon. My father was a demon, and he was good. Still, like all beings, you had the crazies, and then you had the uber-crazies that fed on mortal flesh and blood. Those types of demons shouldn't be walking around in our world when the sun was out.

I stared at my aunts. "No way."

"Way," said Ruth. "*Way*, way."

I pressed my hands on the cool marble top, shaking my head. "Maybe... maybe this was just some powerful spell the killer put on the body after they killed her?" Okay, that sounded like a bit of a stretch but more plausible than day-walking demons.

Dolores wrapped a hand over the strap of her bag. "I don't know, Tessa." Her voice held a faint ribbon of worry. "But this information has to stay between us for now. If the town is already frightened by the fact that one dead girl was found, can you imagine the chaos if they heard that we might have day-walking demons? It would be absolute madness."

"Really, really mad," added Ruth. She scratched the top of her head, adding blue ink highlights to her white, cloudlike hair.

I nodded. "I know. You're right. We need people to remain calm. At least until we've canvassed the town."

"About that," said Dolores. "We'll have to make it quick."

"Why?" asked Iris and I at the same time.

Dolores's eyes flicked to the living room as a peal of merry laughter that sounded strangely like Ronin filled the air. "Well, the town's already in a fret. Word spreads around here like wildfire."

"Uncontrolled and unpredictable," commented Ruth.

"Soon, the town will know that we're looking for the killer. Which means the killer will know too."

Something occurred to me. I straightened. "But you still think the girl was a demon. Do you think the killer is a demon too?"

"Could be. Could be a demon disguised as one of us."

"I don't like that." Ruth rubbed her hands over her arms like she'd just suffered a chill.

"Or not," I said. "We could be wrong about that."

"Which is why it's imperative that we start asking questions. The sooner we do, the sooner we'll get some more information."

"I'll get Ronin." Iris moved past the dining area, and I watched as Ronin tried to get her to climb up on the coffee table with him and his two new lady friends.

"We'll rendezvous back here in four hours," ordered Dolores. "Hopefully, the sluts will be gone by then."

Ruth giggled and followed her tall sister out the back door, leaving me to wait on Iris and Ronin.

My blood pressure rose as I stared out the window, watching my aunts cross the side of the house and then disappear. What Dolores had said was still ringing in my ears like I'd spent a few hours at a rock concert.

But one thing was for sure. I hoped Dolores was wrong about that day-walking demon. Because if she wasn't, things were about to get gravely dangerous.

Like neck deep in the crapper and no one to toss us a life buoy.

CHAPTER

5

"What's the first name on the list?" asked Iris, strolling along the sidewalk.

I halted and checked my phone. "Quinn. Ah... a Geoffrey Quinn. According to Dolores's notes, the guy's a shifter. Apparently, he can change into a giant snake." Yikes. The girl's body had been torn to shreds. A giant snake could have done it using its fangs.

Iris's delicate eyebrows met in the middle, but she didn't say anything. I knew she had her own issues with shape-changing. She'd been cursed by her ex-boyfriend, Adan, to stay in the body of a goat forever or at least until his death lifted the curse. We never talked about it after it had happened. I wasn't sure if it was a sore subject with her, so I'd decided not to push it. If she needed to talk about it, I would let her do it when she was ready.

But I missed the goat. She was so damn cute.

"Does he have to shed his skin every time he shifts?" Ronin laughed at his own joke.

"No idea." The thought of a giant snake gave me the creeps. The idea of a giant anaconda squeezing me to death didn't sit well with me.

We walked along in silence for another minute or so on Hanging Hill Row until we came upon the address I was looking for.

I stopped and pointed to a small redbrick cottage. "This is it. Six Hanging Hill Row."

"Why are the windows boarded up?" asked Iris, that frown returning. She didn't seem particularly interested in visiting this house.

But she was right. The two large windows flanking a black door were indeed boarded up with plywood. Strange.

"I don't know. Come on." We had to hurry this up. We still had many more houses to check before nightfall.

I led the way through knee-high tall grass and weeds. If there'd been a stone walkway at one time, it was gone now. When I moved closer to the house, I could see the right side of the building's windows were also boarded up. So either this Geoffrey didn't like the light, or he was doing something ominous inside and didn't want anyone to see.

I reached the front door, knocked three times, and stepped back.

"Maybe he's not home," said Ronin after waiting a good minute.

"Maybe." I stared at my phone again just as the sound of metal scraping against metal reached us several times, like maybe five deadbolts being unlocked.

"Paranoid much," muttered Ronin.

I had to agree with him on that.

The front door popped open a crack, enough for me to see a yellow eye with a black, vertical pupil.

"What do you want?" hissed a disturbingly snakelike voice.

The hairs on the back of my neck stood on end. I angled my head to get a better look at him, but the door was still hiding most of his body and face. "Are you Geoffrey Quinn?"

"What's it to you? Who are you?"

I pointed to myself like an idiot and said, "I'm Tessa Davenport. Uh… I'm a Merlin here in Hollow Cove."

At that, the door cracked open further, enough for me to see the face of a forty-something male with pale-greenish-gray skin. He squinted in the light, covering his face with his hand as though the sunlight was hurting him. His clothes, which consisted of a pair of jeans and a shirt, were loose on his small frame like they belonged to a much larger man. But that's not what had me tap into my magic. It was the smear of blood around his mouth.

My witchy instincts flared. I reached for the energy of the elements around me and held them. I'd rather be safe than sorry. And something was off about this guy.

Geoffrey stared at me with his creepy-as-hell snake eyes. "What do you want? I'm busy."

"Eating little girls?" offered Ronin.

The shifter's gaze flicked over to Ronin. A gray-forked tongue slipped in and out of his mouth. I didn't like the way he was staring at my friend, wondering what a half-vampire would taste like.

I looked over my shoulder, glared at Ronin, and twisted back around, clearing my throat. "Where were you between nine and eleven this morning?" I waited, expecting the shifter not to answer. But he did.

"Here," answered Geoffrey, his tone rough and scratchy like he didn't use it much.

"The whole time?"

"Yes."

"Eating little girls," repeated Ronin.

I sighed through my nose. "Can anyone corroborate that? Is anyone here with you?"

Geoffrey blinked, and I cringed at his double eyelids. "No. Just me."

I didn't believe him. Now, I had to ask him the hard question. "Can you explain why you have what looks like fresh blood on your face? And I can see some on your clothes."

At that, the shifter's face spread into a creepy, slow smile, cruel as a thorny knife. "I was hungry." He stepped back and pulled open the door. A gust of blood and something foul assaulted my nose. It took a moment for my eyes to adjust to the darkness inside, but then I saw it—the bodies of a least a dozen chickens in all manner of dismemberment. Blood and feathers splattered the walls and a small entry table. Didn't snakes neatly swallowed their food? Guess that rule didn't apply to shifters.

Now that I could get a good look at him, he was covered in blood and *feathers*. Gross.

"I like to hunt my food," said the shifter, blinking fast. "Flesh tastes better when it's filled with fear."

"You've got issues, man," said Ronin, a disgusted look on his face. "Clean yourself up. You look like shit." The half-vampire walked away and grabbed Iris with him, not wanting her to touch anything.

I wasn't sure what to say to the shifter. Should I thank him for his time? I decided to say nothing and walked away to join my friends just as I heard the door slam. Geoffrey didn't kill the girl. He'd been hunting his chickens for what looked like most of the morning. Poor things. I couldn't imagine how scared they must have been, hunted by a giant snake.

I was glad we'd come here instead of Ruth. She would have bawled her eyes out at seeing all those dead chickens. She'd probably have come back and poisoned the shifter with her famous "ten-day diarrhea" potion or maybe even something worse.

"That guy was really creepy," said Iris as we walked along the sidewalk. "Not what I expected."

"Me neither." I didn't know what I expected. Less blood and feathers?

"The guy's clearly unhinged," said Ronin. "But he's not the guy."

"No. He's not." A streak of white and red caught my attention down the road—a bunny. A white bunny dressed in a red suit jacket and gray pants, ran between two houses. He wasn't hopping or running on his four legs. He was running upright, on his two hind legs like how a human would run and walk. Something gold reflected in his hands. I blinked, and he was gone.

"What is it? Did you see something?" Iris leaned over, trying to see what I'd been staring at.

"Uh. No. It's nothing." Because the bunny was gone, and he was probably just a shifter. "Okay. Next on the list"—I swiped the screen on my phone—"are Clara and Sam Rogers.

Eagle-shifter couple." I looked up. "They're just a few houses down."

I stuffed my phone in my pocket, trying to rid my eyes of the images of the dead chickens.

"So, what's up with your house?" Ronin's long legs strolled next to me. He had a curious spark in his eye, like he couldn't wait to get ahold of this information. "Iris says it's purposely not giving you any electricity."

I let out a sigh. "She's right. House is on strike. He's angry. Feels neglected."

Ronin laughed. "A house that feels neglected? How does a house even *feel*?"

"It's a *magical* house," said Iris, as though that should explain everything. It did to me but probably not Ronin. "It has feelings, you know. You can feel it as soon as you walk in. It's usually a very happy house."

I wasn't sure that I felt House's feelings, but I did feel the pulse of energy as soon as I crossed the threshold. Well, at least I used to. Now it was just a dull nothingness, the creaks and screeches of an old house. Like a regular human house.

Ronin was nodding to himself. "That's gotta suck."

"It does." I couldn't help but think of Marcus. The longer House was on strike, the longer Marcus and I were going to spend time apart. If nothing worked, the chief would have to stay at his office, where he could shower and eat something hot.

"That's what I like about you witches," said the half-vampire. "Everything is so *mysterious*." He made a show of his hands. His eyes landed on Iris. "It's so fucking sexy."

I snorted as Iris's face darkened two shades. "Well, at least Iris can stay with you until this is sorted out." If it ever gets sorted out.

Ronin's eyes fell on me. "So... what are you going to do about it?"

"Human sacrifice."

The half-vampire halted. "You're shitting me, right?"

I gave him a playful smile. "I am."

Ronin let out a breath, rubbing a hand through his brown hair. Iris and I both smirked. "Damn. You had me there. I believed you for a second."

"I know." I couldn't stop smiling. "But House does need some sort of payment in the form of cheaters and abusers." I raised my hand at the expression on his face. "I don't know how this all works, but that's what he wants. Magic requires payment. He wants blood, so to speak. My aunts usually handled it, but I guess they forgot."

Ronin shook his head. "How the hell do you forget about that?"

I shrugged. "You'd be surprised." With everything that happened here on a day-to-day basis, it didn't surprise me that my aunts had forgotten to feed House.

We strolled along Mystic Road in silence for a while, all lost in our thoughts. White clouds tracked a blue sky, and the sun shone as a bright yellow disc. I took in the smell of roses, freshly mowed lawns, and the magnolia trees in full bloom. Their light-pink-and-white flowers filled the air with a sweet aroma.

"But having no power is a problem," I said, breaking the silence. "It's Marcus's birthday today. I don't have anything planned yet, but I was going to. Until I realized House was pissed and shut us out. Now I'm out of options."

"You could take him out to a nice restaurant," offered Iris. "There's a really great Cajun restaurant in Cape Elizabeth. They have an amazing jambalaya."

"I thought about that." Dinner at a restaurant did sound good, but I'd wanted to do something different. "But I wanted to try something else. Something special. Something more innovative."

"Give him sex," said Ronin, making me catch my breath.

"Uh... okay," I said with a laugh, feeling slightly embarrassed about having this kind of conversation out loud and not in my head.

"Seriously. All the guy needs is sex," continued Ronin, making the heat rush up my face.

Iris slapped his arm. "*Ronin.*"

The half-vampire shrugged. "What? I'm serious. I'm a dude. He's a dude. All dudes just want to spend time with their girls in the sack. Trust me. Give the guy sex. Best sex you can. It's the best damn birthday present you can offer. He'll remember it forever."

"Right," I answered, my face flaming. Iris giggling next to me only accentuated the heat level to molten lava.

The best sex ever? The thought terrified me. A nice dinner sounded like a lot less of a challenge than sexing up the chief with a mind-boggling sex experience. And now that Ronin had mentioned it, I couldn't get it out of my head. I started to sweat—the nasty stress sweat. Crap, I didn't need this pressure right now.

Thankfully we reached the next house on the list so we could drop the sex talk. The tall, skinny, cylindrical-shaped white house looked like a version of a lighthouse. A circular lantern room fitted below a large cupola. I'd never come down the end of Mystic Road before. I wouldn't have missed this house.

"Someone actually lives in a place like this?" Ronin was staring at the house like it might reach out and bite him.

"It is… eccentric," I said and felt it. It was like nothing I'd ever seen.

"I think it's great." Iris skipped up to the red, oval-shaped front door and knocked, looking like a kid with her arms full of kittens. She reminded me of a young Ruth.

We heard a loud screeching noise before the door swung open.

The skinniest woman I'd ever seen stood in the doorway like her limbs were made of sticks and a strong gust of wind would break her. Annoyance flashed on her long, lean face at the sight of us. Her eyes were red and puffy, as was her nose, as she pulled on the belt of her white feathered bathrobe.

The woman sniffed. "Yes?"

"Hi," said a-way-too-chirpy Iris. "My name is Iris. I work for the Merlin group in Hollow Cove." That was true. "We're here to ask you a few questions. Are you Clara Rogers?"

The woman pulled out a tissue from a pocket of her feathered bathrobe and blew her nose. "Yes. Are you here about our taxes? I'll have them paid tomorrow. I promise. We just… haven't been feeling well."

"Who is that, honey?" came a voice, and then a towering, thin shape loomed next to Clara.

"Tax collectors," said Clara.

Iris opened her mouth and then closed it, looking lost for words. Finally, she looked over at me.

Knowing that look, I took over. "We're sorry to intrude, Mr. and Mrs. Rogers. But can you tell us where you were between nine and eleven this morning?"

"Sure," answered the male shifter. "We were in bed."

I narrowed my eyes, taking in their pasty complexion, dark circles under their eyes, and wet noses and eyes. "What's the matter with you?"

Clara blew her nose again. "Bird flu."

The sound of shoes scuffing the walkway made me look over my shoulder, and I caught Ronin hurrying away as though he needed to distance himself from the Rogers.

I held my breath and took a step back. Was bird flu contagious? Shit. That was the last thing I needed right now.

I tugged on Iris's shirt, pulling her back with me. "Sorry to disturb you. Make sure you drink lots of liquids. Chicken soup is supposed to be good."

I knew that was the wrong thing to say to a couple of eagle shifters as they stared at me as though I'd just instructed them to eat their young.

Biting down on my tongue so I wouldn't laugh, I dragged Iris back to where Ronin was waiting for us on the sidewalk.

He shook his head. "Couldn't do it."

Laughing, the three of us headed back down the street, and I wondered just how many more nutjobs we sheltered here in Hollow Cove. Probably lots.

And that's how it went for another two hours of knocking on doors and speaking to the shifters in question. After we finally knocked on the last door on our list, belonging to Rune and Sybil Zimmerman—bat shifters—every shifter's whereabouts were accounted for. The killer was not among them. But we still had the weres to check. They were next on my list of things to do today.

And that's when we heard the screams.

Screams poured out from everywhere at once, all around us: high-pitched, panicked, and terrified cries.

"What was that?" asked Iris, closing the flap to her bag and making me wonder if she'd picked up DNA samples from the last house to stuff in Dana.

"Over there." Ronin, having superior hearing and senses, compared to us witches, pointed at the intersection between Spirit Lane and Wolfsbane Road, back up from where we'd come.

I lifted my gaze to see a half-dozen paranormals standing around something at the edge of the street. I heard a muffled scream and then saw a female rushing away, wide-eyed with a hand clasped around her mouth.

"Let's go." I ran forward, thinking I might just jump a ley line, but I didn't want to miss anything. Ley lines moved fast. Besides, I was almost to the source of the screaming.

When I reached the crowd, I pushed my way forward and stopped.

The body of a young girl in a red-hooded cloak lay next to a lamppost, on the sidewalk. Her dress and cloak had been torn to bloody ribbons. Her torso, arms, and legs were shredded like they were made of paper. Blood. Blood was everywhere.

Worse was that she looked *exactly* like the girl I found this morning.

"Wait a second." Ronin stared at the body and then up at me. "Is that..."

My heart felt like it was about to launch out of my chest. "The exact same body I found earlier," I whispered.

But that was impossible. Right?

CHAPTER

6

Sometimes our minds can play tricks when we're tired or sick. But I was neither. And for all I knew, this *was* the girl I'd found earlier. But how could that be?

"Tessa?" Iris pulled a worried gaze on me. "What's going on?"

I shook my head and looked back at the body of the girl. "I don't know." I glanced over at the crowd of paranormals who had moved away and given us room but kept throwing us nervous glances. Their faces said it all. They were scared. And they had reason to be because I had no idea what was happening.

This was the second time I'd found a dead girl, just a few hours apart. Judging by the terror that rippled across the faces of the crowd, the news of this situation was going to go viral throughout town, and I could do nothing to stop it.

"This is messed up," said Ronin.

I couldn't agree with him more. "I feel like I just stepped into the twilight zone."

"What are the odds of this repeating?" asked Iris, the hand around the strap of her bag clamped tightly.

Good question. But I didn't have an answer. "Maybe the girl wasn't *dead*, dead? No. That can't be right. She was clearly dead." But I hadn't checked her vitals.

"Maybe she was an undead?" Ronin was inspecting the girl's body. "Like a zombie?"

"That's a horrible thought," said Iris.

"No. I didn't get any zombie vibes." Not that I would know them if they hit me in the face. "Maybe the body disappeared from the morgue and then reappeared here?" No. That didn't make sense. For one, where did the body go during the hours in between?

"You think?" Ronin's eyes rolled over the girl, his face tightening when he reached her shredded abdomen.

I shook my head. "The blood looks fresh. And it's pooled around her. Like she was killed here. Dead bodies stop bleeding after a while. This...

this looks like she was just killed a few minutes ago." I didn't like my answer any better. I sounded crazy. Because deep down, I knew this was the same girl I'd seen this morning.

"Twins?" offered Iris. "Twins that age like to dress the same."

"And die the same, apparently," said Ronin.

I let out a shaky breath. "That's even more disturbing than finding the same body twice." My witchy instincts didn't believe it. "I seriously doubt they were twins. No. This is the same girl."

"Which is impossible." Ronin's face was distant for a moment, his eyes focused elsewhere. "Who do you know that can die twice?"

Good point.

"What do we do now?" Iris looked over her shoulder. The crowd had gathered a following. About twenty paranormals were now watching us, talking among themselves.

I yanked out my phone. "Call my aunts."

"They don't have cell phones," said Iris.

Shit. "Right." I stared at my friends and then at the dead girl. We needed to do something with the body. "Marcus." I tapped his name on the screen and put the phone to my ear. "Voicemail," I said after the fifth ring. "He's probably still with Gilbert and the crowd in the town square."

"We can't leave her like this." Iris's face went through a few emotions until it settled on a mix of distress and pain.

"No, we can't." My eyes darted to Ronin. "Feel like going on a trip?"

Ronin stared at me for a second. "I know you don't mean a *trip*, trip?"

I sighed, my heart starting to pump. "A witchy trip?"

The half-vampire splayed out his hands, a knowing smile on his handsome face. "I'm getting some weird signals. How 'bout you help a vampire out."

I looked between Iris and Ronin. "We need to take this body away. Marcus isn't answering, and I don't know where Dolores and Ruth are. We can't carry her either. That would only bring us more attention that we don't want. So, our only option is... ley lines." I waited to see my friends' reactions. I didn't think they realized what I was proposing.

Ronin gave a shrug. "Okay. So you'll take her with you in a ley line. That sounds reasonable. Where are you going to take her? The morgue?"

"No." I looked at the girl. "If she's going to disappear on us again, I want it to be at Davenport Cottage. We need to run some magical tests. We have to figure out what's going on. And I'll need my aunts' help for that."

"Fine," answered the half-vampire. "We'll meet you there."

I glanced at Iris, who was looking at me with excitement and disbelief. She knew or hoped what I was about to say next. "And you guys are coming with me."

Ronin snapped his gaze to mine, staring at me as though I'd just told him I'd crashed his expensive BMW. "What did you say?"

"This is my dream come true," said a wide-eyed Iris, a grin on her pretty pixie-like face. "Is this real?"

"Yes," I said, and I couldn't help the smile that crept over my face at seeing the Dark witch's excitement. She'd always wanted to ride a ley line with me. I glanced at the half-vampire, who was still staring at me like I'd lost my witch marbles. "I need help carrying her," I told him. "This is the fastest way to bring her back across town without anyone seeing us." I exhaled. "So? What do you say?"

Iris jumped in the air and started to do a little dance. "Yes!"

The crowd of paranormals was looking at her with horror etched on their faces. It looked like Iris was thrilled at the sight of the dead girl. I didn't have time to explain. I just wanted to get the body out of here, fast.

But Ronin didn't look happy. He looked... do I dare say scared? "But I'm not a witch. Won't stepping into a ley line kill me? I thought ley lines were only for witches?"

True. I'd only brought two witches with me in a ley line—that witch who'd killed her husband and tried to blame it on Ruth, and my friend Willis during our Merlin trials. But the thing is, my father, a demon, had been able to appear in a ley line the first time I saw him. He'd even manipulated it with his demon magic. Vampires had demon blood, just like most paranormals. I was willing to bet Ronin could travel in a ley line safely. He couldn't control it, but he could ride it.

"You'll be fine," I told him, knowing this was a risk, but I suspected he'd be okay. "If I feel like something is wrong, I'll let you out." I waited for him to say something, but he just watched me with the same terrified look. "And it won't be for long." I glanced between my friends. "Ready?"

"Ready," said a happy Iris.

Ronin nodded. A frown line marred the perfection of his forehead.

I was going to take my half-vampire friend in a ley line with me. Was I mad? Yeah, I totally was.

I drew in my will and reached out to tap the ley line. A burst of sudden energy hit me like a rushing river. I felt it in my body, my bones, vibrating with the ley line's power.

Holding on to the ley line, I moved over to the dead girl, crouched, and grabbed her by the shoulders. I stood rooted in place for a moment, realizing I'd never held a dead body before like this and not sure how I felt about it. But I had no other choice. The sooner we got her to Davenport Cottage, the sooner we'd get some answers. "Ronin, can you grab her feet? Iris. There's a wicker basket over there. Grab it."

Iris practically skipped as she bent down and snatched up the basket. She hurried over next to me. "Oooh. I can feel it. The ley line's power. It's incredible. Amazing."

I tried not to laugh and looked up at Ronin. "Ronin?" For a second, I thought he wouldn't do it, but slowly the half-vampire knelt next to the girl and grabbed her feet, looking pale and green. If he felt the ley line's power vibrating near him, he didn't mention it. Together we stood, holding on to the dead girl carefully, aware that the crowd was watching us, but I didn't look at them. I needed to concentrate.

I yanked the ley line closer and closer to me, like pulling a rope. I could see it clearly in my mind, like a translucent river. I could see it race across the street, going from one end of Hollow Cove to the other side, and then lost in the distance.

"Iris, hook your arm around mine and get ready to jump," I instructed.

After the Dark witch did as she was told, and before Ronin could change his mind, we jumped.

Ronin screamed like a girl on a roller coaster as the three of us landed together, speeding forward in a howl of wind and colors. I heard the gasps from the crowd as the three of us, well, four, if you count the girl, vanished from sight.

And then we were rushing through town.

Our bodies raced forward. Houses and trees flashed past us in a blur as though we were traveling at warp speed in space aboard the Starship Enterprise.

With my will, I bent the ley line, instructing it where I wanted it to go, where I wanted it to take us. Which was Davenport Cottage.

Iris let out an exhilarated scream, a smile plastered on her pretty face and her dark eyes dancing with excitement. "This is even better than I thought. The best." The Dark witch's clothes and hair flapped in a current, the ley line's power. "Can we ride every day like this?"

"I don't see why not," I told her. The dead girl's head lolled over to my arm, and I pulled my eyes away from the blood on her neck.

"Ronin, open your eyes. Look!" said a delighted Iris, pointing to the blurred houses and street.

Ronin's eyes were closed with a frown on his face, and his jaw clenched like he was trying his best not to be sick. He looked like he was about to pass out. Thank the cauldron, he was still holding the girl's feet.

I'd taken a risk hauling a half-vampire in the ley line with me. So far, I didn't see any signs of distress other than him possibly being sick. So far, so good.

We rushed across town like we were on a high-speed train. Not wanting to miss my exit, I pulled on the ley line, willing it to slow down so I could get my bearings.

Images around me slowed until they weren't blurred anymore and I could make them out.

"We're in the town square." Iris gripped her bag tightly like it was the only thing keeping her from exploding in excitement. "Look. There're your aunts."

Sure enough, I could make out Dolores's tall shape. Ruth and Beverly were next to her. Guess the V party was finished. They stood a little off from a crowd of paranormals who were pointing and shouting at them. Dolores looked like she was about to cast a few curses if they didn't stop. I couldn't hear what they were saying, but I had a few ideas: the dead girl, or girls. I could make out Gilbert standing above the gazebo—the one I was still paying for because I'd accidentally torched the prior one—like it was some throne and he was the king. Little shit. I couldn't see Marcus in the crowd.

And Ronin still had his eyes closed.

I needed my aunts. And they were right there.

So, I did what any clear-minded and clever witch would do in my place.

Angling the girl's body so I was holding her up with one arm, I yanked the ley line around until it was next to my aunts. And then, still clutching the ley line, I tapped into the power of the elements around me, thrust my free hand, and cried, "Trahendum!"

It was a new power word I'd learned, and it did exactly as I wanted.

A force of kinetic energy surged out of my outstretched hand, wrapped around Dolores, Beverly, and Ruth, and yanked them into the ley line.

Dolores splayed out her hands to balance herself as she landed. She blinked at me. "Tessa? What is the meaning of this?"

Ruth was beaming, kind of like Iris. "We're in a ley line!"

"We are?" Beverly grabbed on to her boobs like the ley line might flatten them. "Cauldron, save us!"

I laughed. "Hang on!" With a tug on my will, I leaned forward and pushed the ley line to go faster until the town square was just a blur of color.

My aunts stood behind us like we were on a New York City subway train.

Tessa's Magical Ley Line train. I liked the sound of that.

Ruth sat on the ley line floor, which was just a flat surface of energy we were all standing on, and crossed her legs in a kind of yoga position marveling at the means of magical transport. She was enjoying this.

Even Dolores had the tiniest of smiles until she noticed the dead girl Ronin and I were holding.

"Is that?" she said, pointing. "Is that the dead girl? Where did you find her?"

"That's the thing. She kind of found us."

Dolores stared at me. "What aren't you saying?"

"We think the body's fresh," interrupted Iris. "Like she was just killed a few moments ago."

"But that's not possible." Beverly was still hanging on to her boobs. "Dolores told me about the body you found hours ago."

"I know this sounds crazy," I began. "But the wounds on her were fresh. And the amount of blood suggested she was killed where we found her. On the corner of Spirit Lane and Wolfsbane Road. Not near Martha's place like the first one."

"This is so cool," said a beaming Ruth. "It's like riding a jet plane!" Her voice rose as she started to sing John Denver's "Leaving on a Jet Plane."

I glanced back at Dolores. "If you have a better explanation, I'd love to hear it."

Dolores shook her head, her brows furrowed, but I could see the wheels turning behind her eyes. "Not here. Can you take us to Davenport House?"

I nodded as Shifter Lane blurred past us. "That's where I was planning to go. I'm guessing House won't open the door for us, right?"

"Nope," said Ruth. "He's still very angry with us."

We really needed to take care of that. "Okay. I'll move us to the backyard. Out of sight from prying neighbors' eyes."

I bent the ley line and we surged up Stardust Drive. Then, focusing solely on Davenport House, we shot forward, banked slightly left, and headed for the back of the house.

"Get ready to jump out," I called.

The ley line slowed, and I leaped out, pulling Ronin, the dead girl, and Iris with me to land softly on the grass.

There was an "Oh!" from Beverly as she bent forward, nearly falling, but then righted herself.

Dolores wasn't so lucky and had fallen on her ass.

Ruth held her head high as she expertly walked to a stop, hands on her hips in some version of a superhero pose.

"That was amazing," said Iris, letting go of my arm. "Can't wait to do it again."

My body jerked forward as Ronin let go of the girl's feet, rushed over to a rhododendron bush, bent over, and began puking his guts out. Totally understandable.

I settled the girl gently on the grass. My arms and my front were smeared with her blood, but I couldn't think about that now. Now, we needed answers.

"Quick, before she disappears again," I told my aunts. "We need to do something. Like secure her body in magic, maybe?"

Dolores pushed to her feet. Red spots marked her cheeks, but her embarrassment was short-lived. "You mean like a magical suspension? A pause charm?"

"Never heard of that. But it sounds great." If we could somehow keep the girl from vanishing, we could finally get some real answers. Like, was she the same girl or not? And if she was, how did she die twice?

Ronin hobbled back. "The next time you get one of your bright ideas, count me out." He spat on the ground. "That was *not* cool."

A smile pulled on my lips. "Oh, you big baby. You're fine. It wasn't all that bad."

"He's right." Dolores's eyes narrowed. "Vampires have no business traveling in ley lines. You're lucky he's still in one piece."

"Yeah," agreed Ruth. "Some parts of him could have ended up in Alaska," she said with her eyes round. "Or Madagascar."

"What?" Ronin cupped his manhood. "Definitely never doing that again."

My chuckle was brief when I was hit with the sense that maybe I'd been foolish to have asked Ronin. If something had happened to the half-vampire, one of my closest friends, I would have never forgiven myself. But it was too late.

"Uh... girls?" Beverly pointed to something behind us. Her green eyes flashed with uncertainty and fear. "What is *that* over there?"

We all spun around and followed the direction Beverly was pointing.

A wolf stood across the backyard from us. It stood about seven feet tall and on its hind legs like a human, its claws grazing the earth where it stood, hunched back and waiting. Its fur was dark brown, almost black, with an abnormally large wolf-like head and an elongated snout. Its yellow eyes shone with eerie intelligence. They looked human. The wolf didn't even move, except for its lips pulling back into a nasty snarl, showing off teeth longer than my hands.

And then it hit me as I said, "The Big Bad Wolf."

CHAPTER
7

I realized I was staring at a fairy-tale character, but there you have it. The Big Bad Wolf was in our backyard, looking at us like we were its next meal.

I was going to need a drink after this.

"But that's impossible," said Dolores, her eyes on the beast. "The Big Bad Wolf is just a story written by Charles Perrault."

"I think it was the Brothers Grimm," said Ruth, watching the wolf with interest, and I had a feeling she wanted to go over there and make friends.

Dolores threw up her hands. "Who cares who wrote it first. The point is, how can it be standing there in our backyard? It doesn't make sense. Stories don't materialize into reality."

I shrugged. "Well. This one did." I knew it didn't make sense, but I didn't have time to think about it. "We need to act fast. It looks like it wants to *eat* us." The wolf was a lot bigger than any werewolf I'd ever seen. Like this was the Godzilla of werewolves. Like a werewolf on steroids, but it hadn't gone the way it was supposed to. The thing was disproportionate. It didn't look like a fluffy wolf, more like a grotesque cartoon version.

"Noooo, it doesn't want to eat us," said Ruth. "Look. I think it's smiling."

"No, Ruth. That's just its mouth getting ready to tear you apart," snapped Dolores. "This isn't a cute little puppy from the shelter. This is a deadly monster."

But Ruth wouldn't have it. She looked at the wolf, and then in her "cute voice" she reserved for when she spoke to animals, she said, "You're not a bad boy, are you? You're just misunderstood."

Beverly rolled her eyes. "I swear one day she's going to get us killed. Urgh. What's that smell?" She covered her nose with her hand.

She had a point. "That would be the wolf." The thing let out a stench of rot and sewer.

"You guys just don't understand animals," said Ruth with a frown. And before I could stop her, she was moving toward the wolf. "Here, puppy. Who's a good boy? Awww. You have such cute teeth. You want Auntie Ruthy to brush them?"

"She's mental," said Dolores, shaking her head. "Absolutely bonkers."

"And you're surprised?" said Beverly.

"And she's going to get herself killed." Then, pulling on the elements around me, I readied a power word. And then I was running.

"Ruth! Don't!" Fear and adrenaline sparked through me. I dashed across the lawn, sprinting toward my tiny aunt.

Ruth halted and looked over her shoulder at me. "It's fine, Tessa. See, he doesn't want to eat me. We're friends."

Its features twisted grotesquely. Its lips curled in warning with a steady growl of rage.

Ruth's face fell as she took a step back. "Oh. Okay. Maybe it does."

I pulled on my will and the elements and shouted, "Accendo!"

Twin fireballs shot out of my hands and hit the wolf in the chest. I was amazed at my aim. *Look at me go!*

Unfortunately, my uber-fascinating magic didn't do what I'd expected—like, consuming the wolf in a sheet of red-orange flames.

There was a crack, and my fireballs went out in a burst of black smoke.

Whoopsie.

"What the hell just happened?" Ronin was standing in front of Iris, using his body as a shield. Black talons sprouted from his fingertips, matching the black in his eyes. He'd vamped out.

I swallowed and pushed Ruth back with me. "Looks like my magic didn't have much of an effect." I could see a small burnt mark where I'd hit it. And I *did* hit it. Was the wolf immune to my magic?

Still, I managed to do something to it. I made it *very* angry.

Its yellow eyes narrowed as it focused on me. "Witch. Your powers have grown since we last met."

Huh? "You're confusing me with another witch, *wolf*." Well, if we were going to give each other nicknames.

The wolf's lips parted in what I could only guess was a smile. "I'm still going to eat you."

"Yeah. I don't think so."

Ears pinned and lips curled to show me it meant every word, it came at me. Paws, the size of my head, swiped at the ground as it rushed forward.

There was one more thing I hadn't tried.

A wave of cold energy rippled through my core. My demon mojo.

With my demon mojo awakened, I allowed the cold, wild magic to rush through my veins. And then I let go.

Black tendrils of demon energy roared forth from my outstretched fingers, and I directed it at the wolf.

For a split second, the wolf halted, and I saw the confusion as my demon magic struck.

The black wisps of demonic magic—thanks to my dearest papa—coiled around the wolf like deadly black ropes.

And then, just like my elemental magic, the black strands withered and disappeared.

I cursed. "Well. *That's* not good."

The wolf looked up. "Was that supposed to scare me?"

"Yes." No point in lying. "Yes, it was."

The wolf flashed me its mouth full of teeth. "Interesting."

"Interesting?"

"This is strange magic." The wolf lowered its head. "It doesn't change anything. I'm still going to eat you, witch."

Panic struck me as I realized my magic barely scratched the creature. That thought was particularly galling. How could we stop it if our magic barely had any effect? I wasn't known for my sword skills or my one-on-one combat. Allison showed me how effective I was when she kicked me in the vajayjay.

"Get back into the house!" I shouted at my aunts. At least they'd be safe in there.

"Like hell we are," said Dolores, her fingers and lips moving in a spell. "We're not going anywhere. This is our land. If anyone's leaving, it's that wolf."

The wolf pointed a long finger at Dolores. "I've always liked the tall ones. Meat's tender along those long bones. I'm going to eat you next. Right after I devour this one," he said, pointing at me.

Excellent.

He looked at the body of the dead girl. "You stole my kill, witch."

I caught sight of Ruth disappearing through Davenport House's back door before I turned to the wolf.

The creature stepped forward. "I'm hungry. But you'll do. You're meaty."

My brows shot up my forehead. "Did you just call me fat?"

"He did," said Beverly.

The wolf snapped his attention to Beverly. "Are you Grandmother?"

Beverly's face flashed angrily as she cocked her hip. "Who're you calling a grandmother? You filthy animal."

I laughed, though that was totally inappropriate since we were in the middle of a showdown with a massive wolf from a kids' story turned real who wanted to eat us.

The wolf pointed a clawed finger at me. "You first." And then it hurled its enormous body at me.

KIM RICHARDSON

"Oh, shit." I stumbled back, tripped on my legs, and fell on my ass.

A flash of black caught my eye, and then Ronin was before me.

"You'll have to come through me first, wolf," said Ronin, his body posed and shaking with rage.

The wolf's ears pinned low on its head. "A worthy opponent. Deal."

Both wolf and half-vampire launched themselves and hit with the force of a moving bus. The sound of flesh being torn filled my ears. Blood splattered the grass, but I didn't know if it was Ronin's or the wolf's.

Ronin and the wolf disappeared under a tangle of dark fur and limbs. If anyone could match the strength of a giant wolf, it was Ronin. The next thing I knew, the wolf had Ronin pinned to the ground, and I could see blood spilling from my friend's side.

The wolf opened its mouth like it was about to eat my friend's head. But then, Iris was there the next second, throwing a small brown bag at the wolf's head. It exploded on impact, and black dust fell over the wolf's face.

It backed off, clawing at its eyes.

"What have you done? It burns. I can't see?"

"What was that?" I asked, staring at Iris with admiration.

"Black pepper," said the Dark witch. Iris was a genius.

Ronin leaped to his feet and sliced the wolf's front with his talons. Blood flew as the vampire kept slashing over and over again. The wolf wiped at its eyes and then, with one mighty strike, hit Ronin across the head. My friend stumbled and then collapsed to the ground.

"Ronin!"

The wolf's eyes were red and wet from the black pepper. They rolled around the yard until they settled on me. It growled, promising me pain. "Mine—"

A loud sound of metal striking something resounded. The wolf started forward and stumbled.

Ruth was behind it with heavy iron pans in both hands. "Bad wolf. Very bad." Using her kitchen weapons, she hammered the wolf on the head again, and it crumpled to the ground.

"Ladies. Together." Dolores moved quickly, positioning herself close to the wolf but not too close. Next to her were Beverly and Ruth. I pushed myself up and rushed over.

Their lips were moving, their hands gesturing as their clothes and hair lifted and moved in an invisible breeze. Power surged around me, and I held my breath as I felt my aunts tap into their wills. The outpouring of energy from their auras chimed and resonated.

A gust of fire blew from my aunts' outstretched hands, hitting the wolf. A second later, Iris, drawing her hand from her bag, flung it out and screamed, "Ri errius!" Navy-colored dust roared forth from her extended fingers.

The creature howled as streaks of combined magic hit it. It rolled back and fell to the ground while tall flames coiled around its back. It was still alive. But the more magic we poured at it, the weaker it got.

My turn.

I pulled on my magic—both elemental and demon mojo—grabbing everything I could into a power word and letting it fly.

Fireballs and black tendrils soared out of me and hit the wolf. It flipped over, howling as more flames licked up the creature's body.

Ruth danced back at the heat of the flames, her face tight in anger. More that she'd been wrong about the wolf than it wanting to eat us.

The wolf thrashed madly, letting out a high-pitched whimper and frightened growl as though something was burning it from the inside. Flames and black tendrils reared and coiled around its body like a fire hissing. It flailed madly, clawing at its face and neck and leaving bleeding gouges. Skin sizzled as the creature squealed in pain, its arms and legs shuddering as the smell of burnt flesh soared.

And then it finally collapsed to the ground and was still.

Iris sprinted across the backyard and fell on her knees next to Ronin. "Ronin! Ronin! Wake up!" She slapped his face.

He blinked up at her. "Baby. I love it when you're rough." He grabbed her by the wrists and pulled her down over him.

Chuckling, I walked over to the wolf. The air was thick with the scent of seared flesh and fur, and it was still pulsing with magic.

I stared at the beast. Its maw was open, and blood was trickling from deep gouges across its chest where Ronin had cut it. But it wasn't breathing, and I couldn't see any sign of life.

"Is it dead?" Ruth was next to me. Her iron pans were up near her chest, holding them like boxing gloves, ready to use in case Mr. Wolf was not dead.

"Pretty sure it's dead." But just to make sure, I nudged it with my shoe. The creature didn't even flinch or blink. Grimacing, I took a chance and pressed my hand near its snout. "I can't feel any breath. It's not breathing. Yeah. It's dead."

Beverly joined us. Hands pressed on her cocked hips, she said, "Can someone please explain to me what the hell just happened here?"

I stared at the wolf and then looked over at the dead girl dressed in her red-hooded cloak. "We were just attacked by the Big Bad Wolf."

"Yes, I can see that." Beverly's face was red with irritation. "But why? How can this be real?"

I shrugged. "No idea. But we almost got our asses kicked by a fable."

"Fairy tale," corrected Dolores. "A fable is a short fiction giving a moral lesson at the end. This has all the magical elements of a fairy tale, provided by the imaginary fiction created primarily to entertain."

"Thank you, Professor Dolores," I said, irritated. "Somehow, the wolf followed the girl's body. Like they were connected. Part of the same *fairy tale* or story."

Dolores narrowed her eyes at my tone. "Still doesn't explain why we're seeing this. And why does it keep repeating, assuming the little girl is the same girl you found this morning?"

I exhaled. "This is beyond bizarre, even for Hollow Cove. I mean, I love our crazy, but it's *our* crazy. I'm used to it. This... this is just... wrong."

"Guys!"

We all spun around at the sound of Iris's voice, my heart pounding at the fear in her tone.

"Look!" The Dark witch stood next to Ronin, pointing at the body of the dead girl, or rather, what was left of it.

I stumbled forward, blinking because I was trying to see clearly. The body was transparent, like a hologram or a ghost. And in a blink, it was gone.

"Holy crap," I said, rushing forward. "It's gone. Just like Marcus said. One second it was here and then..."

"Poof," said Ruth as she made gestures with her pans.

"Does this mean it's going to happen again?" Iris watched me, and I wasn't sure if I saw excitement in her eyes or fear.

"No idea." My eyes found the dead wolf. "You think he'll disappear too?"

And then, as if on cue, the wolf's body began to shimmer, and just like the little girl in the red-hooded cloak, I could see right through the wolf to the grass beyond, and then it was just gone.

I made a face. "Okay then."

"Oh, good," said Beverly as she combed a lock of blonde hair from her eyes. "I have a date with Lorenzo. Can't have dead bodies lying around our backyard. First impressions are paramount. You don't want to give the wrong impression."

"Really?" asked Dolores. "I always thought they knew you were a slut."

Beverly rolled her eyes. "Oh, Dolores. If you wax that unibrow, they will come."

Oh dear. "Let's focus on our issue, ladies. Waxing is a whole different beast." God, did I know. Keeping my lady garden nice and trimmed and free of weeds was a weekly endeavor. "I'm assuming this isn't the last we'll see of these two."

"Why do you say that?" asked Ronin.

"Because they've already appeared twice, that we know of, and since we don't know how this happened, we can only presume they'll keep coming until we stop it."

"How do we stop it?" asked Ruth.

I shook my head. "Imaginary characters that can actually kill you? That's a good question." The fact that our magic didn't affect them the way it should had my insides tightening in knots.

Dolores propped her hands on her hips. "The question is, how did make-believe become real?"

Now, *that* was the question of the hour.

Chapter

8

"Any ideas why our magic didn't have much of an effect on it?" I looked across the dining table at Dolores and Beverly, my hands wrapped around my glass of lukewarm water. I'd kill for a cup of coffee, but House was still in a fit and would continue to withhold electricity until he got what he was owed. "Even my demon mojo barely made a scratch."

And that terrified me. What if more were coming? It required all six of us to take down that wolf. And my aunts had some serious battle experience under their brooms. If we'd had to battle more than one of those wolves, I'm not sure we would have made it.

"Because our magic is bound to this world." Dolores looked up from the hefty purple leather-bound tome she'd gone to fetch from her "special" collection the minute we all entered Davenport House. She'd been flipping through the papers for the past twenty minutes. "Wherever this creature came from, it didn't come from our world. It's the only thing I could think of. The only thing that makes a bit of sense"—she exhaled—"is that wolf came from another world."

"Then it should stay there," said Beverly as she crossed her arms over her chest.

"He better not come back," grumbled Ruth as she dipped her hands into a jar of ointment and slapped it over Ronin's chest, smearing it over his wounds a little too aggressively.

"Ow. Careful, Ruth darling," hissed Ronin, balancing back on one of the kitchen island stools. "I have delicate skin."

Iris snorted, sitting on the stool next to him. "You're half-vampire. Your skin is ten times tougher than ours."

Ronin grinned. "Oh, right. Smear away, then." His eyes found the fridge. "Got any cold beer in there?"

Ruth pulled back with a smile. "We've got beer, but it's warm. I like warm beer. You like it warm too?"

Ronin made a face. "Ah… you can keep it. So, still having issues with your house, then?"

Beverly narrowed her eyes. "Don't get me started." She yanked out her compact from her purse and checked herself in the mirror. "I need to keep my face from flustering. No one looks good flustered."

Dolores looked at her sister. "You're not seriously considering going out tonight with this Lorenzo?"

Beverly smiled seductively at her reflection. "Of course I am. You know I always have a date for Friday night. I'm too beautiful to stay in. Gorgeous people need to mingle with other gorgeous people."

"Spare us your vanity." Dolores flipped through another page, not seemingly interested in her sister's social events.

Beverly made a purring sound in her throat. "Lorenzo is tall... dark... handsome, and extremely rich. He's taking me out on his private jet. I'm getting delicious shivers all over my body just thinking about him."

Dolores rolled her eyes. "That's called a fever."

"Are you planning on a cold shower?" I teased, knowing they didn't have any hot water either.

"I don't need to." Beverly looked away from her reflection to glance at me. "Ruth's got a nice, big, hot cauldron ready for me later in the backyard." She made it sound dirty.

Dolores arched an eyebrow. "You're going to bathe in the backyard... in a *cauldron*?"

Beverly perked up. "Yes." She tossed her head back and dragged her hand down her body. "*Glorious* hot water pouring over my *magnificent* naked body."

"You're not afraid the neighbors are going to see?" asked Iris with a smile.

Beverly smirked and proceeded to stare at herself in her compact. "Of course not. They can look all they want. It's not every day they get to appreciate what the goddess perfected."

Funny how conversations boomerang in this house.

My eyes settled on the bundle of black fur curled above the refrigerator. Hildo still seemed upset about the V party. Looked like he hadn't moved from his spot. Poor kitty.

"We're seriously off track here. Back on the topic." I shifted in my chair. "Going back to the wolf and the girl." The idea hurt my head, and I rubbed my temples like I was trying to jump-start my brain. "You said you believe they came from *another* world. What other world?" If they didn't come from the Netherworld and didn't come from here, then... where the hell did they come from?

My tall aunt pulled her eyes from the book. She blinked at me, shaking her head. "I don't know. All I know is that they weren't from any world we know."

I leaned forward. "Are you saying there are *other* worlds?" Holy crap. That was news to me.

Dolores's eyebrows met in the middle. "Who are we to think there are only two worlds? We might not know of their existence, but that doesn't mean they're not there."

"Sounds like Dolores's sex life," snorted Beverly.

Dolores shot her sister a venomous look. "What I'm saying is... other worlds *may* exist beyond our realm. We just don't know. And I can't find any records. It's not like we know someone who's been to another world and came back to tell us."

"Sure we do. That happened to Cedric Sackrider," began Ruth, her face serious and wrinkled, like when she was about to pull some memory from a story.

Dolores exhaled through her nose. "What are you talking about, Ruth? You know someone who's been to another world?"

Ruth nodded and plastered another glob of her ointment on Ronin's chest. His mere look of disgust told me it smelled as good as it looked. "Yes. He told me himself. He said he opened his front door one day and stepped into a world made of cotton candy and toffee."

Dolores didn't look impressed. "Is he still in that world?"

Ruth shrugged. "Oh no. He's in a paranormal mental institute in Boston."

Okay then.

"I never thought of there being other worlds." I really didn't. How could I when I was only rediscovering this one after so many years away from everything paranormal?

"And why would you?" commented Dolores. "Until today, none of us really gave it much thought, I'm sure. But now… now we don't have a choice." She tapped her finger on her tome. "They are not from here. Not after what we've seen. How our magic reacted to that wolf. They can't be."

If they were from another world, I had to warn Marcus. I grabbed my cell phone and texted him.

Me: *Hey. We need to talk. Got some intel on the girl and the wolf. Yeah. There's a wolf too.*

I waited for the three dots to appear, but my screen stayed blank.

I leaned back in my chair, thinking it through. "So when the bodies disappeared, they returned to their world?" My brain hurt just trying to sort everything out.

"That seems logical to me," answered Dolores. "Yes. I think so."

"Like when we vanquish demons," said Ronin. "Their bodies go back to the Netherworld—ouch!"

"Sorry." Ruth looked like she was struggling not to laugh or smile. "Almost done."

I took a sip of my water and frowned at how warm it was. "But why did the little girl reappear? Even if they're from another world, that doesn't explain why she died twice." It was almost like she was trapped in a time loop.

"That, I can't tell you." Dolores slipped her glasses onto her nose and started to read a page from her tome.

"But we can all agree that what we saw today was Little Red Riding Hood and the Big Bad Wolf. Right?" I watched as everyone's attention snapped to me, and I could tell they believed me. They just didn't want to admit it. Because, well, it sounded crazy.

Dolores let out a long breath. "I can't believe what I'm about to say but… yes. I do believe you're right, Tessa. I believe they were characters from a story."

"Characters from a story that were just as real as you and me." I wiped a strand of hair that stuck to my sweaty forehead. "How did that happen?"

"We still need to do some research on that," said Dolores, her expression hard and all business. "I know of spells that can create creatures from myths, like dragons, centaurs, and hippogriffs. As witches, we would have caught on pretty fast that they were just spells, not actual beings. They would have emitted energy. Auras. I don't think that's what these were."

I cast my glance at Dolores. "So, you're positive they were actual beings from another realm?"

"That's what I think, yes," answered Dolores.

"It was Lilith," said Ruth, and I jerked in my seat.

I stared at my little aunt with her fingers covered in the green ointment as though it were the first time I'd laid eyes on her. Why didn't I think of that? "You think Lilith did this?" I knew the goddess got bored frequently, but I didn't see this as her genre of entertainment. Then again, I didn't know her all that well either.

Dolores stared at Ruth. "Not bad, Ruth."

Ruth smiled sheepishly and stared at her feet. "I know." She looked up and added, "Ask me anything. You can pick my brain if you want."

Dolores eyed her younger sister. "How about you leave it alone for a while and let it heal."

Ruth made a face and continued to smear Ronin's chest with her ointment.

"Would Lilith do this?" Iris was staring at me expectantly, like the goddess of hell and I were besties.

I shrugged. "No idea. The goddess is a little unhinged. It's not her style, but what do I know? Maybe she picked up a book on fairy tales and went to town." She had confessed to me once that she enjoyed torturing mortals. Maybe this was her sick idea?

Dolores pulled her glasses off her nose. "Ruth has a point. Lilith, the powerful, charismatic, and wonderful goddess that she is… has the power to create these beings."

Wonderful goddess was pushing it a little. But my aunts had all worshiped her the moment Lilith had restored Davenport House after the dark wizards had burned it down. They all held her in the highest of esteems. Lilith wasn't all bad. But I didn't trust her. And then there was Lucifer… Could he be involved?

The more I thought about Lilith and Lucifer, the more complicated the situation became.

"Maybe you can ask her." Beverly snapped her compact shut. "See if she was just having some fun. A girl needs entertainment."

My aunt and Lilith had that kind of entertainment in common. "It's not like I have her on speed dial."

"Can't you just…" Beverly made gestures with her fingers. "You know. Call out her name or something?"

"I'll think of something," I told her. If this was Lilith's idea of a joke, I wanted to ask her to call it off before people in the town got hurt or worse.

Yet I had the strangest of feelings that it wasn't Lilith. But I still had to ask her, to take her off the list. Did we even have a list?

"All done," said Ruth to Ronin as she tightened the jar's top and placed it on the island counter. "You can put your shirt back on."

Ronin grabbed his black T-shirt from the counter. "Will it leave a scar? My lady happens to think scars are very... virile." He looked at Iris and winked. The Dark witch flushed. Man, she was too easy.

Ruth smiled between the two of them. "No. You won't scar. Sorry. But if you want, I have a potion that can riddle your skin with scars, like third-degree burns," she added with glee sparkling in her eyes as though this were a fantastic idea.

Ronin froze with just one arm through his T-shirt. "Sounds great, Ruth. But I think I'm done for today."

I pushed my glass of water away. "I'm not sure this is Lilith. I'm still going to ask her, but I just think we shouldn't be rushing to that conclusion." Because it seemed way too easy.

"What are you thinking?" asked Iris, turning around and leaning back on the kitchen island so she could see me.

I waited a moment to get everyone's attention. "That somehow these things, these beings, are fairy tales or stories from somewhere else. Maybe they came here by mistake. Maybe they're lost. I don't know. If they did come over from another world or another plane... Why? *Why* did they come *here*?"

The silence that hit me didn't make me feel any better. Guess none of us had any clue as to why two beings or creatures from another place came to our world.

"Maybe they liked our world better," said Ruth, her brows knitted together. "Maybe their world is sick or something."

Dolores snorted. "You've been watching too much TV."

But what Ruth said made an ice chill roll up my back. Because what if what Ruth said were true? If so, more were to come.

"Why Hollow Cove?" said Iris, mirroring my thoughts. "Does it have to do with the ley lines? Was it easier for them to cross over?"

That was an excellent question. "Maybe?" I looked at Dolores, waiting for her to answer.

"We all know Hollow Cove is like a magnet for the supernatural because of the earth's ley lines and magnetic energies," replied Dolores. "It's a possibility."

Iris's question made me think of something. "If they crossed over to our world," I began, "there must be an opening like a Rift or something. Right?"

Beverly nodded. "Yes. That makes sense. Another dimensional pocket."

My thoughts went to Jack, the demon Soul Collector. He'd taken me to a different place, a pocket of another realm, but all within the boundaries of the Netherworld. Not a new world.

Following that logic, I said, "Which means they can continue to pour out of their world since it doesn't seem like anything is stopping them from crossing." My gaze flicked between my aunts and then to Ronin and Iris. "It's going to happen again. Either it'll be Little Red and the wolf or something else entirely. Maybe something a lot worse."

"Don't say that," snapped Dolores, her expression troubled. "It's bad luck."

Ruth nodded. "Like you're inviting the worst to come."

I didn't believe in bad luck, not the way they did. "I just have this feeling we haven't seen the end of this."

"Fine." Dolores laid her glasses on the table. "What do you suggest, then, oh, mighty one?"

I ignored her insult. "I'll speak to Lilith. And if it's not her, we have to find this opening. And when we do, we need to close it."

CHAPTER
9

I closed the front door to Davenport Cottage and gazed around the room. "Still no power, huh, House?" I waited for an answer, though I didn't expect one. I wished I knew another way to satisfy the magical house's hunger instead of providing it with a few cheaters and scumbags. Maybe there was another option. I made a mental note to ask my aunts later. Because right now, I had something else I needed to do.

"Lilith?" I called out, partly feeling foolish. The last time I'd seen the goddess, I'd asked her to swap Ronin and me back to our bodies after Iris had accidentally switched us when trying to perform a black-magic spell. She'd refused, of course. No surprise there. She thought it was too entertaining. Yeah, she was a selfish goddess.

"Lilith? I need to speak to you." Maybe she *was* behind this. Perhaps she and Lucifer had one of their fights, and she wanted someone else to suffer.

I exhaled, moving into the kitchen, irritation making my pulse rise. "Lilith? If you can hear me, I *really* need to speak to you. This is important."

I knew she could hear me. She was a goddess after all. She was seriously mistaken if she thought I was about to offer her a human sacrifice. The longer I waited, the angrier I got until I felt the heat rolling off my neck and up my face.

"Lilith! I swear!"

"All right. All right. Keep your G-strings on," came a voice from somewhere behind me.

I spun around and scowled at the woman sprawled over my couch.

The thirtysomething-looking goddess dipped her head, shifting waves of her long, glorious red hair that shimmered like it was on fire. Her lean body was fitted with designer-looking jeans and a black top under a short red leather jacket.

I let out a breath. "Took you long enough."

Lilith's red eyes gleamed with curiosity. "Why so tense? Is the gorilla not pleasuring you enough? Long enough? You know, you're not getting any younger. Is it dry down there? You might want to explore a little lube."

Ew. "This isn't about him."

Lilith smiled a feline smile with her ruby-red lips. "It's *always* about him. But I have to say I would have been *very* surprised if he was selfish in bed. He's more of an altruistic type. Wereapes are known to be selfless and tender lovers. One day, you'll get bored of him... then... then he's *mine*."

A deep feeling of jealousy, with a dose of overprotectiveness, rose in me. "Never going to happen. So you can stop asking." She'd just arrived and had already started to piss me off.

"No. I don't think I will," she answered, her voice velvet ice, which sent a shiver through me. The goddess flashed her perfect teeth. "You mortals are so impatient. It's because your lives are ridiculously short. I don't blame you. It's just *soooo* dreadfully sad."

"That's nice." I never understood the obsession Lilith had with Marcus. It could just be the want-what-you-can't-have kind of thing. Still, it always rubbed me the wrong way.

Her red eyes glanced around the room, and a frown appeared on her manicured brows. "What's wrong with your house?"

I wasn't surprised she could feel the lack of magical support, if you will. She had reconstructed the main house. "He's on strike."

Her eyes narrowed at my use of the pronoun *he*, but she didn't say anything. "What did you do?"

I walked into the living room. "More like, what didn't I do."

Lilith laughed. "That sounds like fun." She winked at me.

I made a face. "Not that."

"Then what?"

I could tell she wouldn't let this go. I didn't want her in a bad mood. I needed answers from her. "House requires regular payments. He provides us with magic, and in return, we provide him with..." How did I put this? "With males who have been unfaithful. Males who are cruel. Deadbeat dads. You get the picture."

Lilith watched me, and interest flashed in her eyes. "Really? How interesting. And why just males? Females are just as capable of deceit as their male counterparts."

I didn't doubt that. "I don't know. I didn't make the rules. But it seems as though House feels neglected. So, until my aunts give him what he wants, he's taking away our electricity. Hot water. You know... the essentials."

Lilith ran her hands over the couch as though she were petting House like he was a big, fluffy dog. "I love this house. I like how it has a *bad* side."

"House doesn't have a bad side. It's understandable that he's angry." Even though I wasn't thrilled about it. "I'll fix it." But first, I needed answers.

The goddess wrinkled her face. "You smell terrible. And you've got blood on you."

For some strange reason, I wasn't embarrassed. "Been canvassing all around town. Haven't had time to shower yet."

She shrugged like she couldn't care less. "You still stink. Your male won't get anywhere near you smelling like this."

I didn't know how she could smell me across the living room. But she was a goddess. I picked my stinking self up and moved closer until I stood right in front of her. "Listen. I have to ask you something."

Fury, cold and terrible, sparkled in Lilith's eyes. She leveled me with a look. "Careful, little demon witch. I warned you about asking favors."

A cold feeling rolled down my throat and spread into my chest, making it hard to breathe. "I know." I felt a shudder of fear crawl up my back. "It came out wrong. But I'm not asking for a favor… just for you to answer." At her cocked brow and cold stare, I knew that wasn't any better. I swallowed. "Since I'm experiencing some verbal diarrhea, I'm just going to come out with it."

Lilith leaned back on the couch. "This better be good."

I swallowed again, trying to figure out the best way to approach the subject. And not finding anything, I opened my mouth and let the words fly. "Little Red Riding Hood and the wolf, was that you?"

Lilith watched me without blinking. "Is this some sort of riddle?"

I shook my head. "No. Did you create the fairy tale? Did you take that story and make it come true?"

The goddess pursed her lips. "You've lost me again. Don't use such big words, my little demon witch. You don't seem to know how to use them."

Okay, she was going to make this complicated. "The fairy tale. 'Little Red Riding Hood.' Was that you? Did you do this?"

Lilith rolled her eyes like I was the simplest of simpletons. "You're not making any sense. What fairy tale?"

Ah. I realized she might not be familiar with our mortal-human fairy tales. "'Little Red Riding Hood' is a fairy tale, a kids' story written long ago. It's a story of a little girl dressed in a red hood—"

"I'm familiar with the story."

I frowned at her. "But you just said…" I stopped when I caught her smiling. She was playing with me. Of course, she was. "Just tell me if this was you."

"What was me? I need specifics before I incriminate myself."

I reeled in my temper. I didn't want to fight with the goddess. Because, well, I'd lose.

"We had two incidents with Little Red Riding Hood and the wolf. It seems like they're the characters of that fairy tale come true. My aunts and I believe they're not of our worlds."

Lilith tilted her head, looking mildly interested. "Why do you think they're not from our worlds?"

"Because of how our magic affected them," I said, recalling what Dolores had said. "More like how little it did. And then the bodies just disappeared like they never existed."

"Disappeared?"

"The girl, the Little Red Riding Hood, we first found her mangled body this morning. And then her body vanished at the morgue. And then the exact same dead girl appeared later, but someplace else. We brought the body back here to do some tests. The wolf must have followed us or the girl's scent. Anyway, they both vanished." I was rambling. I observed Lilith's expression and body language. She didn't come off as sly as someone who'd just orchestrated this. She was more curious and, dare I say, anxious?

"And you think *I* did this?" Lilith's expression was slightly entertained, as though she was happy I was blaming her for this, which was a little odd and unsettling.

"I'm not sure," I answered, keeping my voice steady, not wanting to set her off. "It's why I wanted to check with you first. And? Did you?"

"No."

"No? That's it?"

"Why would I do that?" said the goddess. "What does it bring me? Nothing. It's not hunting humans for sport or sex. It's just sad, really. And kind of boring. Lacks originality if it needs to steal from an old story."

"I get it. But you're the only one I know who has that kind of power to transform fictional characters into real life." I thought about it. "Lilith? Have you ever heard of something like this before?"

Lilith stared at her red, manicured nails. Her silence didn't make me feel any better.

I tried a different tactic. "Can gods, goddesses, turn make-believe into reality?"

Still nothing.

"Are there other worlds?"

At that, the goddess turned her eyes on me, and a wicked smile crossed her perfect features. "If I say yes, will you give me an hour with your male? *Please* say yes."

Not this again. I looked away from her unsettling stare. "No. But please answer the question." Okay, so my voice was a bit rough and really not the smart way to talk to a being who could snuff the life out of me with a snap of her pretty fingers. But this obsession with Marcus set me on edge every time.

Lilith laughed, the sound throaty and like she knew I wouldn't accept. "Okay. Yes. Yes, there are other worlds."

Huh. I was not expecting her to answer. "Really?" My pulse raced. "How many?"

Her red eyes rolled over my face. "Three hours with your male, and I'll answer."

"Forget it. Aren't you with Lucifer now? Wouldn't he be upset if he caught you or knew you were having relations with other men?"

Lilith draped a long strand of red hair behind her shoulder. "Why would he? We have an open relationship. It's just sex. It doesn't bother us like you mortals who can't seem to separate animalistic desires from the heart. It just goes to show how weak you are."

More like we had some standards. "You're right. We are much weaker than you. Can you tell me how many worlds?" I figured stroking her ego might loosen her tongue.

Lilith giggled like this was a game she was enjoying. She leaned forward, eyes wide with delight. "I'm not telling."

"Fantastic."

Lilith laughed. "You're such a sarcastic little demon witch. It's why I like you so much. Why we're friends."

Yeah, I was still not sure about that. She thought we were friends. I wasn't convinced.

I stared at her. "You say we're friends, so as friends, answer me this. Is it more plausible that one of these worlds found a way into ours than some witch or wizard giving life to fairy tales? Like a crack or a hole is leaking into ours?" It made more logical sense to me since, according to Dolores, if these characters had been created by magic, our worldly magic, our powers would have defeated them much easier and wouldn't have disappeared like that. So that's what I was going with.

Lilith's eyebrows twitched. "Not bad, my little demon witch."

"So, I'm right?" Holy crap on crackers. "There's a hole somewhere?"

"It appears so."

I frowned at her. "I'm assuming you knew all along. You could feel it. This opening. Am I right?" When she shrugged, I added. "Why didn't you tell me?"

"Because it's much more entertaining to make you guess. Where's the fun in telling you?"

I swear, if she wasn't a goddess, I would have grabbed her with one of my ley lines and kicked her ass all the way to Antarctica.

Anger bubbled to the surface of my mind. "If you know this, do you know how it came to be?

How a hole from a different world managed to break through to our world?"

Lilith's expression tightened, all smiles gone. "I think that's enough questions for today."

Something wasn't right. I didn't know her well, but I knew enough to recognize when she was uncomfortable. Something about my question bothered her. Why? She wouldn't look so tense if it was just an unfortunate crack caused by maybe the ley lines. No. If I had to guess, this was something else. *Someone* else.

"Someone did this," I told her. "And by that look on your face, you know who. Who did this, Lilith?"

The goddess stood, and I got a whiff of spices. "I think I'll be leaving now. Your questioning is starting to get tedious."

I couldn't help but notice she was avoiding my eyes. But I was pissed. She knew who'd done this and wouldn't say who.

Anger coursed through me. I stepped closer to her. "Tell me!"

Her hand jerked. Some unseen force wrenched my body still as though I'd been turned to stone.

Oopsy. Now I'd done it.

This wasn't the first time Lilith had trapped me with her magic, and it still scared the crap out of me. I was helpless against the unseen strength of her power, which she'd imprisoned me in. My magic was useless against hers. And she knew it.

My body lurched. I felt a sudden release, and I could move again. My breath came in with a jagged gasp as her power lifted from me.

"I won't warn you again," said the goddess, a turmoil of anger in her tone. "I wouldn't think twice about ending you. You're nothing to me."

That I did believe, which was why I didn't believe the friend thing. It was more like she thought we were friends, but only when she wanted us to be: the goddess's fair-weather friend, if there was such a thing. She made her own rules as she went.

I let out a breath, trying to calm the storm of emotions welling in me. "Okay. Sorry. I shouldn't have said that. But if you know something, as *friends*, shouldn't you tell me?"

I blinked, and she was gone. A slight whiff of spices remained, the only indication that she'd been here.

"Great."

But it wasn't great. Lilith knew something. Worse, it was pretty evident by her reaction that someone had opened the door to another world on purpose, and she knew who it was.

And me, well, I was going to find out just who that was.

I gave my armpits a sniff. But first, I needed a shower.

CHAPTER
10

I really did need a shower after the day's events. And the logical, simpler way would have been to pop by my mother's place and shower there. But I wasn't in the mood for her constant yapping about the wedding plans. The truth was, we hadn't had time to dive into them. And the idea of seeing her right now was making me claustrophobic.

Which explained why I was packing some clean clothes and towels in a bag, hoping to catch a quick shower at the Hollow Cove Security Agency. I knew there were showers there. And the bonus was that Marcus, though not answering his phone, was most probably there as well. I needed to speak to him since my phone was about to die.

But right before I made my way to the chief's office, I decided to swing by Davenport House to give my aunts an update on what I'd learned from Lilith.

I'd made it about ten feet and stopped cold.

A massive iron cauldron sat in the middle of the backyard. And yes, Beverly was in it.

"Hey, darling." Beverly waved at me, the bubbling, hot water covering just below her breasts.

"Hi," I laughed. I had no idea how she got the water to wave and gurgle as though jacuzzi jets were in there. Yeah, it was spelled.

"Want to come in? The water's great," said my aunt, gesturing for me to come over.

"Thanks. Maybe some other time." I pulled my eyes away from Beverly's naked body and popped in through the back door. Seeing Dolores and Ruth stooped over a display of books on the kitchen table, I quickly told them what I'd learned from Lilith.

"From what I'm understanding, you think someone did this?" Dolores asked.

"I do. And Lilith knows, but she's not telling."

"Why not?" Ruth's face screwed up.

"My guess is because this person is someone she cares about." It fit. But it still didn't help me with knowing who that was.

"Oh." Ruth's face lit up. "I know. We'll give her an offering. She'll tell us if we do."

I shook my head. "Not with the way she was acting. I don't think it'll work. I'm sorry. I thought I'd get more out of her."

"But you did." Dolores pursed her lips. "We know this wasn't a magic trick. And we know this hole was created by someone very powerful."

I stared at Dolores. "Who?"

"Another god or goddess," said my aunt. "Only they have the power to open doorways to other worlds. And I'm not talking about the actual crack in the Veil of our world. I'm talking about *other* worlds we know nothing about."

I thought about it. "Then we need to figure out which god or goddess did this. Maybe if we knew, we could ask them why they did it and if they could please shut it down." Before it got worse.

Dolores let out a fake laugh. "Gods don't listen to us mortals."

"So what, then?"

"The only thing we can do is figure out where this hole is and attempt to close it."

"Attempt?" I didn't like that she used that word as though we wouldn't be able to shut it for good.

"There's still a lot we don't know," said Dolores. "There's more research to be done. It'll take time."

"Are you going camping?" asked Ruth, staring at my carry-on bag.

"No. Just going over to Marcus's office to take a shower." I adjusted the strap on my bag. "Okay. Well, I'll let Marcus know. Is there a way we could make a spell that could detect this opening?"

Ruth slapped one of the books with the palm of her hand, and excitement flashed across her face. "Already working on that. It'll be like a tracking spell… only bigger."

"That's great. How soon will it be ready?"

"By tomorrow, we should have it up and running," answered Dolores.

Singing caught my attention, and I looked out the kitchen window to see Beverly with a glass of red wine in her hand, singing "Staying Alive" from the Bee Gees.

"Well, I won't keep you." I walked past the dining room and then spun around. "If you discover anything else, I'll be at Marcus's office."

I shut the front door and headed down Stardust Drive. Lilith was right. I smelled ripe. Hopefully, I could sneak in and shower before Marcus found me.

I crossed Shifter Lane a few minutes later and stared at the gray brick building with the sign HOLLOW COVE SECURITY AGENCY, before making a beeline toward it.

I pulled open the glass door and wandered through the lobby. I could see other doors that

124

led to more offices and one that led to a gym where Allison had beaten me. I was almost expecting to see the gorilla Barbie smiling at me. But then I remembered Marcus firing her ass, and I felt all giddy inside. The showers were just off the gym.

Scarlett and Cameron were nowhere in sight. Neither was Marcus.

The only person here was the old lady seated behind a desk across the lobby.

"The chief isn't here," barked the older woman. Her frown made the wrinkles around her eyes more pronounced.

"That's okay, Grace," I told her, and I was glad he wasn't. "I'm just here to use the showers."

Her face went slack. "Excuse me? You can't just come here and demand to take a shower? What's wrong with yours?"

"It's broken." I moved past her to the door that opened to the gymnasium where Marcus and his staff trained and kept in shape for their work.

"I'm going to tell the chief about this," said the older woman, giving me a disapproving stare.

"Fine. You can bill me for the hot water."

I pushed open the door and crossed the gym. A sign with black letters that read SHOWERS hung above a doorway. The door was open, so I poked my head in. A vast room with gray tiles

125

from floor to ceiling appeared. I counted four individual showers, all without shower curtains or anything that would keep the showerer concealed. Just a wall of tiles separated them.

I pulled my head back and looked around. "Okay, no separate showers for women and men." Looks like Marcus's crew all showered together. I wasn't a prude or anything. I just wasn't accustomed to showing off my lady bits to strangers.

I'd come all this way. And I definitely didn't want to go to my mother's place. Plus, I wasn't about to take another ice-cold shower. So with my mind made up, I opted for the last shower stall on the left, where if anyone came in, you'd get less of a naked view of my butt than the others.

"Looks like it's going to be a two-minute shower." I stripped, put my dirty clothes in a neat pile on the floor, and pulled out my towel. I left it on my bag next to the shower stall, just in case I needed to wrap myself quickly.

I stepped into the shower, wincing at how cold the tiles were against my feet, and turned on the shower water. Water splashed my face. It was already hot—no need to wait.

"Lucky bastards." I moaned as the deliciously hot water splashed over my face and body. Not forgetting where I was, I quickly grabbed my bodywash and loofah and began scrubbing.

"Hi," said a voice.

"Ah!" I spun around and shot my loofah—straight into Marcus's face.

He blinked as it slowly slid off his cheek, leaving a thick, soapy trail.

"Damnit, Marcus. I almost took out your eye!"

"Not quite." He laughed.

"You scared the living crap out of me."

"Sorry I scared you. Grace told me you were in here." He put a hand on the shower wall and leaned over. His eyes slowly rolled over my now soapy body. "I wanted to come take a peek."

Heat ballooned over my body. I grinned. "Peek away."

The chief chuckled. "I got a better idea. How about I join you."

Excitement fluttered through me. Nothing was hotter than taking a shower with this sexy male specimen with expert hands. Hell, he was just lovely to look at naked. But then...

"Anyone can come in," I said, more horrified than I wanted to sound.

The chief grinned as he tugged on the belt of his jeans. "I locked the door."

"Really?" I hadn't even noticed. I looked at the room's opening, and sure enough, the door was closed. I could see the knob of a lock. When I looked back at the chief, he stood there in all his naked glory as though the goddess herself had sculpted him and had taken her time with all the delicious details.

"Nice," I told him. As my grin widened at his smile, I realized something. "You wereapes stay nice and fit for a long time. Right?"

"That's right."

"So, I'll be married to a really hot grandpa."

Marcus laughed, the sound making a hot splash over my skin that had nothing to do with the hot water. "That's right."

I grinned like an idiot. "Come to granny, boy."

The chief stepped into the shower and crushed his hard, solid body against mine. He leaned forward and pressed his lips against my mouth, rough and wanting. I moaned into his mouth as our tongues danced a tango. He dragged his hands down to my hips and cupped my ass, causing a surge of heat to rush inside my body.

I pulled away, running my hands over his back and finding the ridged muscle under his warm skin while we let the water splash between us. "So what happened at the town square?"

"The usual. Gilbert's making everything worse. We have a panic on our hands now. And he still wants to go ahead with this oyster business." His voice was rough, his eyes dark with desire.

"Of course. This *is* Gilbert we're talking about. It's always about what he wants and how good he looks in that stupid bow tie."

Marcus chuckled. "I heard you found another body. I got your text. I wrote back."

"Yeah, my phone's dead."

He leaned forward and sent kisses down my neck. I had to resist rolling my eyes back in my head.

"We did find another—or rather—the *same* body." At his questioning frown, I added, "I think the dead girl's part of a fairy tale that, for some strange reason, repeated." I recounted what we'd discovered, that I'd brought the girl's body back with us in a ley line, and that the Big Bad Wolf found us.

My heart skidded into high gear as his hands moved around my front and caressed my thighs.

"So, tell me about the wolf," he demanded. "Your magic didn't work?"

"It did. Just not as it should. It was like he was resistant to it. And it took all of us to take him down."

"And then they both disappeared." His mouth was on my neck again, nibbling while going south.

"That's right. My aunts think it's because they're not from our worlds. Somewhere in our world, there's a hole. Kind of like a Rift. And that fairy tale came leaking out. Lilith agrees."

Not exactly. I knew the goddess was hiding something: the someone behind all of this.

Marcus pulled back, concern showing over his handsome face. Wet strands of his dark hair splattered over his eyes, cheekbones, and jaw, making him all the sexier. "You spoke to Lilith."

"Mhm. And I have a feeling she knows who's doing this. But she's not telling."

The chief's gaze turned dark. "Lucifer?"

"No. I don't think so. That's not what my gut told me." I remembered her face, the worry in her features. It wasn't for Lucifer. This was something or someone else.

Marcus ran his big, calloused man hands over my butt again, and I was very aware of his manhood standing at attention. "Am I to assume this hole is going to keep leaking out more versions of the Little Red Riding Hood and the wolf?"

"Probably," I said, moaning as he bent down and kissed my left breast. "It's creepy and sad that we have to witness her death repeatedly. And that wolf was like nothing I've ever seen before. But the truth is, I don't know if it'll only just be that specific fairy tale or if there'll be others." We all knew there were much fouler and darker fairy tales. I shuddered at the thought.

The chief's shoulder muscles tensed and went stiff and quiet for a moment. "I'm sorry I wasn't there to protect you."

My heart warmed at the raw emotion in his voice. Any man who wanted to protect his woman was a winner in my book. I was a very lucky woman.

"None of this is your fault."

When he met my eyes again, he had that sort of calm before the storm. Then his eyes darkened with a hurricane of emotions. "I would have ripped apart that wolf." His tone vicious, menacing.

My heart did a somersault in my chest. "I know."

"I don't care where it came from. I would have ended it."

"I know that too."

"No one touches my girl," he said, some of the tension leaving his shoulders, but his voice trembled with uncontrollable rage. He yanked me closer until his hard chest crushed against my breasts, and I could barely breathe until we were one unit.

His intense overprotectiveness didn't rub me the wrong way. Some women would have construed this as macho behavior. Me? It turned me the hell on.

"What we need to do is find where they're coming out from," I said, wanting to veer away from the talk of the wolf. "My aunts are working some tracking spell. Should be ready tomorrow. Then we'll find it."

"How are you going to close it?"

"Good question." I breathed in his scent of male and some musky cologne that was exhilarating. "I don't know yet. I haven't thought that far ahead just yet. I'm sure my aunts are thinking about it too."

"Maybe it's like closing a Rift," said the chief.

"Could be. But I've never done that, and I wouldn't even know where to begin." But I felt my aunts knew all too well how to close Rifts, the cracks in our Veil that enabled demons to cross over. "Let's find it first, and then we'll see what the next step is."

"Good plan."

"I know."

He dipped his head forward and assaulted my lips with his. I met his attack with my witty tongue. A stab of desire went right to my middle as a low, guttural moan came from him. All cohesive thoughts had left the building, and my body wanted nothing more than to rub up against him.

"Dinner at your mom's place tonight," he said as he pulled away slightly.

I frowned. "I forgot about that. I wasn't planning to go."

"You said you would." His hands drifted down my waist, holding me there. My hands touching his skin sent a sliver of heat tingling through my fingers.

"Did I? I can't remember." I did not want to think about my mother at the moment. It was kind of a mood kill.

"She called me about twenty minutes ago," said the chief. "She couldn't reach you, so she called me."

"Total stalker."

"I promised we'd go," said the chief, his gray eyes staring at my lips like he was about to devour them. *Please devour them.* "I'm a man of my word."

I let out a sigh, my body pumping with desire. "The things we do for love."

Marcus smiled, the kind that promised a few orgasms. "But first, I need to take care of something."

And he did. Twice.

CHAPTER
11

I'll admit, having superhot shower sex with Marcus lifted my mood a few octaves, yet it did nothing to warrant time with my mother. However, seeing how important his word was to him, I reluctantly agreed.

I tossed my bag in the back seat of Marcus's burgundy Jeep Grand Cherokee and then climbed into the front passenger seat, all clean, all postcoital.

Marcus climbed behind the wheel and fired up the engine. "Give me your phone," demanded the chief.

I handed it to him and watched as he pulled out a charger from a USB port on the dashboard and plugged it in. "It'll take longer this way, but it'll give you some juice until we get to your mom's. I don't like the idea of you not having a working phone. You never know when someone might need to reach you."

"Yes, sir," I teased.

Marcus laughed as he pulled his Jeep from the curb and headed up Shifter Lane. I leaned back into the soft leather seat, enjoying the constant hum of the Jeep's engine. I closed my eyes for the briefest of moments, thinking about how quickly my life had changed in just over a year.

Today was also Marcus's birthday, but I had nothing to show for it. Did the sex in the shower count?

Having dinner with my mother wasn't how I wanted to spend the rest of the evening. Yes, she did rub me the wrong way—all the time—but that wasn't the reason I didn't want to see her. I was more avoiding her because I knew she would harass us with questions about our wedding. The fact that *we* hadn't even discussed it yet had me on edge. What if Marcus and I had completely different ideas? I wanted a small wedding, like just immediate family. What if he wanted a big, fat, witchy-wereape wedding? After meeting his mother, and knowing mine, I was sure they wanted a huge wedding, and I'd be outnumbered. I felt a flush of nerves inside my belly just thinking about it. I hated lots of attention. I knew I would hate a big wedding.

I shook my head, literally *shook* it, and pushed away those thoughts. It wasn't like the wedding was anytime soon. I had lots of time to freak out about it. Just not at this very moment.

The thought of seeing my father brought a smile to my lips. He was just the demon to change my mother's mind. They were stupid cute, these two. And I was glad they'd found each other again after all these years. It just went to show, you couldn't put timing on love.

"What's going on here?" came Marcus's growl-like voice. He slammed on the brakes, jerking me forward.

"What the—" My eyes tracked the scene. It was so strange and happening so fast that it was hard to concentrate on just one thing at a time. So, I started with the biggest, most prominent one.

The ship.

Scratch that. Not just a ship, but a giant, massive traditional wooden galleon of the fifteenth century sat in the middle of Crystal Row. Three masts sprouted from the main deck about a hundred and twenty feet in length. A black flag with a skull-and-crossbones symbol flapped in the breeze, the name *Jolly Roger* written on the front sail. From what I could see, it was armed with bombards that fired granite balls.

"It's a ship," said Marcus, his jaw slack, and I could see the utter shock on his face.

"The *Jolly Roger*."

"What?" Marcus was still staring at the ship like it wasn't real. Like this was just a dream.

It kind of felt that way, but I knew whose ship this was. My adrenaline spiked.

Damn, damn, damn.

Marcus leaned forward in his seat, staring out the windshield. "Are those... *pirates*?"

I scanned the ship. I could make out about a dozen men dressed in vests, shirts, and coats with dark pants. A few had colorful cloth tied around their necks and tucked in front of their vests, like neckties. Even from a distance, I could see their weathered skin, like those exposed to the elements most of their lives.

"Yup. And that one over there is Captain Hook." I pointed to a thin man with curly, black hair draped over his shoulders, with the largest maroon hat I'd ever seen. A prominent hooked nose rested above a thin, black mustache. He wore a frilly, white shirt underneath a red coat with gold lining and maroon cuffs. From what I could see, an orange sash over his right shoulder held his sword scabbard at his left hip. His maroon pants looked almost like tights, and he paired them with white, knee-high socks.

And it looked like I'd answered my own question from before. It wasn't just *one* fairy tale that slipped into our world. There were more.

Marcus glanced at me, disbelief written all over his face. "Are you saying this is..."

137

"Another fairy tale come true. Wait—what's happening?"

Six pirates on the main deck were running around in a frenzy. And then I understood why.

A granite ball exploded from one of the bombards. The sound was like nothing I'd ever heard, as though thunder detonated right next to my head.

My ears rang as the black granite ball sailed into the air and hit one of the houses.

The Jeep shook as the house exploded in a cloud of wood fragments, brick, plaster, and dust like it had been rigged with a bomb. The thunderous rumble echoed up through the Jeep.

The house, which I'd admit I had never really paid any attention to before, was gone. Obliterated. Only a mountain of debris, chunks of wood, and shattered brick stood in its wake. Metal rebar stood up like the legs and arms of a giant skeleton as a soft pattering of dust sifted down from the air.

If anyone was in there, no way could they have survived.

Cauldron help us.

"Fuck!" Marcus leaped out of the Jeep, me right behind him.

Front doors to neighboring houses burst open as paranormals clambered out to see what the blast was. Hell, probably the whole town had heard the explosion.

"Where's Peter Pan?" howled a voice that I presumed was Captain Hook. My eyes went to the skinny man in the maroon hat stabbed with a tall, white feather. He stood at the edge of the forecastle deck, glowering down at us. "I want Peter! Bring him to me! Come back here and fight me, ya coward! Or I'll find ya wherever ya are, ya hear me, Peter Pan?"

"Oh, crap." I looked at Marcus. "He thinks we have Peter Pan."

"What happens when we don't give him Peter?" Marcus hauled off his leather jacket.

A chill went through me. "He'll slap us with his good hand?" I didn't even know if Peter Pan was here. But if Captain Hook was, I wagered Peter was around here somewhere.

"Prepare the piece!" shouted a voice from the ship, followed by the sound of grinding metal, and then, "Prick and prime!"

I didn't know what they were saying, but I knew it wasn't good.

"I need backup on Crystal Row," Marcus said to someone on his phone. "Now!"

Captain Hook snarled and then beat the air with his hook. Yup, the severed hand with the gleaming sharp iron hook.

"*Fire!*" he howled.

Oh. Shit.

"Get down!" Marcus crushed his body over mine, and the next thing I knew, we both hit the hard pavement.

139

Another deafening blast echoed around us. The ground trembled as though an earthquake had hit us.

I pushed myself up enough to see over Marcus's arm, where a massive pile of rubble was all that was left of the house that had been blown to smithereens a moment ago. Damn. Another house destroyed. Hopefully the owners had run out, but I hadn't seen anyone coming out of that house.

A weight lifted off me, and the next thing I knew, Marcus grabbed my arm and pulled me to my feet.

"We have to stop them before they destroy the whole town!" cried Marcus, his eyes on the ship as he ripped off his shirt and pants. I glimpsed a very fit, golden-brown body, rippling in muscles, followed by bright light. Marcus's face and body heaved, stretching his features and body strangely. Then I saw a flash of black fur accompanied by an awful, tearing sound and the breaking of bones.

A snarl came from the four-hundred-pound silverback gorilla next to me. He slammed his fists on the ground. "Ill distraac dem. Yoo desstroy de sshhip," he shouted. His vocabulary had improved tremendously in his beast form.

"Okay. But you better get your ass out of the way of that ship when I'm ready," I told him, pulling on the elements around me. Okay, Captain Hook had a mighty ship, but he had nothing on us. We had magic. I just hoped it would work better this time.

I blinked as the gorilla pushed off at incredible speed toward the ship. He climbed up the hull like it was something he did regularly, and there he was, on the deck, pounding the head of some pirate.

"God, he's hot."

"Who's hot?"

I turned and saw Ronin and Iris rushing over.

"Hey, is that Captain Jack Sparrow?" asked Ronin, staring up at the ship.

I wished. I loved me some Johnny Depp. "Nope. This here is Captain Hook."

The half-vampire put his hands on his hips, his eyes glancing from what was left of those two houses to the massive pirate ship. "Houston. We have a problem."

"The fairy tales aren't stopping. Are they?" asked Iris, waving her hand at some of the dust and debris falling around us.

"No." I cast my gaze toward the ship again and spotted Marcus swinging from one of the masts like it was a jungle gym built for him. Pirates swung their long, curved swords at him, trying to slice the wereape, but he was too fast for them. Too skilled. If I didn't know any better, I would have sworn he was having fun. Was that a grin on his gorilla face?

"What in the blazes is going on here!" Gilbert came running forward as fast as his grubby little legs would allow, staring at the ship like it was an alien craft that had just landed. That would have been just as plausible.

"We're being attacked by pirates," I told him.

Our town mayor stared at the two piles of rubbish that had once been family homes. "But the Pirate Carnival isn't for another two months. I'm dressing up as Captain Jack Sparrow."

No one wanted to see that.

"Did I miss something?" asked Gilbert.

"Yeah. This isn't your carnival. These are *real* pirates." Sort of. "And they're going to kick our asses if we don't stop them."

As if on cue, Captain Hook stood at the edge of the main deck, pointed his iron hook at the line of houses that hadn't been destroyed yet, and shouted, "Why, you blithering blockheads! Think you can hide Peter Pan from me!" He cut the air with his hooked arm and cried, "Fire!"

"Get down!" I yelled as I fell to my knees, Ronin and Iris doing the same, though Gilbert had stayed frozen in his spot.

A blast roared around us as another granite ball rocketed past, nearly clipping Gilbert and hitting what was once a cute, light-blue bungalow with white shutters. With an earsplitting blast, the house exploded like a piñata.

The paranormals in the streets screamed, grabbing their children, and running for their lives. That was smart. What wasn't smart was staying put and trying to figure out how to get out of this clusterfuck, which was what I was doing at the moment.

"Damn it," I said, straightening. "I think I'm going deaf."

Gilbert grabbed me by the shoulders. "You're a Merlin. *Do* something!"

I wiggled out of his grip. "I will. I'm thinking here. I need a plan. Can't just go running into battle without a plan." And this was a real battle.

"What's there to think about?" Gilbert's eyes were round with fear. He pointed to the ship. "Kill them."

"It's not that easy. My magic doesn't affect them like I wish it did."

The owl shifter stared at me, his eyes accusing. "What are you saying? You can't help us? You're useless."

Irritation flared. "I don't see you trying anything."

Gilbert's face flashed an ugly red as he tugged the sleeves of his jacket. "I'm the *mayor*, not the hired help," he added, staring at me like I was just a grunt.

I glowered at the smaller man. "If this was the land of the witless, you would be crowned king."

Gilbert's face twisted into a sour expression, but he didn't say anything.

I knew he would use whatever came next to deduct my pay. I needed the money. My job. Especially if I had a wedding coming up. "I'm going to stop this."

The sound of metal grinding echoed around us as the ship's bombards rotated slowly and aimed at new targets.

Gilbert whimpered. "I can't stay here." With a flash, a large, tawny owl took flight, leaving a trail of feathers in his wake.

I narrowed my eyes at the owl flying away. "Figures. Once a coward, always a coward." I turned my head toward the ship and found Captain Hook staring right at me. "Okay, weird."

He snarled and pointed his iron hook in my direction. "How's ya gettin' on me, old cock!" cried Captain Hook.

Ronin laughed. "Did he just call you a cock?"

"Possibly." My adrenaline soared as I saw the bombards being armed with new granite balls. I needed to think of something fast before he blew up the whole street and moved on to another part of town.

"Tessa!"

I whirled to find Dolores, Beverly, and Ruth running toward us, their eyes wide and focused on the massive ship.

"Oh, my," said Beverly, staring up at the vessel. She fanned herself. "Are those pirates?" She pushed up her breasts, staring at the grungy, dirty, sweaty pirates like this was one of her dreams come true. Probably was.

"Aye-aye, Captain, arrgh," grunted Ruth. She smiled at me and said, "I've always wanted to be a pirate."

"Not now, Ruth," snapped Dolores. Her face was set in determination as she observed the ship. "We'll have to combine our magic and hit it with everything we've got."

I didn't like how unconvinced she sounded. "You don't think that'll be enough. Do you?"

Dolores didn't look at me as she said, "Let's pray that it is. Ladies."

Together, my aunts formed a front line, facing the ship. They joined their hands, and their lips moved as they chanted, calling up the earth's magic.

I looked at my friends. "We need to evacuate the people in those houses." I pointed to the row of cute cottages painted in different colors. "Can you do that?"

Iris tapped her bag. "We're on it. Ronin, come." I watched as Iris and Ronin made for what was left of the cottages on Crystal Row.

I turned back around and joined my aunts at the front line with fear gnawing in my stomach. I couldn't see Marcus anymore. "Marcus is on the ship." Damnit. He needed to get off.

Dolores's head whipped my way. "Then you better hope he gets off right about now."

I cursed. "Marcus!" I shouted, but over the screams of the townspeople and the those coming from the ship, I doubted he would hear.

"Don't worry." Dolores's focus was on the ship. "We'll send a warning shot first. He'll get the message." My aunt lifted her free hand and cried, "Fuasurt!" A yellow-and-orange fireball blasted out of her hand.

The fireball hit the bow of the ship. Flames rose, spreading deeper into the front of the vessel as though it were being fed with gasoline.

"Fire on deck!" cried Captain Hook. But his eyes were on us. "Witches. Hear me! I'll burn all of ya."

Pirates scrambled toward the fire with buckets of sand. But they didn't need to. As soon as they tossed the first bucket, Dolores's fire went out. I could see some damage on the wood boards, blackened by the fire, but the flames had just died. Just like with the wolf, our magic wasn't enough. Either that, or we needed a boost.

Captain Hook threw back his head and laughed. "Aha! Yar devil's work does not work on my ship. Blast these devils!" he ordered, and to my horror, the bombards slowly turned in our direction.

I blinked. "Oh, crap."

"I was afraid of that," said my tall aunt. "That was Marcus's warning shot. He better get out now."

I couldn't see the wereape. I just hoped he'd gotten the message.

"Together now," ordered Dolores, anger etched across her brow. She pulled off her shoes, rooting her bare feet in the small patch of grass that bordered the street. Ruth and Beverly followed. I figured this was more of a direct way of tapping into the elements.

"Let's show this mangled idiot who he's dealing with." She grabbed my hand, and I flinched at the power. I felt like I'd just gotten an electric shock, but I didn't move away.

Thunder rumbled, and the air buzzed with raw energy, pulsing through the clouds as my aunts and I tapped into the power of the elements. My hair and clothes lifted around me in a gust of power. I could feel the energy in the soil, grass, trees, lakes, and oceans. All four elements were interacting.

My skin pricked as our combined magic flowed through us. We were badass witches. This captain didn't know who he was messing with.

Holding on to the magic, my eyes tracked the bombards as they pointed at us like metal fingers.

"Now!" shouted Dolores.

With a burst of strength, I pulled on the earth's magical elements. I jerked as a giant slip of that power ripped through me. Our collective power, our magic.

And we all let loose.

A burst of yellow, orange, and red light blasted from our chests and hit the ship's side.

I blinked into the bright light. Most of the vessel was hidden by it. Wood cracked as fifty-foot flames engulfed the ship. Screams that sounded like they were being burned reached us. I wasn't thrilled about that. I didn't like killing anyone, even evil pirates from another world.

But they'd attacked first.

Relief washed over me. This was going to work. We were going to blast this sucker back to wherever the hell it came from.

But then, the light subsided. And when the fire went out, the ship was still in the same position. The only evidence we'd hit it was the blackened scorch marks on the ship's side. Even the sails were intact.

"It didn't work," said Ruth.

"I have eyes," snipped Dolores.

"But why didn't it work?" Ruth looked at Dolores, expecting an answer.

However, whatever Dolores was going to answer was interrupted by the shouting of the captain. "*Fire!*"

I blinked as a granite ball came straight for us.

Oh, crap.

CHAPTER
12

What does a witch do when a cannonball is fired at her head?

She runs.

"Get cover!" I shouted as the four of us scrambled for our lives.

I leaped as far as my legs would allow — which was about four feet — and crashed to the ground face-first. The air moved, and I felt something zoom past me just as I flattened myself against the pavement.

Boom!

My body jerked as the ground vibrated under me, my ears whistling with the sound of a blast as though a grenade had just detonated next to my head. At that point, I realized I couldn't hear anything apart from the constant whistling.

I pushed myself up and looked around. The spot where I'd been standing moments ago was now a massive, ten-by-ten crater, like a meteor had just landed. If we hadn't moved when we did, we'd have been obliterated.

Holy shit.

I glanced over at the ship. Captain Hook and a handful of his pirates jumped up and down, victory written over their faces. Their lips moved, but I couldn't hear a thing. My eardrums were shot, but I didn't really care. What I cared about was Marcus.

Where the hell was he?

Something grabbed my arm, and I jerked, my leg up and ready to nail the bastard who had grabbed me, in the balls. But it wasn't a male.

"Dolores?" I said, though I couldn't even hear my own words. Maybe I'd thought it but hadn't actually said anything.

My aunt's lips moved, and I waved a hand at her. Then I pointed to my ears and shook my head.

Dolores nodded, her lips still moving, and then the next thing I knew, she'd pulled me with her into a jog. The witch was strong, and those were some serious manhands. But I'd never tell her.

She steered me away from the hole in the ground to the area behind a large maple tree. Beverly and Ruth looked up as we arrived.

They were both flapping away with their lips. I just shook my head.

Dolores was saying something to them. And then they all looked at me.

"What?" I think I said.

Ruth pulled something out of her bag and handed it to me. I took what looked like a small glass vial with a black liquid inside with a constituency of tar.

Ruth made a gesture of drinking with her hand to me.

Right. Bottoms up.

I winced. Yup. It tasted like tar. "That was nasty… hey… I can hear." I stared at my aunts, hearing the distant screams and shouts over my heart pounding.

Ruth smiled, grabbed the vial, and stuffed it in her pocket. "We all had to take a shot of *clear-ears*," she said, and I wondered why she was carrying that type of potion with her in the first place.

"Now what?" I leaned over and peered around the tree. The ship was still there, almost unscathed, but it had suffered some damage by the looks of the charred sides. "We can keep hitting it, but by the time we actually make a difference, they'll have blown up the whole town."

Dolores wiped some dirt from her long skirt. "Well, whatever we decide, let's make it quick. But we won't be able to sustain our powers forever. A hit like that takes the same amount of hit on us."

True. All magic required payment.

"Is that Marcus?" Beverly was pointing at the ship, her perfect face scrunched up like she was having trouble with her eyesight.

When I turned around, my heart got stuck somewhere in my throat.

My wereape fiancé stood on a wood plank. His thick gorilla arms were bound with chains, and iron cuffs were shackled to his ankles. Captain Hook stood behind him, a long, gleaming sword pointed at Marcus's back.

My pulse quickened, and I strained with the effort to keep my hands from shaking from the shots of adrenaline.

"Give me Peter, or the monkey dies!" shouted the captain, a manic glee sparkling in his eyes.

"He's a gorilla, you idiot," I called out.

A frown appeared on the captain as he worked out what I had just said. Then his dark eyes broadened as he cried, "Give me Peter, or the *gorilla* dies!"

"Not too clever, that one," I said.

"What'd you expect? He's just a two-dimensional character from a book," said Dolores.

"Right." I took a breath. "I have to save Marcus."

Before they could talk about it, I ran toward the ship. Toward the thing that could kill me and everyone around me with just one of those granite balls.

Hook saw me. And with an angry grimace, he lifted his sword high above him and then brought it down—on Marcus.

My magic might not do actual damage to these guys. But I just needed a little bit.

"Inflitus!"

A blast of kinetic force fired out of my hand—and hit Marcus.

The gorilla was thrown off the wood plank just as Hook's swipe went wide. He landed with a loud thud and a moan.

Okay, firing magic at your man is not the way to win points. I might have broken a few of his ribs, but at least he was off the damn ship.

I ran over to him. I couldn't help my smile as he looked up at me. "Sorry. But I had to do something."

"Uuu itt me." The gorilla's shoulders started to bounce, and a deep laugh sounded in his chest.

"I know. It was the only thing I could think of. Let's get you up." I grabbed his arm and pulled. Yeah. There was no way I could lift a four-hundred-pound beast. It was like trying to raise a car with my pinky finger.

I let go as he managed to get to his feet. "What kind of manacles are those?"

The gorilla shrugged. "Sstrong."

"Mmm. Probably can't rip them apart like you normally would." I looked over my shoulder. "Let's get you to Ruth. She might have something in her bag that'll melt this stuff." Hopefully.

"Ood ideeaa."

I looked him over. "You don't look like you were hurt that badly. Just a few cuts. What the hell were you doing in there?"

"Bying timmme," said the gorilla. At my frown, he added, "Sawbaatage."

"Ah." I stared at the ship. Okay. That explained why they hadn't fired on us again. Yet.

"Witch! I will behead ya!" cried a voice.

I glanced up and saw Captain Hook glaring at me. He punched the air with his iron hook like that was supposed to mean something.

So I gave him my version of what I believed that meant.

I grinned and gave him the finger.

"Come on."

I ran beside the gorilla, and even though his hands and feet were bound, he still managed to go way faster than me.

"That was very foolish of you, Marcus," scolded Dolores. Giving him one of her infamous scowls, kind of like a teacher who caught a student cheating. "You could have been killed. What the hell were you thinking?"

"He sabotaged their bombards," I answered for him. "Should buy us some time."

Dolores pursed her lips. "Well, then. Why didn't you start with that?"

I bit down my remark. This was not the time to start a fight with my Aunt Dolores, even though a part of me wanted to slap that dignified smirk right off her face.

"Don't move. I've got just the thing." Ruth pulled out what looked like a saltshaker and sprinkled orange dust on the gorilla's wrist cuffs. A soft pop was followed by the smell of burnt tires, and then the metal melted away like ice on a hot day.

I knew it.

When she was finished doing the same with his ankles, Ruth straightened, a smirk on her face. "You walked the plank," she told the gorilla excitedly, and maybe a little jealous it hadn't been her.

The gorilla grinned. "I knooo."

She gave him a covert thumbs-up.

I rolled my eyes. "Okay. So now what? How do we destroy a pirate ship from another world?"

Ruth shrugged. "Beats me."

I looked over the gorilla's shoulder to the ship. I could see Captain Hook flailing his arms at his pirates, red-faced. Probably pissed that he couldn't blow up another house. It gave me an idea. "We need a bomb."

"Did you say bomb?" asked Beverly.

"To blow up the ship."

"What makes you think it'll work?" Dolores looked from the ship back to me. "It might have no effect at all. Our magic barely scratched the surface of that vessel."

"You got a better idea?" My voice was rough, but I didn't care. "I don't know how much time we have left before—"

Another loud boom echoed in the air.

"Duwnne!" cried Marcus as his gorilla body tackled mine.

My breath escaped me as we hit the ground, just as the sound of something exploding blasted over our heads.

The next thing I knew, the gorilla had me back on my feet. The first thing I noticed was that the big old tree had a gaping hole right in its middle, as though a giant had punched his fist through it.

The gorilla turned to me, his face terrified. "Runnn!" he shrilled. The sound of cracks and wood splintering came from above me, growing louder.

I glanced up and saw half of the massive tree tipping down in our direction.

Swell.

"Iss waaay," said the gorilla, pulling up my aunts and ushering them away from the wreckage and the deadly tree that would flatten us all.

We ran. There was a loud crash behind us, which I knew was the tree. Blinking through the tree dust and debris, I saw Captain Hook clap his hands, well, his hand and hook. Bastard. He was enjoying the idea of killing us.

Captain Hook looked our way and shouted, "*Fire!*"

With his hand on my arm, Marcus pulled me along with him, my aunts following closely behind.

Another boom shook the air. And the house and car to our left blasted into a haze of dust and flames.

Together, we burst through the smoke of debris. I could barely see as thick clouds of dust filled the air. But the gorilla never faltered, dragging my ass along with him.

Another boom.

How many of those damn balls did that ship have? Were they everlasting?

A wave of dusty debris rolled over us again, clogging my lungs and making my eyes tear. Choking, I pushed myself into a staggering, ugly run. I never said running was my forte. My chest tightened as I heard my aunts struggling behind me.

This was insane. We couldn't keep running like this. Sooner or later, one of those granite balls would be for us. We had to do something. *I* had to do something.

I just didn't know what at the moment. It's hard to plan things when you're running for your life.

We strode over the rubble before us, kicking rock and rebar. Marcus swore, and I slid, panting to a halt. Two bodies lay in our way.

I recognized one of them—a young paranormal male who worked at Gilbert's grocery store. Next to him was the body of a female paranormal, older, but I didn't recognize her.

"Kome on," growled Marcus. And then we were off again.

Shoulder to shoulder, we rushed through the mix of concrete boulders and brick that was once someone's home. Debris was everywhere, piled in with bodies.

We spilled out into the next street over. The night was coming in fast, but I could still see the ship, aided by the cars and houses still ablaze. Horror struck me at the destroyed homes and the loss of lives.

I heard the scream of a young child. Following that, I saw a family struggling to climb over the rubble to get to safety. And then I saw the ship aiming its bombards toward the family.

And lost it.

Call it my witchy instincts or the overwhelming desire to protect the innocent, but I saw red, and I just knew what to do.

I moved away from the gorilla and my aunts, focusing solely on the ship and the assholes inside.

"Tessa? What are you doing?" Dolores stared at me.

"The only thing we haven't tried." We'd tried our elemental magic, and I'd even attempted my demon mojo, which hadn't had much effect on the ship or the beings from that other world.

"What's that?" asked Ruth, her eyes curious.

"Tessa?" Beverly looked at me, worried.

I glanced at them and then pulled my focus back on the ship. "Ley lines."

I didn't know if they guessed what I was going to do, but none of them spoke while I tapped into the ley lines, letting my anger and fury spill into me and feeding my magic with my raw emotions.

I'd never tried this before. Hell, it might not even work. But I was out of options.

Adrenaline pumping, I drew in my will and reached out to tap the ley line. A burst of sudden energy hit as it answered, and I could feel its vibrating energy beneath the pavement.

I took a breath, trying to steady my hammering heart and knowing this might not turn out as well as I hoped.

As I held the ley line, I heard my aunts shout my name and other remarks I couldn't make out over the roaring white noise in my ears. I felt Marcus the gorilla watching me, but I didn't look at him. I couldn't. I knew what I'd see on his face—fear and worry. If I saw that, I'd lose my focus. If I lost my focus now, I'd be ripped in half with what I was about to do.

And I kinda liked myself in one piece.

Here goes nothing.

And then I did something I'd never done before.

Holding on to the ley line, I reached out and tapped into *another* ley line.

Searing pain bit into my flesh, and I stumbled. Hissing, I nearly let go of the first ley line, but I didn't.

The only thing I let go of was a nervous fart.

Grinding my teeth and straining with my will, fueled by my deep hatred for that enemy ship, I held on to two ley lines. The sounds of battle blared in a combination of cries and shouts, making my ears ring with constant pressure.

Someone was shouting my name. Dolores? Marcus?

The power of the ley lines raged inside me, throbbing and radiating through my middle and limbs. I could clearly see the two ley lines, like gleaming, semitransparent, rushing rivers. I held on. One on each arm. One to the east and one to the west.

With my will, I bent the ley lines, pulling them, yanking them, until I had them exactly where I wanted—one on each side of that damn ship.

I could see the captain clearly, aided by the ley line's magic, no doubt, even the victorious grin on his face as he shouted orders to obliterate that young paranormal family.

Please, let this work.

And then I pulled the two ley lines *together*.

A deafening sound of wood and metal tearing hit the air. The ground shook as the great ship lifted, banking and tipping like it was caught in a great sea storm. Then it spun around like a top, faster and faster, light exploding from inside the ship as screams erupted from somewhere inside it. I'd lost sight of Captain Hook. I didn't care.

And then, the ship started to bend, folding on itself in the middle, like a sea god was folding it with his giant hands. Then with a final pop, the ship was no more.

"Oh, my cauldron. She did it!" clapped Ruth.

"Tessa? Are you all right?" Dolores was next to me, along with Marcus in his human form.

I opened my mouth to tell them how badass that was, how amazing it had felt to hold such power, but blackness clouded my vision. And then, the next thing I knew, everything around me disappeared.

CHAPTER
13

"You passed out. Marcus carried you back." Ruth handed me a mug. "Drink this. It'll give you some energy."

I leaned over in my seat at the kitchen table and grabbed the mug. "It's hot. How did you manage that?"

"I've got my cauldron going outside," she said. "Dolores won't let me start a fire in the potions room." She laughed.

I remember the cauldron going with a certain Beverly inside it. "Is this from the same cauldron that Beverly…"

Ruth snorted. "No. It's not from the *same* cauldron, silly. No one wants to drink *that* water."

"Good to know." Knowing that Ruth was an expert with her healing potions and tonics, I took a big gulp, surprised at the citrus taste. "Mmm, good. Thanks."

Ruth beamed. "You're welcome."

"Where's Marcus?" I looked past the dining room into the living area, expecting to see the chief.

"He went to help with the rescue effort," said Ruth. "People are trapped in some of those houses."

My gut clenched. "Oh my god." What a horrible thought.

"Not to mention all the dead," said Dolores, holding a candle. "Lots of work to be done. They'll have to remove all the wreckage. The bodies too."

"Will they rebuild the houses?" I knew how devastating it was to lose a home. We'd thought Davenport House was a goner when it had burned down to nothing but ash.

Dolores thought about it. "Probably. But not for a while."

"Where will they stay? Those who've lost their homes but survived?"

"The library for now," said Dolores. "Thankfully, only seven houses have been destroyed.

163

Thanks to you, Tessa. It could have been a lot worse."

I sighed. "Yeah. Still, it should never have happened."

Ruth came over and stood beside me, her hip hitting the table's edge. "How did you think of that?"

"Of what?"

"Using *two* ley lines. We all felt them. I didn't know you could do that," said my Aunt Ruth. I could tell by the excitement in her tone, she would have loved to experience that herself. My Aunt Ruth had first told me that I could ride the ley lines. She'd encouraged me to do it, and I would never forget that.

I shrugged. "I didn't either. It was just a thought." And I was glad it worked.

"You think they'll come back? The ship and the pirates?" asked Ruth after a moment.

"I don't know. I hope not." But the fact was, I had no idea if they were *dead* dead or if I'd just sent them back to wherever they came from. "At least we know we can use the ley lines."

"Not for a while, you won't." Dolores gave me a pointed look. "You passed out. But it could have been worse. Ley lines are enormously powerful and onerous. One is powerful enough. Two, two is like playing with something nuclear. If you try that again too soon... you'll kill yourself."

I didn't doubt her. "You're probably right." I'd learned from my past to listen to those who were wiser than me, especially Dolores.

Dolores raised her chin proudly. "I'm always right."

Beverly let out a groan. "The self-righteous sasquatch strikes again."

"What's the matter with you?" Dolores thrust the candle she was holding at her sister like it was a wand.

Beverly pulled out a chair, set a wine bottle with four glasses on the table, and sat. "I had to cancel with Lorenzo. Look at me. I'm a disaster. I smell like smoke and cauldron knows what else. No one wants to see Beverly Davenport in this state. I'm unpresentable."

"I'm sure he'll understand," said Dolores, lighting another candle and setting it on the counter. "We were trying to save our town."

"Doubt it." Beverly poured herself a generous amount of red wine. "He told me he was taking Maria instead. That won't go well."

Okay, I'll bite. "Why not?"

Beverly took a sip of her wine. "Her breasts are too small."

I had that coming. "Do you ever think of finding the right man and settling?"

Beverly snorted. "Me? Settling? Why would I keep this gorgeous body for only one man? The other available bachelors have a right to Beverly Davenport too."

Okaaaay.

"Relationships are hard enough," said Dolores, and I was wondering if she agreed with Beverly's polyamorous dating style.

Ruth leaned in and said, "The secret to a long-lasting relationship is to hate the same people."

I burst out laughing. "Ruth, I think you're right."

Dolores moved to the kitchen table and set out three large candles. She snapped her fingers, and flames sprouted from the wicks.

"You need to teach me how to do that sometime," I said, taking another large gulp of Ruth's healing tonic, already feeling much better.

Dolores looked at me. "A witch never reveals all her secrets."

I laughed, but I still wanted to learn that. I stared at the flickering flame from the candle nearest me. We were still in the dark, regarding House giving us back power. And I knew if I brought it up, it would only add more stress to an already stressed situation.

Speaking of stressful situations...

The sound of the front door opening and closing reached us. Shoes clapped along the wood floor, and then—

"Do you hate me so much that you won't even come to dinner?" My mother stormed into the kitchen, her face flushed and angry.

Oh, crap. I'd totally forgotten.

"Uh..."

My mother made a face. "*Uh...*" she repeated. "That's all you've got to say? I *slaved* in the kitchen all day to make you your favorite dish, and this is the thanks I get? You stayed here? With them?"

"I have a favorite dish?" That was news to me.

My mother looked on the verge of tears, angry tears. "How could you, Tessa? Your father was waiting for you. We both were."

Ah, hell.

"Relax, Amelia. Tessa was out saving our town," said Beverly. "Angry doesn't look good on beautiful people." She wiggled her fingers at her. "You're ruining your face."

My mother threw her glare at her sister. "Shut up. What do *you* know? You don't have children."

Uh-oh.

Beverly stilled, except for her eyes, which looked like mini hurricanes were spinning in them. She stood very slowly. "You don't want to start a fight with me, Amelia. Not after the night we just had."

Ruth made wide eyes and hurried over to the sink, pretending to be washing dishes with imaginary hot water.

"*Your* night?" my mother howled and fisted her hands. "What about me? What about all *I* had to go through and put up with to make this dinner happen."

167

Here we go.

I chucked the last of Ruth's healing tonic and then poured myself a glass of red wine. I guess that was the wrong move, judging by the angry eyes my mommy dearest swung my way.

"And you're drinking wine?" My mother looked like she was about to explode. "You and that ape never even bothered to show up. And now I find you here *drinking*."

I swallowed my wine. "Careful, Mother. I'm in one of those moods where I can't control myself."

My mother's eyes narrowed. "You're a selfish, spoiled little girl."

Now it was my turn to stand. "I'm many things, but selfish is not one of them."

"She's not a little girl either," muttered Ruth and then ducked when my mother glared her way.

"Amelia," said Dolores, approaching her younger sister. "We were out fighting. Protecting the town. Didn't you hear the commotion?"

My mother shook her head, looking livid. "No. I was working in the kitchen. Or haven't you been listening?"

"We were fighting pirates," said Ruth, beaming.

"Really?" My mother was shooting daggers at her sisters. "Liars! All of you. You think I'm a fool? I'm not." If she could do magic, which she couldn't, I had the feeling she would have cursed her sisters by the way she was staring at them, like they were cockroaches she wanted to squish.

"You do look like a fool right now," said Beverly, who was staring at her sister with the same amount of animosity.

My mother's lips shook like she was struggling to say something. "Fine." Her eyes met mine. "I can see how little I mean to you. Fine. But I thought you cared for your father. He'll be hurt when I tell him how little love you hold for your parents."

I wanted to slap her, but when I saw the tears, *actual* tears falling down her cheeks, all anger evaporated.

Damn it. "Mom." I walked over to her, unsure whether to hug her. We weren't the hugging type. I opted to grab her hand instead. "I forgot. I'm sorry, but it's the truth." I tried to make eye contact with her, but she refused to look at me. But she didn't let go of my hand. "And we were attacked. I can't explain it. But these people from another world breached ours and have crossed over. First, it was Little Red Riding Hood—"

"And the Big Bad Wolf," interrupted Ruth.

"And now it was Captain Hook and—"

"Pirates," added Ruth, with that strange smile returning. "Arrgh, arrgh."

"And his battleship. He was using his bombard balls to destroy the town. People have been killed. We were there, Marcus and I, trying to save our town. We honestly forgot."

My mother sniffed, still avoiding my eyes. "You did?"

From the corner of my eye, I saw Beverly sit back down and take a mouthful of her wine. "Yes. And we were on our way to your place. I swear it. You can ask Marcus." I stared at her. "You really didn't hear anything?" That would be surprising. She was only a few blocks from where the ship was catapulting granite balls at houses.

My mother shrugged, finally meeting my eyes. "I heard something. But I just turned the music louder so it wouldn't distract me. I had everything planned. I..." Her words got all choked up in her throat. Whatever she wanted to say wouldn't come out now.

My eyes burned at seeing her all emotional like this. I knew then how important this dinner was. And now I felt like a real asshole because I hadn't wanted to go. I'd dismissed it like it was nothing. If it hadn't been for Marcus pushing me to go, I wouldn't have gone and not even thought twice about it.

"I'm sorry."

"Everything's ruined now. Cold. Wasted."

I sighed. "What about Obiryn? Is he upset too?" I felt bad enough with my mother crying about this dinner. I didn't want to think about how upset he'd be too.

My mother wiped at her eyes. "He's fine. He said you'd probably have a good reason for not even calling."

Ouch. "My phone died." It was true. "I don't have power at the cottage." Also true. "And we were on the way, so we didn't need to call. Everything happened so fast. I'll make it up to you. I promise."

My mother just shrugged but said nothing. She was still holding on to my hand, and that sent all kinds of weird emotions through me. Yes. I had been selfish. I'd never thought about the work she put into this special dinner. She was far from perfect, my mother, but so was I.

And you only had one mother.

The front door slammed shut, and I jerked, blinking fast. I'd never heard it open.

I let go of my mother's hand. "Marcus?"

I heard feet running, multiple sets. The entryway was dark, lost in shadow. But then, a moment later, Iris and Ronin came dashing through the living room area to the dining room.

Fear slammed into me at the worry on my friends' faces. "Did something happen to Marcus? Is the ship back?" Cauldron, I hoped not. Dolores had said I couldn't use the ley lines again. Not if I wanted to live.

Iris shook her head. "No. The ship is not back. Marcus is fine."

"That he is," said Beverly, and she winked at me as she proceeded to sip on her wine.

"We saw what you did, by the way, to the ship," said Ronin. "And let me just say... that was awesome." He started to clap.

I smiled at the half-vampire. "Thanks. It's something new." I'd moved two ley lines at once. Damn. No one had ever said I could do it. And I'd never read it in any book or my little black book of ley lines. It just came to me.

And it had also caused me to black out.

I pulled my eyes back to Iris. "What's going on? Why do you look like something's happened?"

Iris looked over to Ronin before answering. "People have gone missing."

"Gone missing?" Dolores came to stand next to me. "What do you mean 'gone missing'?"

"I mean *gone* missing. Vanished," said the Dark witch.

"Maybe she means those who died," said Beverly from the table.

Iris shook her head. "No. I'm not talking about them. These people aren't dead. They're just gone. They disappeared without a trace."

"Does Marcus know?" I asked, knowing he'd want to be informed of this.

"Yeah. We just came from the battle site. That's where we were when they started to show up," said Ronin. "Townspeople came to Marcus for help. Looking for their loved ones."

"He asked if we could help him with this while he's trying to sort out all the damage," said Iris. Her face took on a sad cast. "They've pulled out more bodies."

"Oh, no," said Ruth. "How horrible."

"Of course, we're going to help," I said, glad I wasn't there retrieving those bodies. I wasn't fully recovered from my ordeal with the ley lines, but I had enough energy for this.

"You shouldn't be going anywhere, missy. You're only just recovering." Ruth came around and pointed a wooden spoon at me.

"I feel fine. I'm all better."

Ruth narrowed her eyes. "Hmm. I'll get you another dose, then. Better have more in you. Otherwise, you'll pass out again." The sound of her bare feet slapping the wood floor arose as she disappeared through the back door.

"What does she mean, 'pass out again'?" My mother was watching me. "Did something happen to you?"

I nodded. I didn't want to lie to her. "Yeah. I kind of bent two ley lines at the same time."

"And destroyed the pirate ship," added Ronin proudly.

My mother looked at me, confusion and then worry framing her pretty face. "What?"

"I'll explain later." I turned to look at Iris and Ronin. "How many people are we talking about?"

"Seven," answered Iris. "Seven, so far."

"Seven?" I was not expecting the number to be so high. "That's a lot of missing people. And they all disappeared recently?"

"Yup," said the half-vampire. "All in about three hours."

Dread made my stomach clench. I looked over at Dolores and Beverly, who mirrored my fear.

I turned to the sound of the back door banging shut. "Here. I've put it in a thermos so you can drink on the go." Ruth handed me a pink thermos with the words GET YOUR WITCH ON etched in black.

"Thanks, Ruth." I smiled and took a sip. The same citrus taste coated my tongue and throat as I swallowed. "Let's go."

"Now? But it's dark out." My mother crossed her arms over her chest. "How can you possibly find anything at this hour? You should wait for morning."

"We have to go now." I glanced at my mother's worried face. "Marcus is relying on us, on me. He can't be in two places at once. And he's busy." Besides, as a Merlin, this was part of the job. "The longer we don't do anything. The more people will disappear."

"How do you know this?" asked Dolores, a questioning brow on her face. "You know something we don't?"

I licked my lips. "Just a hunch. But this portal or doorway to that other world has something

174

to do with this." Yup. I didn't believe in coincidences. The two were connected. "We need to find that opening."

"We haven't finished our tracking spell," said Dolores. "Won't be finished until tomorrow. It needs a few more hours to brew. For the charms and ingredients to dissolve and take form."

"I know. I'll have to find it some other way. Find those who've gone missing, and we find that portal." It was just a theory, but I was going with it.

These missing townspeople were connected to the fairy tales that plagued our world. I just didn't know how.

But I was going to find out.

CHAPTER

14

Who goes looking for a portal to another world at night?

This witch.

But I wasn't alone. Iris and Ronin were with me. I couldn't ask for better, more loyal friends, and I felt extremely lucky. I couldn't do it alone. I needed help and was glad to have an experienced Dark witch and a half-vampire on this quest.

Hollow Cove, our quaint, quirky little town, was a dangerous place now with these fairy-tale stories coming true. The wolf and the little girl hadn't been that bad. But the pirate ship had been a devastation. Just to show how bad things were, before things got better, they always got worse. Speaking from experience, of course. We didn't know what lurked in our world, what leaked out from another realm. So, investigating during nighttime wasn't exactly the best move. But we couldn't wait. I couldn't wait.

Yes, we were on our way to investigate the missing persons, but first, I needed to check on my wereape.

Knowing him well, I knew he'd be taking this hard. The loss of life. The destruction of all those homes. He'd feel guilty. Blame himself for not protecting the people of his town. It was in his DNA. He couldn't help it. I didn't want him to tear himself up for something he had no control over.

I'd left my phone in Marcus's Jeep. I'd used Iris's to call him, but the chief wasn't picking up, which was why I'd asked Ronin for a detour to seek him out.

"I never thought I'd see imaginary characters come to life." Ronin slowed his BMW at the stop sign.

"Me neither," I answered, staring out the window from the back passenger seat. "But here we are."

Ronin pressed on the gas, and the car sped forward again. "Yeah. But are they the Disney version or Guillermo del Toro's?"

"Ooooo. *Love* him," said the Dark witch. She turned in her seat, and I saw a sparkle of admiration in her eye. "He's a genius."

I laughed. "I think he's awesome too," I told her, really meaning it. "But I'd rather not see *his* fairy tales here. Thank you very much." Yeah. His versions were more like lesser demons with only one mission—to eat as many mortals as possible. I was not up to fighting any of those. Not tonight.

"We're here." Ronin pulled his car next to the curb.

I leaned forward and stared through the car's windshield. "It's worse than I remember."

Tall portable lights were placed around the damage, giving us a complete view. It was like a bomb had been dropped on the street. Chunks of wood, brick, and rubble littered the roads. The devastation was horrible. I didn't know how anyone could survive if they were still inside when a granite ball hit.

I climbed out of the car. The scent of burnt wood prickled my nose. "He's over there," I said, pointing to the chief talking to a male paranormal I didn't know. I headed over, Ronin and Iris following behind me, though they were hanging back a bit and giving me space.

Marcus looked up as I approached. He tried to smile but couldn't, like his facial muscles were paralyzed.

"I'll get the first trucks in," said the male paranormal. He was taller than Marcus, but where the chief was dark and thick, he was lean and pale. His blond hair was tied back in a low ponytail. He glanced at me quickly before walking away.

"That's Lars," said Marcus. "He came from New Hampshire to help. Brought some friends too." He gestured to a group of equally tall males, hauling chunks of debris and tossing them in waiting trucks.

I sighed. "Good. We need all the help we can get."

Marcus glanced at Lars, who was talking to someone in one of those trucks. "We do."

"Here." I pulled out another thermos, this one a bright orange with the words THIS WITCH BITES, from my bag. "Ruth made this for you. It's one of her healing tonics. I promised I'd get it to you."

The chief took it. "Ruth loves to spoil me."

"She does."

Marcus put the thermos to his lips and took a mouthful. "How you feeling?" His gray eyes rolled over me like he was looking for wounds. "You passed out. I had to carry you back."

I smiled. "So I've been told. Thank you for that."

Marcus didn't smile back. "You shouldn't be here. You should be resting." His gaze darted behind me to Iris and Ronin, who had stopped and were talking to each other.

"You asked for my help, so here I am."

"I was asking for tomorrow. Not tonight."

Iris hadn't mentioned that. Probably lost in translation. "Has to be tonight."

"Why?" Marcus took another mouthful of Ruth's tonic.

"Because I believe those missing persons are connected to that portal or whatever is helping these fairy tales cross over. I *think* the longer it's open, the greater the chances of more people disappearing."

Marcus's jaw clenched as he thought over what I'd just said. "This is a disaster."

"I know. But the sooner we find this doorway, the sooner we can close it."

The chief frowned. "Have you figured out how to close it?"

I shook my head. "Not yet. But I'll figure something out."

Marcus reached out and clasped my hand. My heart skipped a beat at the roughness of his calloused hand. "Then I'm coming with you. This doorway... we don't know anything about it. It's dangerous. I don't want you taking any unnecessary risks."

"I won't."

The chief raised a brow that said it all. He knew me too well.

"I promise I won't do anything stupid." That was a stretch. "This is a search-and-discover mission. First, we need to figure out what happened to these people. What's the connection with the doorway? Anyway, you're needed here. I can do this. I've got Iris and Ronin with me."

The chief intertwined his fingers with mine. "Okay. But don't stay out all night."

My heart swelled at the emotion in his voice. "And you? I can see that you're beating yourself up because of this." I searched his face. He looked tired. "You know this isn't your fault."

The chief pulled his lips into a short smile. "I know what you're trying to say. But this is my town, Tessa. If I can't protect it, who will? This is what being the chief is all about. Protect the people who live here. I failed."

"You didn't fail."

"I should have figured out a way to stop the bombards firing."

"You tried."

Muscles pulled along his neck. "Not good enough."

I squeezed his hand and moved closer until my front rubbed against his hard chest. "This is a new evil that none of us were prepared for. You can't blame yourself."

"Sure I can."

I knew it was hopeless. Whatever wereape hormones were programmed in him to protect

were raging inside right now and weren't listening. "Fine." I leaned in and kissed him, pulling
on his bottom lip as I pulled away. For a moment, desire flashed in his eyes, but in a blink, it
was gone, replaced by that haunting, angry
look. "I'll keep you posted if we find anything.
My phone's in your Jeep."

Marcus gestured with his head to the right.
"It's still where I left it."

I looked over and spotted his burgundy Jeep.
"See you later." I stepped back, but the chief
drew me closer, crushing his lips on mine again.
The slip of his tongue over my bottom lip sent
heat pooling into my chest.

He pulled away and said, "Be careful."

"I will."

"Here." Marcus yanked out a piece of paper
from his jacket. "Here're the names and ad-
dresses of those who've gone missing in the last
few hours. And where they were last seen."

I took the list. "Thanks. I hope we find them."

"So do I," said the chief, but his voice lacked
conviction.

I let out a breath and made my way toward
the Jeep. Part of me wanted to stay with Marcus
and help, but we needed to find those missing
persons. And the portal was our best chance at
stopping this mess. I needed to find it.

I yanked open the door, grabbed my cell
phone, and headed back to where Iris and Ronin
were patiently waiting.

I waved my phone. "Needed this."

"Where to, boss?" Ronin had his hands jammed in the front pockets of his jeans.

Using my phone's flashlight, I glanced at the list of names. "Not far from here, actually. Just two blocks. Scarecrow Road. It's where Neil Stevens was last seen. We can walk." I figured we'd miss important stuff if we used Ronin's car to drive around town. We needed to be outside with our senses on alert.

"I know that guy," said Ronin as we walked up the street. "One of my renters."

"Really?" I folded the list and carefully stuffed it in my shoulder bag. "What can you tell us about him?"

The half-vampire shrugged as he walked. "Not much. All I know is that he looks like a loner. Gaming type. Doesn't go out a lot. Looks angry all the time."

"Sounds like Dolores," I muttered.

Iris laughed. "She does look angry a lot."

"Who reported him missing?" asked Ronin.

"His girlfriend," I answered, remembering seeing it written next to his name.

We walked for another few minutes. All the while I sent out my witchy senses all around me and kept an eye open for possible attacks from wolves or pirates. No doubt my friends were doing the same.

Little Red Riding Hood and the wolf appeared twice. Well, I'd only seen the girl the first

183

time, which meant they might appear again. Or even the pirate ship. When they died here, did that mean they died in their home world as well? Would the pirate ship come back? I had no idea.

"Here it is," I said, pointing to the small green bungalow with a red roof. "This is the girl-friend's house and the last place Neil was seen."

Again, I set out my witchy senses, but I didn't get any paranormal vibes. But would I? I hadn't felt much with the girl or the wolf. Would the portal be the same?

"I'm not feeling anything," I said, looking over at the row of houses lit softly in the street-lights.

"Me neither," answered Iris. "If there was a portal, I'm pretty sure we'd feel it. It's energy, right? Energy that we're not familiar with, but still energy. And all I feel is the power coming off the electrical poles."

"God, you're sexy when you speak geek," said Ronin, and I could see the blush on Iris's face.

I exhaled. "You're right. It's not here. But if he was heading home from her place, then" — I turned on the spot and pointed — "he'd be going in that direction."

"Good call. Let's go." Ronin strolled down the street, his long legs making me and Iris jog to catch up.

And after several minutes of fast walking, I was, one, sweating profusely, and two, shocked that we'd made our way back to the center of town. I hadn't sensed anything out of the ordinary the whole time we'd walked over. Neither did Iris. She would have said if she did.

"Maybe it's not in Hollow Cove," said Ronin. "Maybe it's on the outskirts of town."

"It's here." I wasn't a hundred percent sure, but something about the fact that these events had happened in this town had me betting the doorway was here somewhere.

I was going to find the damned thing.

"Maybe we should wait for your aunts' spell tomorrow." Iris gave me a weak smile. "It might be easier in daylight."

I shook my head. "I'm not going anywhere. Besides, I wouldn't be able to sleep." Not when Marcus was out there, hauling out dead bodies and having to contact next of kin. If he was out working, I was too. I yanked out the list. "Hang on. These other people…"

"Yeah," chorused Ronin and Iris.

I looked up. "They all went missing around here. Around the downtown area."

"Really?"

"This Abigail was last seen on Mystic Road. Danny's buddy reported that they last saw him on Warlock Drive. And these two, France and Tyson, both were last seen on Twilight Street."

"That's just up here," said Ronin.

185

I stared back at the list, looking over the last few names and the locations where the missing had been last seen. And then it hit me. "So, if you draw a perimeter around these locations, they all point to somewhere around Enchanted Drive and Shifter Lane."

"X marks the spot," said Iris.

"Let's go." Ronin jogged east toward Enchanted Drive with Iris rushing behind him.

Me? I was starting to feel a little bit woozy, light-headed and weak, like I was getting a cold or something. But I couldn't stop now.

Gathering my strength, I rushed after my friends. When we hit the intersection of Enchanted Drive and Shifter Lane, I felt it.

It wasn't much, at first, like a soft hum that slid over my skin. But something was *definitely* here.

I turned on the spot. "This way," I said, moving toward where I felt a stronger pull of energy.

I slipped between two commercial buildings, the Hairy Dragon Pub and Practical Magick, the bookstore I loved and wished I could spend more time in, all the while feeling that prick of energy growing stronger.

Squeezed at the end of a short alleyway was a crooked shed that had seen better days, with gray siding stained by moss and the elements. Its double doors were open.

And inside the shed was a large, golden disc.

The disc undulated in the air, and energy pulsated all around us, its glow pushing back the shadows and highlighting the alley in light.

You didn't have to be a rocket scientist to know what it was.

We'd found the portal.

CHAPTER
15

"**W**ell, cover me in jam and tie me to an anthill. Is that what I think it is?" Ronin bumped my shoulder as he came to stand next to me.

"That's the portal or whatever it's called."

The golden disc hummed with an incredible amount of magic and power. I'd never felt anything like it before, like the motherlode of power. It didn't feel ominous or like anything untoward. The energy radiating from it was warm and inviting, like an old friend offering you a nice cup of hot coffee.

Come to think of it, it looked like the exact opposite of a Rift, where the Netherworld's dark magic pulsed with cold and stinging energy with the promise of pain if you dared enter. Instead, this doorway glowed in golden hues and warmth with a friendly smile attached to it. Weird.

"Can't believe you found it," said Iris, giving me a proud smile. "And you didn't even need your aunts' help. Go you."

I snorted and glanced behind me, seeing no one. "Makes you wonder how long it's been here. Waiting like this." And the better question was, who the hell created it?

"So, now what?" Ronin eyed the pulsing disc curiously.

I searched the pavement, found a sizeable rock, and grabbed it. "Let's see first." I tossed the stone into the mouth of the portal. I wasn't sure what to expect. A burst of light? A deafening sound? Something. Just not... nothing.

The rock just slipped through with a slight ripple like I'd tossed it in a pond. "Well, that was underwhelming."

"What were you expecting?" asked Iris.

I shook my head. "No idea. Maybe a sound or something? I wanted to know if I could hear the other side."

"Well, it's not big enough to spit out a pirate ship." Ronin stepped closer to the portal, his face highlighted by the golden glow. "How do you explain that?"

"I can't," I answered. "I've no idea how that pirate ship got there. But it did. All I know for sure is that it has something to do with that." I took a careful step closer, the hum of whatever magic, tingling over my face and my body. Not unpleasantly. Just different. "But it's big enough for a little girl and a wolf to walk out." I stared at the disc. "And someone to walk in."

Iris sucked in a breath. "You think those missing people went through there? Like they just blindly walked in?"

"Yeah. I think so. Makes sense, right? This thing appears, and people start to disappear. I don't have proof. But I'm willing to bet they're on the other side of where this thing leads."

Ronin whistled. "Poor bastards."

"But why would anyone do that?" Iris was staring at the disc like she wanted to take a sample to stuff it inside Dana.

I shrugged. "I don't know." But something about this glowing disc had people trusting it enough to walk through. I might be wrong. Maybe those missing people had been killed in the pirate attack or even by the wolf, and we just hadn't found their bodies yet. But my witchy instincts told me they'd entered the doorway.

"Maybe they were kidnapped." Ronin moved closer to the portal. He looked over at us. "It's possible that something else came through here and picked a few people for their dinner."

"Gross." Iris made a face. "Don't say that."

"He's right." I hadn't thought of it, but being taken made more sense to me than just wandering mindlessly into a portal. "Maybe something came out and took them."

"Like Jack the Ripper," said Ronin.

"Jack the Ripper wasn't a fairy tale," said Iris. "He was real."

Ronin edged closer. "Boogieman, maybe?"

"Don't get too close," I warned, adrenaline gushing through my body. "We don't know what's on the other side of that thing."

"It's okay," said Ronin. "I'm not that close."

But it *wasn't* okay. I didn't want us to get too close. I didn't trust it. It might feel welcoming and warm, but that had all my warning flags rippling.

Yeah, we'd found it, but there was still a huge problem. "We shouldn't leave it open. It's too dangerous. We leave it like that, and we risk more people walking in or things walking out. We have to close it." The sooner we got it closed, the better off we'd be. I didn't want to risk another episode with the pirate ship or something worse.

But that was beyond my skill. I didn't have a power word or the magic to shut the door to another world. Not to mention I wasn't in tip-top shape.

"What about the people on the other side?" Iris's face was full of horror, as though I'd just said she couldn't do Dark magic anymore.

"I'm afraid it's too late for them." I didn't like saying it, but it was the truth. We couldn't go

get them, not when that meant traveling to another realm, and that's even if we survived.
What if we couldn't breathe the air? What if just
crossing over killed us? The truth was, those
people were most probably already dead.

"They're already dead," said Ronin, pulling
the words out of my head. "Tess is right. We
have to think about us. The people here, now."

Iris blinked fast. "Those poor people. What
will we tell their families?"

I shook my head. "I don't know. We'll think
of something once we get rid of this doorway.
But first, we need to figure out a way to destroy
it."

"Hang on." Iris rummaged through her bag.
When she pulled back her hand, she had a small
cloth bag the size of her hand.

"What's that?"

"Grave dirt, gnome testes, and dry demon
blood," answered the Dark witch. She stared at
what I assumed was my questionable frown
and added, "It's like a bomb. It can be used to
shut down Rifts."

Ronin whipped his head around at us. "Told
you she was hot. My girl makes gnome testes
into bombs. It doesn't get better than that."

I laughed. "You guys are nuts."

"And we *use* nuts." Ronin smirked.

I laughed harder.

"Better than being boring and ordinary." Iris
moved closer to the glowing disc, right up to

where Ronin stood. Her lips moved as she mumbled what I assumed was a spell. And then she tossed the bag into the portal's mouth.

"Duck!" screamed Iris as she knelt, holding on to her head.

"What? You didn't mention that part!" I howled back, dropping to the ground with my head touching the cold pavement while Ronin laughed.

After a few seconds, Iris lifted her head. "Nothing happened."

I looked at her. "Is that good or bad? I can't tell."

The Dark witch stood. "I'm… not sure. But if you wanted it closed or destroyed, it didn't work."

"Don't worry about it, baby," encouraged Ronin. "You can make more gnome gonad bombs when we get home."

I snorted and stood. "Well, that was all kinds of fun." I blinked into the portal, trying to get a glimpse of what was on the other side, but it was like thick, muddied glass. I saw traces of shapes, but that could be my eyes playing tricks on me. I was freaking tired.

"We need my aunts," I said finally. "This is beyond my skill and knowledge." And I wasn't embarrassed to admit it. We needed Dolores. My eyes moved along the shed. "First. Let's get those doors closed. It's best to keep it hidden until we figure something out."

"I got it." Before I could object, Ronin walked over to the shed and grabbed the door panel on the right. He started to shut the door and then just froze, his eyes fixed on the shimmering disc.

A slip of fear grabbed my throat. "Ronin? You all right?"

The half-vampire didn't answer. Instead, he just kept staring at the disc like he could see through it to the other side.

"Ronin?" called Iris, the worry in her tone doubling mine. "What's the matter with him?"

"I don't know."

"Ronin!" shouted Iris, her voice now filled with panic.

"Someone's calling me," said the half-vampire in a dreamlike tone. "I can hear her. She's calling my name. I think... I think I know her... and she knows me."

"What?" My heart slammed in my chest. I eyed the golden disc warily and took a careful step forward. Something wasn't right. "Ronin. Step away from there. Ronin!"

Ronin leaned forward until his face was only a foot away from the shimmering portal. "It's my mother. My mother's calling me."

Oh shit. "That can't be. Your mother is dead, remember? The dead don't talk back." Unless they're ghosts or revenants, but that's not what was happening here. What the hell *was* happening?

"I have to go. She's calling me." Ronin let go of the door and lifted his hands in an embrace, seemingly in a trance or something. I held my breath as he trailed his fingers over the edges of the disc.

"Ronin! No!" Iris sprinted forward.

"Iris. Wait!"

Too late. By the time I'd opened my mouth and uttered the words, she was already next to him. She wrapped her hand around his arm. "Ronin. Come with me… come with…" Her attention snapped to the glowing disc. And then, just like Ronin, her face went slack, her eyes focused on the gleaming portal like it was the most wonderful thing in the world.

"It's so beautiful," she said, her tone matching her dreamlike expression. "I've never seen anything so wonderful. It wants me to go. I have to go. It's just so beautiful."

Ah, hell. It was as though they were both high as kites.

"My mother's there," said Ronin. "Can you see her?"

"Let's go," said Iris, tugging Ronin's arm. "It's so beautiful. I want to go."

"Guys? Snap out of it. It's tricking you." That's right. The pretty glowing disc was as evil as a Rift, possibly worse.

I watched in utter horror as my two best friends moved toward the light, like the end of the tunnel you supposedly see right before you die.

But I wasn't about to let them cross over.

I rushed forward, trying to stay farther back, but too late. When I skidded to a stop, I was nearly as close as they were. I braced myself for the voices or the pull that Ronin and Iris were experiencing, but I didn't hear or sense anything from the portal except its continual thrumming of power. No time to dwell on that.

I tapped into the elements around me and shouted, "Trahendum!"

A blast of kinetic energy fired out of my hands. It wrapped around both Iris and Ronin like an invisible rope. And then, with all the will and strength I had left, I pulled.

Iris and Ronin sailed back and landed a good ten feet from the shed. Better than nothing.

Dizzy, I exhaled, letting go of my magic. My head throbbed, a giant migraine on the way. I shouldn't be doing any kind of magic. But I didn't have time to think about the repercussions.

"I'm coming, Mom," said Ronin as he whirled around and reached out to the portal, his arms up like a walking zombie.

Uh-oh.

"Beautiful," said Iris as she got to her feet and followed him.

"Seriously?" Fear and anger soared. I would not lose my friends. Hell no.

I raised my hands, rammed my will through the last of my magic, and shouted, "Trahendum!" This time I didn't let go. This time, I poured it all out.

The kinetic energy, once again, wrapped around my friends, and with a combination of adrenaline and whatever strength I had left, I pulled their asses away, hard.

Iris and Ronin soared in the air and hit the exterior wall of the bookstore.

Oops. That was a little harder than I'd expected, but at least they were away from the shed, a good thirty feet.

"Ow." Ronin rubbed his head. "What the hell just happened?"

I let go of the hold I had on my magic. "I just saved your asses. That's what happened."

Iris pushed herself to a sitting position on the alley floor. "Oh my god. Did we almost... Did I?" She wrapped her arms around herself. Her eyes were round as they fixed on me. "I almost walked through there."

Ronin cursed. "Me too." He looked away, slightly embarrassed at his loss of control. He raked his fingers through his hair. With his jaw clenched tightly, he cleared his throat. "Man. That was intense."

Ronin's eyes were red, and I felt a stab in my heart. Whatever he heard or saw did a real number on him. After what he'd gone through years ago, his parents were a touchy subject.

197

"You're okay," I told them, trying not to think about what would have happened to my friends if they'd crossed over. I would have never seen them again, that's what.

"Thanks to you." Iris frowned at the portal. "I can understand how those others crossed over. The closer I got… it was like…"

"The easier it had you in its web," I said. I'd seen it with my own eyes. That thing had an unnaturally strong pull on anyone near it. "It's dangerous. Anyone with a curious mind could get sucked into it." And I wasn't about to leave it like that for the next wandering fool.

I glared at the shed and cried, "Ventum!"

A gust of wind fired out of my hand. It hit the shed's doors and blew them closed. The rattle echoed as the doors slammed shut. I couldn't see a lock or anything to keep the doors from opening again. It would have to do for now.

"It's not permanent," I said, panting. I had to struggle to keep myself up and not flat on my ass. I was glad to have the portal covered. "But it should hold until we talk to my aunts and figure out how to shut it for good. Or at least, keep people out."

Because that's exactly what I was going to do.

I was going to destroy this portal if it was the last thing I did.

But now, after downing all of Ruth's tonic drinks, I needed to pee.

CHAPTER
16

Dolores waved a dismissive hand at me. "Stop babbling and spit it out. You're not making any sense."

I smiled. "Well, you know my babbling capabilities are infinite."

"Don't be a smart-ass," snapped Dolores.

We'd arrived at Davenport House only a few moments ago and thankfully found Dolores and Beverly gathered around a candlelit table, working out what I could only guess were incantations for that tracking spell, which we didn't need anymore. Ruth was in the kitchen and looked like she was trying to magic the faucet to work.

"We found the portal, the gateway to that other world," I said, slowly this time. I recapped how I found it and what happened *after* we found it.

The three sisters shared a sidelong glance, not saying anything for about thirty seconds. That doesn't sound like a long time, but it is when you're freaking out because you've almost lost your best friends.

I looked over at Iris and Ronin, who watched my aunts like they were expecting them to have all the answers. Hell, I did too.

"Guess we won't need this anymore." Dolores closed the tome she'd been copying from. She folded a piece of paper with writings and symbols, no doubt the spell they'd been working on.

Beverly grabbed a candle, stood, and held it in front of Ronin's face. "Are you still hearing voices? Have an uncontrollable need to walk into that death trap?"

Ronin leaned back in his chair. "Uh… that's a *no*."

Next, Beverly did the same to Iris. "What about you? Does the light want you back? Do you hear it calling?"

I laughed. "It's pretty safe to assume they're okay. I think you have to be near it to feel its pull." I'd felt a pull, but nothing like my friends.

Beverly shrugged. "Fine." She pulled out her chair and sat, setting her candle on the tabletop.

"But don't blame me if they change their minds later. You never know what lingering effects that portal might have on them."

Good point. I looked over at Ruth. This was one of those times when she'd say something along the lines of, *I knew so and so who lost their minds because of something or other.* But Ruth was strangely quiet by the kitchen sink. I wondered why that was.

"We feel fine," said Iris. "Maybe just a little bit shocked and embarrassed, but I'm not hearing any voices, if that makes you feel better."

"It does," said Dolores. "Hearing voices is *never* a good thing."

I could attest to that. Hearing the voice of the queen of hell in my head had been a pretty traumatic experience for me. One I didn't wish to repeat.

"Those missing people. They went through." I was positive now, especially after seeing Iris's and Ronin's reactions to the portal.

"This is very bad, Tessa," said Dolores. The shadows from the candlelight created deep crevices around her wrinkles, making her look over one hundred years old.

"You mean worse than almost losing your best friends, bad?"

Dolores stood slowly and hunched over the table. Her hands splayed out. "From what I know of portals and doorways to other realms, what I've read over the years, and the wisdom that has been laid upon me from generations before…"

I leaned forward in my seat. "Which is?"

My aunt's dark eyes pierced mine, and I had to strain to keep from looking away. "Doorways to other realms are treacherous."

"We know," grumbled Ronin, still in disarray at what had happened. The entire walk back to Davenport House, he'd remained silent.

Dolores looked his way before continuing. "The fact is, the longer they stay open, the bigger the damage to our world, and the harder they are to close."

"In what way, damage?"

"Think of a Rift." Dolores spoke to me, her voice deep and filled with unease. "If Rifts were allowed to exist, if they didn't disappear when the Veil repaired itself, well, what do you think would happen? We would all die. Our world would die, replaced by things that live in the Netherworld."

Except for my father. He was a cool demon. "And you think this is what would happen to our world if we don't destroy it soon?"

She nodded. "I'm afraid so, yes. It's only logical. With a portal the size of a small shed, it enabled a giant ship to appear in our world in only a matter of hours. Maybe just under one day. Imagine what would happen after three days. A week. A month? Our world as we know it would cease to exist."

I stifled a shiver. "I get the picture." I glanced at Dolores. She was still frowning the way she did when she still had lots to say. "And? What else?"

"This… this pull you mention concerns me," she said finally.

"In what way?"

Beverly snorted. "Because she's never heard of it, that's why."

Dolores sent a glare in her sister's direction. "It's more than that."

My heart was hammering now. I didn't like this. "Keep going, Dolores. What is it?"

"A portal that allures one into its depths, well, that is something very clever but equally frightening." She leaned back and waited until she had all our attention. "And if a Dark witch and a vampire couldn't resist this… this pull… that indeed is very vexing."

I couldn't agree with her more. "So, let's get rid of it and be done. I don't want anyone else to disappear and die."

"I'm not sure they're dead."

We all stared at Dolores.

"They may be still alive," she answered.

I leaned forward, trying to see her face better in the light of the candle. "You sure about that?"

"No. I'm not sure of anything that has to do with that portal. But if those beings traveled to our world and survived, it's plausible to think the other world might support the paranormals that crossed over."

"I'm not going in there for a rescue mission," said Ronin. "You can count me out." His face held traces of pain and guilt. My friend was battling with his emotions. I felt sorry for him.

Dolores shook her head. "I don't want anyone going in there. That would be unbelievably foolish. But we must close this doorway."

I grabbed my phone. I only had one bar of battery life left. "I need to tell Marcus. He has to know about the portal." I moved my fingers across the screen as I texted him.

Me: *Found the portal. It's in the shed behind Hairy Dragon Pub and Practical Magick. It's dangerous. It pulls you in. Need to set up a perimeter around it. Keep people out. Call you later.*

I waited and saw the three dots appear, knowing Marcus was texting back.

Marcus: *Okay. Going to check it out.*

I set my phone on the table. "So, how do we close it? Iris tried one of her... bombs, but nothing happened."

"It would have worked if it had been a Rift," said the Dark witch.

Dolores sighed, her brows pinched together, a look she got when her brain worked overtime. "We'll need some time to think about it. This is something we've never faced before. But some spells can affect the Veil, which is what is happening now. It is more difficult to close than to create a hole. So, we might find something following that direction." She flicked her gaze at her sisters. "Looks like we won't be getting any sleep tonight."

"That was the plan with Lorenzo." Beverly let out an exaggerated sigh. "All that mind-blowing sex I had planned for tonight was going to keep him *up* till morning." She caught me looking and winked.

I tried not to visualize that in my mind's eye. Too late.

"I'll need the cauldron, Ruth." Dolores looked over toward the kitchen. "Ruth?"

Ruth jerked at the sound of her name. And that's when I saw it—no, *her*.

A tiny female human, the size of my hand, sat on the edge of the counter next to Ruth. Fair-skinned, she wore a green, strapless dress that hit just above her knee. On her feet, she wore green flats with white puffballs on her toes. Transparent, butterfly-like wings sprouted from her back. Her shoulder-length blonde hair was worn in a bun, revealing her pointy elf-like ears.

Her baby-blue eyes met mine for a second. She looked oddly familiar.

I blinked. "Is that... Tinker Bell?"

"What?" Dolores looked over at Ruth, her eyes wide in disbelief. "What is she talking about?"

Beverly giggled. "I have the most adorable Tinker Bell outfit. It's really just me and my glorious naked body with these sparkling wings."

Ruth expertly hid the little fairy with her body and smoothed out her expression to the best innocent face I'd ever seen on her. Hell, she deserved an Oscar.

"Huh? I don't know what you mean," said Ruth, cleverly avoiding all eye contact.

She'd lost her mind. I rushed forward and looked behind Ruth. Sure enough, a tiny little human with wings sat on the counter's edge. "Oh my god. Did you kidnap her?"

Son of a nutcracker! My aunt stole Tinker Bell.

"You kidnapped Tinker Bell?" Dolores pressed her hands against her head as though it might explode. "Cauldron help us. This is the craziest thing you've ever done. What's the matter with you?"

Ronin whistled. "That is one hot fairy. Just saying."

Tinker Bell's face flushed a bright pink. Okay. So she understood us.

Iris had expertly moved next to me, watching the tiny fairy with interest, and I knew she wanted to snip a part of her wing to stash in Dana.

Tinker Bell flew onto Ruth's shoulder, leaving a trail of golden fairy dust behind her. She smiled at me, embarrassed, and then hid in Ruth's white hair.

"You can't kidnap a fairy," said Ruth, like we were the idiots. "You'd be cursed by the foulest curses. Might even die. Fairies have powerful magic. They don't let you take them. They go where they want."

A growl and a hiss had me turn back to the counter. Hildo was poised with his head and shoulders down and his hind legs up, ready to pounce.

Ruth shot him a glare. "Bad Hildo. She's not a toy. You can't eat her."

Hildo's ears flattened, his yellow eyes tracking the fairy. "Wanna bet?"

Well, that wasn't good. I had no idea if cat familiars ate tiny fairies, but I didn't want to get into that right now.

"How did she get here, Ruth?" demanded Dolores, staring at her sister as though she wasn't sure who she was looking at.

Ruth's face lit up. "She followed me home."

Dolores smacked her palm against her forehead. "She's lost her damn mind."

"That's nothing new," said Beverly, trying to catch a glimpse of the fairy.

Ruth made a pleading face. "Oh, can't we keep her? She's just so cute. And she hates it over there. She told me she wants to stay with me. She wants to stay here with us."

I tried to see Tinker Bell's face, but she kept it hidden. "She told you that?"

"Yes," said Ruth. "So, we can keep her?"

A few pieces sliced off my heart at what I saw on my aunt's face. She truly loved all creatures, big and small. And that included tiny fairies from imaginary worlds.

"She's not a kitten from the shelter, Ruth," said Dolores. "She's a fairy. And she's not from here. She needs to go."

Ruth's face flushed an angry red. "So what you're saying is that if you're not from here, you don't belong?"

Dolores let out a puff of exasperated air. "No. That's not what I mean." She licked her lips and tried again. "We don't know what the effects of her being in our world will be. She could just as easily live happily as she could die."

"She's fine. And she's staying here." Ruth turned away, grabbed her piece of leftover cheesecake in the shape of a male appendage, from the party, walked to the dining table, and sat.

Damn. This was not going to be easy.

I followed Ruth to the table and pulled out the chair next to her. "Can I talk to her?"

Ruth tipped her head, and I could see Tinker Bell whispering something in her ear. Then Ruth looked at me and said, "She says yes. She'll talk to you."

With a flutter of wings, the glowing, golden fairy flew from Ruth's shoulder and landed on the table.

I had a moment of stunned silence. "Hi. I'm Tessa. I understand that you want to stay with us here in this world?"

Tinker Bell opened her mouth. A sound, like a light jingling noise reminiscent of a bell, came spewing out.

"What?" I leaned forward. "What did you say?"

Tinker Bell blew out a frustrated breath. She opened her mouth again, and the same bell-like sound came spilling out.

"I think she's trying to say something," I said. "I don't think she can talk."

Tinker Bell glared at me. Then her entire body turned fiery red. Huh. That was interesting.

"She said, yes, she wants to stay," said Ruth.

"You can understand her?" asked Dolores, who'd joined us at the table.

Of course, if anyone could understand a fairy from a fairy tale, it would be Ruth. And I'm guessing why she was feeling the need to protect and keep her.

Ruth nodded. "Yes, of course I can understand her, silly."

"Ruth." Dolores folded her hands on the table. "This is not like the time you started that carpenter-ant farm under the porch. We can't just burn her. This is a tiny human. Not to mention that her being here might reap repercussions."

Ruth shrugged. "Like what?"

"Well, for one. Won't her own people get worried? They might come looking for her."

"Then we'll just have to wait and see." Ruth stood. "Come on, Tinker Bell. Let's go to my potions room. I have lots of stuff to show you." And with that, Ruth left the kitchen and headed through the door, a tiny golden fairy trailing after her.

"I'll be needing that cauldron, Ruth," Dolores called. She stared after her sister, shaking her head. "What a mess. She'll have to get rid of that fairy eventually. She doesn't belong here with us."

My head started to pound at that moment. "Well, if you don't need me for a little while, I think I'll go have a nap."

"Me too." Iris moved over and joined Ronin. "I think we all need a bit of a nap. I'll stay with Ronin tonight. You know..." She looked around the kitchen and dining room at the candles. "Since there's no power and all."

I waved at my friend. "I'll see you guys later." I watched as Ronin and Iris made their way down the hall and out the front door. "Come get me when you have something," I told my aunts.

"We will," answered Beverly. "Go have a rest before you pass out again."

She wasn't wrong. That's exactly how I felt.

Without another word, I stepped out the kitchen's back door and shambled my way to Davenport Cottage. I was too exhausted to put up a fight with House. I just had enough energy to climb into my bed.

I grabbed my phone and texted Marcus one last time before the battery went out. Knowing Marcus, he probably went straight to the portal's location. I'd been terrified, seeing my friends lose their minds like that so quickly under the portal's spell. The fear that something might happen to him plagued my mind.

Me: *Be caref—*

And then my phone went out.

CHAPTER
17

Pressure pushed my face. Pricks, like needles, assaulted my forehead, cheeks, and nose. Was I dreaming? Nope. Pain didn't exist in dreams. Or so I thought.

I snapped my eyes open as a black, furry body walked over my visage, *literally*, taking his sweet time.

"Hildo, seriously!" I pushed the cat off my head and pulled myself to sit. "You do know we mortals consider walking on our faces as rude?" What was up with cats walking on their humans' faces while they slept? And why did they think it was acceptable behavior?

The cat blinked. "You were snoring."

"So, you thought walking on my face with your pointy nails was a good way to stop that?" Did I snore? The thought of me snoring next to Marcus was mortifying. I hoped the cat was lying. What if I *was* a snorer? Or worse, a *drooler*.

I looked the cat over. His silky black fur was ruffled and sticking out, the result of natural survival instincts designed specifically to ensure our kitty cats looked larger to whatever was threatening them.

"What's your problem? You look a little rattled."

The cat sat on my thighs. His tail curled around his paws. "I hate her."

I rubbed the sleep from my eyes. "Who? Ruth?"

Hildo's yellow eyes sparkled with what I could only describe as deep hatred. "No, not Ruth. Ruth is wonderful. Ruth is the epitome of good. I couldn't ask for a better witch." He lowered his head, his eyes narrowed. "I'm talking about the rat with the wings I'm going to feast on."

Tinker Bell. "Come on. It can't be all that bad. What could she possibly do to you? She's just a tiny fairy."

The cat's ears rotated back behind his head. "*That* she is *not*. I don't trust her. She whispers things to Ruth. Evil, dangerous plots to end my life. I know it."

"Guess you can't understand her either." I reached out and rubbed under the cat's chin, enjoying the purring that sounded the second I did. I smiled at the cat familiar. "Aren't familiars immortal?"

"It needs to die," hissed Hildo, ignoring my question.

I laughed. I couldn't help it. He was just so cute, all angry and bothered. "Hildo, are you jealous?"

"No."

He'd said it too quickly. "You are. You're totally jealous."

"I'm not jealous of a flying rat."

"Yeah, you are." The poor cat felt like Ruth had replaced him. "But you shouldn't be. Ruth loves you. The two of you belong together."

The cat moved away from me and went to sit at the edge of my bed, his back to me. "Doesn't look like it."

"Why do you say that?" Even if you had sharp teeth and claws, and you hissed and spat, Ruth loved you. It didn't matter if you came from another world.

Hildo looked over his shoulder and said, "She forgot to feed me this morning."

Uh-oh. Okay, that was bad. "I'm sure it's an honest mistake. I'll make you something. Wait—morning? Oh, crap. What time is it?" Instinctively, I grabbed my phone to check the digital clock, but I was met with a black screen. Right. My phone was dead.

I looked at the window, seeing how bright it was. It was indeed morning.

"It's nearly one in the afternoon," meowed the cat. "And I haven't had my breakfast. So there you have it. I'm finished. Replaced by a buzzing insect."

"Thought you said rat with wings."

The cat shrugged. "Same difference."

"Come on. I'll get you something to eat." I yanked the covers off my legs and hurried to the bathroom. I had expected to see the toilet soiled with my business from yesterday, but the bowl was sparkling clean as though it had just been scrubbed with bleach. I cocked a brow. "Looks like you don't want to be dirty, huh?" I told House, not that I expected him to answer.

Like yesterday, I brushed my teeth with whatever water I could find, pulled on some clean clothes, and headed for the big house with Hildo running ahead of me.

He waited at the back door for me, and I wondered how he opened the door to Davenport Cottage. But familiars were magical beings. He probably used his magic. Or not. Cats were clever creatures. I'd known some who could open doors. Seemed even regular cats possessed some kind of magic.

I caught sight of Ruth hovering over a large cauldron the size of a pasta pot bubbling over a fire next to the garden shed.

She looked up as I approached. "How are you feeling today? Did you sleep okay?"

"Better. I slept well." Until Hildo clawed my face. Guess a few hours of sleep rejuvenated my body, probably with the help of my aunt's healing tonics.

Tinker Bell sat on Ruth's left shoulder, her legs hanging over the larger witch's clavicles. The tiny fairy smiled at me and waved. I waved back. She was *really* cute, and I totally understood why Ruth loved her. But Ruth also loved spiders and worms and all sorts of creepy crawlers. I wanted to ask the fairy how she felt, not knowing how her body reacted to our world, but I wouldn't understand her. I was also still half-asleep and didn't want to get into the whole translating thing with Ruth.

My stomach growled, and I realized I was just as hungry as Hildo was. The cat waited patiently for me at the back door, his eyes on the fairy. Probably contemplating ways to kill her.

I leaned over the boiling substance in the cauldron. A lime-green liquid bubbled, and acrid air wafted up, teasing my nostrils.

I pulled back, grimacing. "Smells like bum and feet."

Ruth laughed, and a sound like wind chimes erupted from Tinker Bell. Was she laughing too? Yes, she was.

"It does. Doesn't it?" Ruth gave her mix a whirl with her pink spatula. "But that's when you know it's working." Ruth's white hair was piled on top of her head in a messy bun stabbed by a kitchen fork.

"Is that part of the spell to close the portal?" We needed to shut it down like yesterday. I felt a bit guilty that I hadn't stayed up to help my aunts, but my body was in no shape to do anything but sleep.

"Yes," answered my aunt as she sprinkled what looked like blue crystals into the mix. "Iris gave us the idea last night." She beamed, an excited gleam in her eye as she said, "We're going to *blow* that sucker up!" She threw her hand with the spatula in the air, sending green globs of goo splattering over her front and hitting my face. It smelled much worse up close and personal. She didn't seem to notice.

Tinker Bell clapped. Yeah, these two were perfect for each other.

I wiped the side of my face and flicked the goop to the floor. "Sounds like fun."

"Oh, you just wait. It will be." Ruth jabbed the spatula back into her potion. "No more pirates. It'll be closed for good."

I looked at Tinker Bell, trying to guess her reaction to having that doorway closed forever.

217

She'd never be able to return to her homeland, wherever that may be. But she just kept smiling and staring at the bubbling potion.

"What about Tinker Bell?" I couldn't help myself.

"What about her?" Ruth kept stirring, her eyes on her potion. But the fairy's eyes snapped to mine.

I knew she could understand me. "Maybe you should let her go home before you... you know... blast the doorway?"

Ruth didn't look at me as she said, "She wants to stay here."

"You sure?"

"Of course I'm sure." Ruth gave a mock laugh, still avoiding my eyes.

I looked at the fairy, and she gave me a shrug. Somehow, that didn't convince me. But the fairy wasn't a hostage, and she could leave whenever she wanted. So, why did she stay with Ruth?

"Do you know if any more... imaginary characters came through since last night?" I asked my aunt.

Finally, Ruth's blue eyes met mine. "Not that I know of. I think you did good by shutting those doors." She dropped some more crystals into her mix. "I heard Marcus was there all night. At the portal. Keeping an eye on things. Such a good, young wereape. Very much like his father. Did you ever meet him?"

I shook my head. "Not yet." Hopefully I would before the wedding. The *wedding*. Damn. We still hadn't thought of a date.

My insides roiled at the mention of Marcus. I hadn't heard from him since his text last night. And with my phone dead and my aunts' landline not working, thanks to House, I had no way to reach him. Obviously, he didn't come home last night. He was either still guarding the portal or had slept at the office. I was pretty sure he was still guarding the portal. I'd have to find him and talk to him in person.

A loud meow interrupted my thoughts. I looked over at Hildo, still waiting for me by the door, but now he was standing up, his tail flicking back and forth in irritation.

"I think I'll feed Hildo before he gives himself an aneurism."

Ruth looked up at me. "Oh, would you? I've been so busy. I haven't stopped since last night." She lowered her voice and added with a tiny smile, "I think he's angry with me. Because of Tinky."

"Tinky?" Okay, I'd admit, that was a cute name for the fairy. "I'm sure he'll get over it." Not a chance. "Well, I'll see if Dolores needs help. See you later, Ruth. Tinky."

Tinker Bell waved at me again, and it was hard not to like that little fairy. But once we shut down the portal, would she stay? I had a strong feeling Ruth would be heartbroken if the fairy went back to her home world.

"Took you long enough," growled the cat as I climbed up the steps to the back door. "Didn't you see me here? Are cats invisible?"

"The annoying ones." I opened my mouth to tell him that I knew he could open the door himself, but I resisted the urge. The cat was going through something. I didn't want to make it worse.

Yanking the back door open, I let Hildo in and walked into the kitchen to find Dolores sitting in the same chair I had seen her in last night. She was bent over some book, a pen in one hand as she scribbled away with her eyes on the book, not the pen.

Wow. That took some serious talent. Wonder if she could teach me that.

"How's the spell going? Ruth says it's supposed to detonate or something?" I moved over to the table. Books and scrolls that weren't there yesterday littered the table, some piled on top of one another in tiny book towers.

Dolores didn't bother to look up. Her expression was laced with a tired irritation. "Going. Still lots to do. We need to create a discharge large enough to weaken the portal and then seal the opening at the same time."

That sounded like a lot of work. Was that sweat on her brow? "Is this like the time we sealed the vortex? When we combined our powers? Is that what we're doing?" It was that time when the Sisters of the Circle had tricked me into letting Lilith out by creating a vortex. Not that I thought keeping Lilith in a prison was a good thing. I just didn't like being used and lied to. And those witches creeped me out.

"It is. There's a lot of improvising," answered Dolores. "We've never had to face this before."

"Where's Beverly? Is she still sleeping?"

"She stepped out for some errands early this morning," answered my aunt. She finally glanced at me. "You really think Lilith is involved?"

By her tone, I knew she wanted me to say no. "I do."

Dolores slanted me a demanding look. "I'd hate to think our lovely goddess is implicated somehow."

Our goddess? "I think she knows who did this." I spied a batch of muffins sitting in a box with the words *Flying Piggies Pastries* written on the sides.

"Why do you say that?"

I grabbed what I believed was a blueberry muffin, peeled the top, and stuffed it in my mouth. "A pretty good hunch. Mmm. Is it me, or is this the best muffin I've ever tasted?"

"Don't be ridiculous," said Dolores. "All muffins taste the same."

"Don't tell my muffin that." I swallowed. I felt Dolores's eyes on me, and when I looked at her, it was almost like she was trying to punch a hole through my forehead to peek inside my mind. "She was avoiding the question. I asked her if she knew who had the means to open a doorway to another world, and she got all quiet. I know her enough to know she's protecting someone. Or, at the very least, she knows who did this." The problem was, how did you make a goddess blab? You didn't.

"I'm not sure I feel any better with that bit of news." Dolores tapped the pen on the piece of paper. "It means whoever did this has it in for us. For Hollow Cove. It means they did this on purpose."

Dolores was silent after that. I could see the wheels of her big brain working through her eyes.

"Can I help? I'm not great with spells, well, other than my power words, which I think are spells, just really short spells—"

"You can stop talking, for one," snapped my aunt. "I'm trying to concentrate here."

I frowned at the witch. "I'm only offering help."

"As you can see, I don't need it right now." Dolores kept reading through the book and writing simultaneously at unmatched speed.

I bit my tongue at the slight. I knew she hadn't slept, which accounted for the layer of grumpiness this morning. So, instead, I focused on the cat. If she needed my help, she'd let me know.

I looked down at Hildo and rubbed my hands together. "Okay. Feed the cat." I moved to the pantry and peered inside. "What does Ruth make you for breakfast in the morning?"

"Eggs and Canadian bacon," said the cat. He leaped up onto the counter. "Extra crispy."

Such a princess, that cat. Without power, I couldn't make him eggs and bacon. I grabbed a can of tuna I spotted on the shelf. "Looks like it's your lucky day. Tuna, it is."

Hildo didn't argue as I peeled open the can and dumped the tuna on a plate. "I'll get you something better for dinner."

"It's okay," said the cat, his mouth full. "Tuna's pretty good. Ruth buys only the best for me. Always wild tuna."

"I'm sure she does." Ruth loved Hildo. We all knew it. Guess the kitty was just struggling with some insecurities.

I finished my muffin. "I should go find Marcus. See how he's doing." I was the worst fiancée in the world now that I realized I'd completely forgotten his birthday yesterday. If there was an award for the worst fiancée who ever lived, it would have my face on it.

I made my way around the kitchen island. "I'll be back soon—"

Screams rushed to my ears from outside.

"Now, what?" Dolores slammed her pen on the table. "What is that racket?"

We heard a few more screams and a few startled exclamations before the screaming repeated itself, closer this time.

I sprinted to the front entrance like a greyhound, Dolores right behind me.

When I yanked the front door open, Dolores and I both cursed.

"Holy hell."

The street was teeming with men dressed in red coats, high boots, black helmets, and sashes. They marched in perfect unity in their striped trousers. I counted maybe fifty, some armed with rifles, some with swords.

Their movements were… jerky and stiff, like stop-motion animation characters. When one of the men came closer, chasing down a poor paranormal woman I recognized as one of our neighbors, Mrs. Deville, I realized his face was flat, his features painted.

These were not men. They were made of wood.

"What is this? What are they?" Dolores's tall frame stood next to mine, and energy prickled around me as I felt her pull on her elemental magic.

"These are the Nutcracker toy soldiers," I answered, shaking my head in disbelief. "And they're attacking Hollow Cove."

CHAPTER
18

I'd heard of the Nutcracker ballet over the years. I knew you could see it performed by humans. I just never imagined a wooden version would be so deadly.

But they were.

Not to mention that this was probably the creepiest thing I'd ever witnessed.

They were big, human-sized versions of the toy soldiers. Their movements were rigid, like clockwork soldiers, something straight out of your worst nightmare.

A sea of red coats as far as I could see. It wasn't just a few soldiers like I'd first thought.

It was an *army*: a massive army of toy soldiers. Of *armed* toy soldiers.

But then the realization dawned on me. If we had toy soldiers, that meant that the shed doors were open. Something had happened.

Marcus.

A choking, wet cry caught my attention, and I looked over to see a wooden soldier yank out his sword from the abdomen of a male paranormal. He collapsed to the ground.

The same toy soldier walked over the dead male and proceeded to run, more like walk fast on stiff legs after a female paranormal who'd run into a house.

Looked like I wasn't going to get a break anytime soon.

"Keep working the spell," I told my aunt as I ran down the front porch. Right now, closing that damn portal was the most important thing.

"What are you going to do? You can't fight them all?" Dolores watched me with round eyes. "Our magic has limited effects on them."

"I know." I spun around, tapping into my well of magic.

"If you use your ley lines like that again…" Dolores didn't finish what she intended to say. It didn't matter because I knew what she meant. If I pulled on my ley lines again like I'd done yesterday, it'd probably kill me.

"I've got this. Just… keep working the spell."

"Are those toys?" Ruth appeared next to Dolores. "Why do they look like the Nut-cracker?"

"Because that's what they are, you nitwit," snapped Dolores.

Ruth said something to her older sister that I didn't catch. I'd already turned around and headed toward my first toy soldier. That sounded crazy.

As I got closer, the toy soldier was even spookier up close. He had large painted eyes, thick black brows, and a black mustache above a hinged jaw that opened at the sight of me, like a ventriloquist puppet—not that those were any less disturbing. They weren't.

The soldier's painted eyes tightened in what I could only assume was hatred and the need to kill.

Yup. Totally creepy.

He raised his arm with a sword high above his head, and then he brought it down.

I wasn't just going to stay there and let him.

I yanked on my magic and thundered, "In-flitus!"

A push of kinetic force slammed into the toy soldier, forcing him back. The toy soldier lost his footing and fell.

I didn't stop there.

"Accendo!"

A fireball flew out of my hand and hit the toy soldier. High red-orange flames wreathed into

227

the air, the smoke filling my nostrils along with the scent of burning wood.

I staggered as a ripple of nausea hit, the magic taking its payment. Okay, so I wasn't fully recovered. But I was still fit enough to burn me some toy soldiers.

Through the flames, the toy soldier looked up. His eyes narrowed into slits.

And then he rushed me.

Oh, shit.

An armed, human-sized toy soldier was bad enough. But a *flaming*, armed human-sized toy soldier was worse.

"Ah!" I wailed like a little girl and started running in the opposite direction. What? I'd just suffered temporary brain fog. I'd forgotten my power words. How the hell did that happen? Was this the result of using too many ley lines? I didn't have time to ponder it. I was too busy running for my life.

"Tess! Duck!"

I did.

Ronin came out of nowhere and pitched himself at the flaming toy soldier in a savage show of strength, talons, and hate.

My heart stopped for a second, flabbergasted that my half-vampire friend hurled himself against the flames. But Ronin was fast, like blink-and-he-was-gone kind of fast.

The flames danced and bowed with the toy soldier. And then the fire vanished, just like when we'd hit the pirate ship and the wolf.

I spotted the toy soldier's face and body, blackened by my fire as he stabbed with his sword. The half-vampire flew sideways, evading the toy soldier's sword as it came whipping down. Both arms were extended in front of him, his talons tearing up the wood soldier's body and face like he was carving him into a sculpture until the thing had no more face and was just a bare wood surface. Ronin spun and kicked out with his legs, catching the soldier's ankles and knocking him down.

Finally, I recovered from my brain fog. "Evorto!" I whipped out my hand as a kinetic force hit the toy soldier. With a pop, the soldier blew up in a cloud of wood fragments and dust.

Black spots dotted my vision. I let out a breath and bent forward, feeling another wave of dizziness. I was not in good shape.

Ronin let out a sigh, spread out his taloned hands, and stretched. "This is not Disney's version of *Toy Story*."

I straightened. "Nope. But it's *someone's* twisted version."

I looked around, my pulse thrashing. Everywhere I looked, I saw red—a sea of toy soldiers. It was as though the earth had split open and was vomiting them from her belly because she didn't want them either.

The only thing we had on our side was the daylight. I didn't know how we could have fought these things in the dark.

My eyes found Iris. She stood feet apart, her hands fisted at her sides. A toy soldier came at her, and she thrust out her hands. A cloud of shimmering black dust flew over the soldier, like black fairy dust. With a sharp sound, like the clap of thunder, the soldier's hateful gaze froze in place, his wooden jaw wide as his body went rigid like his clockwork had malfunctioned.

Without stopping, Iris met the solidified toy soldier, poured liquid over his head, and then jumped back.

I stared wide-eyed while the toy soldier melted as though his body were made of wax. Ripples deformed his face, pooling around his shoulders until all that was left of the soldier was a puddle of red and black.

Good. At least they weren't invincible. Was it because the portal had been opened for a while? It made sense. Maybe they would be more susceptible to our magic.

"Keep it up, honey," cried Ronin, clapping his hands. "My dirty, deadly witch. You kill like no other, darling."

I watched in horror as rows upon rows of toy soldiers split into separate groups. Some ran into the streets while others disappeared beyond the trees. Worse were those that opened doors and walked straight into houses.

And they just kept on coming. More and more of the same toy soldiers appeared in the street.

"Where are they all coming from?" Ronin's gaze was on the nearest horde of toy soldiers.

"From the portal. From the damn portal."

And as luck would have it, a crap load of toy soldiers came straight for us.

We didn't have time to run for cover. We didn't have time to do anything but fight and pray to the goddess that my witch-ass survived this onslaught of wooden bastards.

They were a mass of twitchy, stiff, horrid, wooden toy soldiers as mindless and nasty as a school of hungry piranhas, just a hell of a lot creepier.

"You good?" called Ronin, angling his body and getting ready to hit some more toy soldiers.

"Excellent," I lied. I felt like I were the clothes in the dryer.

In a flash, the half-vampire was gone, lost among the toy soldiers. I heard the distinctive *pop-pop-pop* of gunfire. And for a horrible moment, I thought Ronin was hit. But then I caught a glimpse of him, spinning around, tearing up toy soldiers as he went, like he was a wood chipper.

Groups of paranormals hit the streets. Some were in their animal forms, attacking and beating the toy soldiers with everything they had. The toy soldiers were pushing hard, not giving the paranormals a chance to escape. There were just too many of them. We were out-numbered twenty to one. It would be a massa-cre if we didn't find a way to stop them.

A clicking sound reached me, and I spun. Two toy soldiers advanced, pointing their rifles at me. The click of the rifle was my only warn-ing.

Gathering my will again, I cried, "Protego!"

A sphere-shaped shield of protection rolled up over my head.

The bullets hit my sphere, and I ducked. I found myself on my knees, the top of my hair brushing against the energy of my shield.

My shield wavered as they kept firing. Five? Six shots? How many rounds did they have in those?

My shield rippled and then popped.

Super.

Their rifles clicked empty. With jerky, stiff motions, both toy soldiers began to reload.

My chest burned with hatred, but I could feel my magic running low, possibly to nothing at this point. "Where are you from?" I asked. I wanted answers. I wanted to know who let them in so I could go and kick their ass.

The nearest toy soldier's eyebrows lowered. His jaw flapped, but no words came out.

"Mute, human-sized toy soldiers? Excellent."

Clicks sounded again, and both soldiers raised their rifles at my chest.

Okaaay.

Their wooden fingers pulled on the trigger—

"Tessa! Move!"

Before I could do anything but blink, someone grabbed me from behind and threw me sideways.

Pop. Pop. The shots went wide.

Marcus was there. And in his hand was a... *chainsaw?*

It was like watching a version of *Evil Dead*, where one of the characters had attached a chainsaw to his severed arm and started cutting down the dead.

Well. Only in Hollow Cove.

Marcus had a strange gleam in his eye as he swung that chainsaw, meeting the closest toy soldier and sawing him in half. The top part of his body slipped off his hips and landed with a thud on the ground. There was no blood or anything that would suggest a living creature, just sawdust.

Without stopping, Marcus lunged forward, dropped the chainsaw on the other toy soldier's head, and dragged it down, severing the soldier from the top of his hat all the way to his boots. The toy soldier blinked, and then slowly, his severed left and right sides pulled apart and toppled to the ground.

"They can be defeated," I said, impressed and finding my man beast really hot with that chainsaw. Was that wrong? Probably.

Marcus exhaled, rolling his shoulders and making a show of his muscles popping. "Looks like it."

"You're rocking that mountain-tree-logger thing. All you're missing is a plaid shirt."

The chief flashed me a smile that did all kinds of things to my lady garden. "Thanks, babe. Fire doesn't destroy them?"

I shook my head. "Not initially. But I think they're weaker. I think it has something to do with how long the portal's been open." I looked back at the chief. "The portal?"

"I asked Scarlett to take over around four this morning. Something must have happened. She's not there anymore."

Damn. I liked Scarlett. I hoped she didn't get sucked into the portal.

"I'm counting at least a hundred of these things," said the chief, his eyes on the surrounding streets. He looked at me and said, "We need more chainsaws."

He wasn't wrong.

"It's ready!"

I turned to see Dolores running, her long legs propelling her forward with ease, with Ruth running behind her, trying to catch up. When Dolores reached us, she held up what looked like a small linen cloth bag. "We need to get this to the portal right away."

"And this," gasped a panting Ruth. A glass vial hung in her hand. I looked her over, searching for the fairy, but I couldn't see Tinker Bell anywhere. Maybe Hildo had gotten his wish and had eaten her.

Ronin and Iris followed, both red-faced but seemingly unscathed.

I stared at my aunts. "Where's Beverly?"

Dolores cast her gaze over my head. "She's still not back yet, but we'll be fine without her. We need to go now before more of these wooden things come through."

Ruth smiled and let out a small giggle. "I think they're cute."

"Cute and deadly. Let's go."

And then we were running.

I was sweating, and my lungs felt like, no matter how many deep breaths I pulled in, I wasn't getting enough air. I would need to rest for a week after this.

A row of toy soldiers stepped in our way, pointing their rifles at us, execution style.

Marcus and Ronin sprang forward. The half-vampire ducked and spun with in-your-face movements, forcing the toy soldiers to turn their attention on him. He was acting as a distraction as the chief swung his chainsaw and dismembered the toy soldiers even before they could shoot.

That could work.

"Come on!" urged Marcus as he moved ahead of us, cutting a clear path through the wooden toy soldiers.

Thankfully, Hollow Cove wasn't a huge town. We didn't have far to go, maybe a five-minute jog, but my thighs burned by the time we reached the shed.

We dashed through the narrow alleyway to find the shed doors wide open. Not at all like I'd left them last night.

The golden disc shone just as it did the night before, well, with just a little less luminescence in daylight.

"Ruth!" ordered Dolores as she walked over to the shed.

"Coming." Ruth hurried after her.

I rushed in between them. "Careful. Don't get too close." I didn't know if Scarlett had been tricked into crossing over, but I wasn't about to let my aunts be fooled.

Dolores planted her feet about ten feet from the shed. "This is close enough. Ruth…" She turned her head toward her sister. "As soon as I'm done with the spell, you toss your potion at it."

Ruth set her jaw in determination. Her face was red and blotchy from all the running. "Don't worry. I've got this sucker."

I stepped back and joined Iris and Ronin as I watched my aunts prepare their spell. Marcus hung back just a little, guarding the entrance to the alley with his chainsaw.

Dolores stood with her arms outstretched. The air around the alley was suddenly filled with crackling energy. She'd just pulled on the elements.

A wind rose, following the incantation by my aunts.

"In this darkest hour," chanted Dolores and Ruth in unison, "we call upon the goddess and her sacred power. Seal this path; block the way; lock its hold forever."

A wash of energy fell on us, my skin erupting in goose bumps as it dropped down into the ground like rain.

The portal hummed. Its edges buzzed with energy, and I could see tiny electrical sparks along its sides. It shuddered as though it were being forced by a giant hand to shut down. It was shrinking.

It was working!

"Now, Ruth!" ordered Dolores, her clothes and hair flapping in the wind.

Ruth arched back with her hand clasped around a vial containing a lime-green sub-stance, and then she hurled it forward, bending her body like a seasoned pitcher.

The vial flew out of Ruth's hand and was swallowed by the disc.

I braced myself, expecting some sort of mag-ical explosion.

And it was.

An explosion of brilliant purple light echoed around us. The concrete heaved around my feet. I stumbled several steps back and watched as segments of the shed shook, loosening up. The shed rumbled as wooden panels fell. The shimmering golden disc began to shrink on itself until it became half its size.

"It's working," I called out, feeling a flicker of relief.

There was a sudden loud noise like a shriek, and the portal jerked and heaved until it grew back to its original size. The golden disc rolled and shimmered as though we hadn't just tried to destroy it.

It didn't work.

Ruth looked at Dolores and shrugged. "Whoops."

Dolores took a step forward. "I don't understand. It should have worked. I know it. I did everything right. I didn't make a mistake."

"Well, that was a kick in the dick," said Ronin. "Looks like we're back to the drawing board."

Iris looked at me, and I knew what she was thinking. If Dolores and Ruth couldn't close this thing, we were out of options.

Echoes of screams reached us from beyond the alley. The toy soldiers were still attacking our town. "Let's get rid of those soldiers. Then we'll come up with another plan." We had to.

We couldn't just leave that portal open. It had to be destroyed. I tugged on Dolores's arm, dragging her along with me. "Come on. They need our help."

"She's right," agreed Ruth as we joined Ronin and Iris in the alleyway. "We'll think of something. We always do."

I hoped she was right because, so far, it didn't look good.

"We should close those doors," came Marcus's voice.

I walked a few steps and then froze. "Marcus, hang on—"

But the chief had jogged over to the shed. The chainsaw still hung in his hand. He made to grip the left door panel—

And a golden, mist-like, giant hand slipped out from the portal and wrapped itself around Marcus.

"Marcus!" Fear gripped my throat.

The portal-hand—I didn't know what else to call it—drew back into the glowing disc, Marcus in its grasp. I blinked, and the chief was gone. Just gone.

Heart pounding wildly in my chest, I let out a wordless scream that shattered my core.

"*No!*" I pitched forward. I'd gotten five steps when I was abruptly stopped by an iron hold around my arm.

"Tessa, stop!" shouted Dolores, her grip hard and painful. But I didn't care. All I cared about was Marcus.

"Marcus!" I shouted, bucking and kicking as I tried to free myself from my aunt's death grip. *Oh. My. God. Marcus.* The last image of him being swallowed up by the portal drove fear from the primitive part of my brain that began a madness. All I could think of was going in there after him.

"Tessa, stop! Think! You can't go in there!" my aunt repeated, but I wasn't listening.

"Marcus! *No!* No!" I kicked and made contact with my aunt's leg, hard, but the damn witch wouldn't let go.

I did the only thing I could.

I tapped into my magic, the power of the elements, until my body shook with adrenaline, fear, and raw power.

"Let me go," I growled. "Don't make me hurt you."

Dolores's hold tightened. "I won't. You can hurt me. But I won't let you go."

"You go in there, and you won't come out," said Ronin as he and Iris put themselves in front of me like a wall.

"Please, Tessa, just stop," said Ruth, joining them.

"It's Marcus!" I yelled. "Don't you understand? I have to go. Let me go!"

"You can't," said Dolores, and I felt her body thrum with her own magic.

"It's Marcus," I cried again. My wereape, my chief, my everything…

"I know," said Dolores. "But you can't go in there. Not yet. We need to think about this. Do you hear me? You go in there without a plan, and we'll never see you again. I don't think this is what Marcus would want. He wouldn't want you to rush in after him. What if you never come back?"

Her words finally settled over me. I let go of my magic, and then my legs felt like they were made of water. I slumped to the ground with tears flowing down my face as a sob broke from my lips. "But… he's not dead. He's not dead!"

I went somewhere far, far away from myself. Silent tears slid down my face and neck, puddling around my clavicles. My body shook. I couldn't stop it.

Dolores knelt next to me. She gripped my shoulder with her hand. "I know," she said, her voice soft and full of emotion. "He's not dead. And we *will* figure this out. We just need a plan. A much better one this time. If there's a way to get him back safely, we'll figure it out."

"Maybe we'll find someone who knows more about those doorways than we do," added Ruth. She pulled back a strand of hair from my eyes. Her eyes were red, and by the way the muscles in her face kept shifting, I could tell she was trying hard not to start crying. "It'll be okay."

It wouldn't. Not yet.

But Ruth's words gave me hope. Because there *was* someone who understood portals better than anyone.

And that someone was my father.

CHAPTER

19

I was running—again.

Technically, I shouldn't have been capable of running. My body was already worn out and weak from the magic and the previous running around. But my fear, the spike in energy, pushed my legs hard and as fast as they would go. It didn't matter that I sucked at this specific physical activity. All that mattered was that I kept going. If I wanted to save Marcus, I needed to keep going.

Images of him slipping into that portal plagued my mind over and over again. It was all I could see. Hell, I was barely aware of where I was going.

I didn't think I'd ever run this hard, this fast, for this long, in all my life. Maybe I was pushing my mortal body a bit too hard. I didn't care. I only had room in my head for one thought.

Marcus. I had to save him.

My shoes slipped. I scrambled on all fours and pushed myself up again, my palms searing from where I'd scraped them on the pavement. My throat burned with every breath, but I didn't stop. I couldn't. The longer Marcus was trapped in that world, the worse it was. What if he couldn't breathe? What if that hand had crushed him? What if… what if Marcus was already dead?

No. I wouldn't do this. I wouldn't let the despair take over. If Tinker Bell could breathe our air and was, from what I could tell, healthy, I had to believe Marcus was too. I had to.

"You're going to give yourself a heart attack if you don't stop." Ronin jogged alongside me, not even out of breath or breaking a sweat. I hated him right now.

I just shook my head. I was afraid if I spoke, it would slow me down. And I was almost there.

"Can I ask where you're going?"

I shook my head, irritation flowing in my veins. If he stopped my momentum, I might have to kill him.

"If you'd told me, I could have carried you."

I pressed my lips together and kept sprinting, but his presence was a distraction, and I felt my legs slowing. It didn't matter, though. I was here.

The quaint gray cottage boasted white trim, next to mature lilac trees. Rows of rhododendrons and Anabelle hydrangeas encased a wraparound porch.

I ran up the porch, and without bothering to knock, I yanked the door open and rushed in.

My mother turned from her seat, a cup of tea in her hand. "Tessa? Are you here to apologize? I think I deserve a much better apology than you barreling in here looking like a vagrant…"

The rest of her words were lost to me as I headed toward the basement door beneath the staircase to the right of the entrance.

"Hi, Amelia," I heard Ronin say, followed by his tread as it came closer to me. "Sorry to just pop in like this. Tess's not feeling so hot at the moment."

I faced the basement door. My head was spinning from all the running and all the emotions. I should be sitting down with a bucket of water, but I didn't have a single second to waste.

I reached out, grabbed the door handle, and yanked it open. "Dad!" I shouted, my voice scratchy and parched. "Dad! This is an emergency!"

Just like in Davenport House and Davenport Cottage, my father had created a portal with my mother's basement door, where a replica of this same door also existed in his apartment in the Netherworld.

"What emergency? What's happened? Tessa?" came my mother's voice from behind me.

"Marcus went through the portal," answered Ronin. "He went bye-bye."

"What portal?"

"The one that let in the pirate ship and those toy soldiers," answered the half-vampire.

My mother was silent as I listened for an indication that my father was on his way. I looked down at the wooden stairs, hoping to see him, but he didn't show.

"Dad! Please! You need to come right now!"

I felt a hand on my shoulder and spun around to find my mother standing next to me. "Tessa, please tell me what's the matter?" She was staring at me like I had a few screws loose. Maybe I did.

The stairs to the basement creaked, and when I turned back, my father stood on the threshold, wearing a cobalt-blue suit and a worried expression. "Tessa? What's happened?" A pair of luminous silver eyes stared back at me, set around a handsome face with dark graying hair and a matching trimmed beard.

I opened my mouth, but nothing came out as I was hit with a massive emotional wave. My lips quivered as if I was cold, and my eyes suddenly swam with tears.

My father took my hand and steered me to the living room. "Sit. Tell me everything." He pulled me down next to him on the soft beige couch. He looked up at my mother. "Some water for her."

I was surprised my mother didn't object to being ordered around as she hurried to the kitchen. If I'd demanded water or anything, she would have stayed put, and the only thing she would have given me was a defiant glare.

I took a breath and tried again. "It's Marcus."

"What happened to him?" asked my father, and I saw Ronin lean on the wall between the living room and the kitchen, his arms crossed over his chest.

"He went through a portal—no, he was *pulled* into one. Taken." I gave him a quick summary of the events since I'd first found the dead Little Red Riding Hood to when Marcus was taken.

"Here, Tessa. Have some water."

I looked up and grabbed the tall glass of water my mother held out for me, her face worried.

"Thank you." I took the glass and drank, nearly choking on the first gulp. But the water soothed my throat, and I took another sip.

The front door banged open, and Dolores, Ruth, and Iris rushed in.

Dolores panted, holding her side like she had a cramp. The redness in her face made her look like she had a bad sunburn. "The next time you think of running, a little warning would be nice."

"I think she coughed out a lung," laughed Ruth as she crossed the entryway and joined us in the living room.

Iris was staring at me from the doorway, a pained expression on her face that said it all. She was sorry for me, and she didn't think I'd ever see Marcus again.

I pulled my eyes away. I couldn't, *wouldn't* think about that right now.

When I looked back at my father, I didn't like the concern that showed on his face. "What do you know about other worlds?" I asked, focusing on the major issue here.

Obiryn ran his fingers through his beard. "I haven't experienced the existence of other worlds myself, but I do know they exist."

Ronin whistled. "We are not alone."

"What about portals?"

"I'm very familiar with portals, as you know. I used one just now to get here, just as you experienced a similar one when you came to my home. You might even say I'm an expert at them."

I nodded. "I was hoping you'd say that."

My father frowned, not sure of my meaning, and he continued, "Most magic portals and time corridors allow travel through time and space. And portals can be ring-shaped, with a watery 'event horizon' or doors, like the ones I've installed here." He pointed to the basement door. "You also used a portal when you worked with the Soul Collector. He took you through one."

"I remember." And I remembered how sick it made me feel the first time. I wasn't sure I'd ever really get used to that.

Long seconds passed as Obiryn gazed silently at me, thinking who knew what, and I worried that he wouldn't help. "How close did you get to this doorway?"

I thought about it. "I don't know... close. Why?"

"Did you feel anything?" asked my father.

"I did." Iris moved to the living room. "It talked to me."

"You heard voices?" I asked, knowing that Ronin had. When I looked over at him, he'd shut down again, reliving that experience, no doubt.

"No," answered Iris. "Not in the way you think of sounds. But like... I *felt* it. It was a feeling of ecstasy, of beauty, and it *made* me want to go."

"Were you closer than Tessa?" My father eyed her, waiting for an answer.

Iris looked at me before answering. "Same, I guess. She came to pull us away. Me and Ronin."

249

My father's silver eyes fixed on me again. "And what did *you* feel, Tessa? Did you feel a pull? Did you hear a voice?"

"I didn't hear anything. But I did *feel* something. Barely. But nothing like Iris and Ronin. It was just a hum of energy. Nothing more. I was probably too far away from it." I *was* a tad behind Iris and Ronin. Too far for the portal's grab? My gut was telling me this was something else. The portal didn't react to me the same way it did other people. And I was hoping I was right about why that was. "And judging by that tight expression, this portal is different. Am I right?"

My father glanced down at his hands. I saw something else on his features, but I wasn't sure what that was. Worry? Fear? "All these portals we're accustomed to, well, they're all gateways within *our* worlds. They don't lead to realms, only doors to different parts of ours. And this one—"

"The one that took Marcus," I said, a ripple of fear running through my gut.

"Yes. That one is *different*. First, well, I've never heard of a portal that creates a hand and snatches you away."

"But it did."

"And that's what worries me."

I set the glass of water on my lap. "In what way?"

"Well, for one, it means someone created it and is still controlling it. It means whoever made the doorway is keeping an eye on things. On this town. Its people." He looked at me, and I could tell he wasn't sure if he wanted to say what he'd intended to say next.

"What? Say it," I pressed.

"Yes." Dolores folded her hands before her. "If you know something, Obiryn. Please tell us."

My father glanced at Dolores for a second before answering. "Why would this gateway reach out and take Marcus?"

I shrugged. "Maybe he was too close?" A hand didn't come out and grab Iris and Ronin, and they were about the same distance from the portal as Marcus had been.

"Maybe it didn't like that he was sawing through those wood soldiers," offered Ronin.

My father tapped his chin, and tension crossed his features. Clearly, he knew something was not right. "And maybe it's because it knew if it took him, *you* would go in after him."

I felt the blood leave my face. "Are you saying this is my fault?"

My father shook his head and let out a breath. "No. Demons, no. But I think it *wanted* that reaction from you. For you to go in after him."

"She almost did," said Dolores.

I didn't look at her. I was still angry. Not at her. At the situation. She'd held on to me, and for good reason.

251

But what my father was implying was insane. "You think the portal wants me to go in? Why?" To be trapped in there forever? Who would want this? Why?

"I don't know. But I feel that you're involved in this somehow. I don't know how exactly, but you are."

I tried not to let his words bring me down into despair. No matter what this portal was, it wouldn't stop me from going through with my plan. "This world, this place with storybook characters come to life... Have you ever heard of it before?"

"I've heard of a place similar to the one you describe," said Obiryn making my mother suck in her breath.

My heart thrashed. "Tell me about it. Who created it? Why did they create it?"

My father cocked his head to the side like he was contemplating what to say next. "All I know, which is all from rumors passed on over the years, is that there was such a world, a world of fairy tales and stories. It was a world created to escape to. To be in the company of what only dreams could be."

I leaned forward to get a better look at his face. "Who created it?"

"Well, the only ones who can create other worlds are gods. Gods and goddesses."

I knew it, which only accentuated my ongoing theory of Lilith being or knowing someone involved.

"Since you're so knowledgeable about portals," I said. "How do we destroy it? We can't leave it open. Look what's happened in only a day or so. These characters will wipe out our town if we don't shut it down."

"But what about Marcus?" My mother stepped in front of my line of sight. "He's in there."

I looked away from her, still focused on what I needed to know from my father.

"We tried a nullification fusion spell and tossed in a mushroom poison hex. It's like a virus. It should have infected the portal and forced it to shut down. But it didn't work." Ruth looked at me, and it was almost like she blamed herself for what had happened to Marcus. I knew she loved him dearly, but none of this was her fault.

My father shook his head. "It wouldn't. It's not like your usual Rift. You can't just blow it away."

"Too bad," muttered Ronin.

"You need to hit it at its source." My father glanced at Ruth. "You need to hit the core. The heart of that world."

"So, what you're saying is, with my aunts' same spell, I could have destroyed it, but only if I'd hit the core of this place? Is that it?"

My father was silent for a moment. "Yes."

"But won't that destroy that world? If I hit the core, won't it wipe out the world and all of its inhabitants?"

"Not necessarily."

"Not necessarily?"

"I'm not sure, but I believe you cannot destroy a world with only a spell. But you can *infect* it. The mushroom poison hex, as you say, would have been sufficient. And it should be strong enough to close any portals."

It wasn't really reassuring. I didn't want to be responsible for destroying an entire world. I hoped he was right.

"I'm not following." My mother rubbed her arms together. "How can you infect a world? Where is this core? How does that even work?"

"Because"—I flicked my gaze to my mother—"I'm going in."

"What? Are you insane?" Dolores came right up to the couch, and I had to let my head fall back to look at her face. "You can't go in there. You might not be able to come back?"

"I know that. I'm willing to take that chance."

"You don't know anything about that place," cried my mother. "What if something is waiting for you? To take you. To kill you!"

"I'm going."

Dolores pointed at Iris. "Look what it did to your friends. You'll lose yourself to it."

"I won't." Well, that was what I was hoping. I looked at my father. "I'm not affected the same way. Am I? So, I know I'm the only one who can go through and still keep my senses. Right?" It was the only logical thing, the only thing that made sense.

"Right." My father's face was serious.

I nodded. "So, I'm going. I'm going after Marcus. And I'm going to find the core and blast it with that virus."

"Tessa." My father reached out and grabbed my hand. "Before you go. You need to know something."

"What?"

"Once you find the core and transmit that virus, you'll have maybe… minutes to get out before it shuts down. If the portal closes with you in there… you'll be stuck in that world for the rest of your life."

Fantastic. "How long will I have?" I didn't know how big this world was, but I hoped it wasn't that big. Maybe the size of a large city. I hoped.

"Fifteen, twenty minutes, maybe? A half hour, tops. But I wouldn't bet on it."

"Okay then. I better get going." I stood up, my father standing with me.

"Well, I think it's a terribly stupid idea," said my mother. "You're not going."

I gave a mock laugh. "I'll be fine. I know what I'm doing." Not really. "I wouldn't go if I didn't think I was going to come back."

"You better come back," said my mother. "You owe me a nice dinner."

"I know."

"You're not going anywhere until I have a look at you. You're going to need some more healing elixir." Ruth examined my face. "We don't know what the effects of pulling two ley lines did to your body."

"What's this about two ley lines?" My father watched me closely, and I could see a proud smile forming on his lips.

"She annihilated a pirate ship with two ley lines," said Dolores.

"Saw it happen," added Ronin. "Fucking awesome."

I smiled at my father. "I'll tell you all about it later."

My demon father beamed, though I could see a tinge of fear flashing across his face. "I can't wait."

I glanced away before my father's fears imprinted on me. I needed to focus. Because if I lost my focus on the plan, I might just change my mind. I couldn't do that. Because I knew Marcus would do it for me. He'd cross into another world to save me. I would do it for him too.

Yes, crossing into a portal to another world—possibly a perilous world—was not a smart thing to do. It was crazy. Good thing I had just the right amount of crazy to go through with it.

I didn't know if I'd make it back. But hell, I was going to try.

Hang on, Marcus… I'm coming…

CHAPTER
20

I stood before the glowing disc, waiting to see if one of those giant portal hands would reach out and grab me. It didn't.

I bit back my disgust at it. I hated it. Hated that it had taken the one man, the only man, who'd ever made me happy. Who didn't flinch at my imperfections, he embraced them. Loved them. A man who loves your cellulite is a damn keeper. I wasn't about to let him go. I just prayed to the goddess he was okay.

"We'll be right here waiting for you to get back," came Dolores's voice from behind.

I glanced over my shoulder, seeing her and Ruth about twenty feet from me. Iris and Ronin stood shoulder to shoulder next to them. They were all very different in their appearances and personalities, but right now, they all shared the same look: the Tessa-is-crazy-to-go-in-there look.

When we'd headed back to Davenport House, the streets were littered with the remains of the toy soldiers. Bonfires were flaming on the roads, and I'd seen wooden arms, legs, and heads among the burning wood. I didn't see one toy soldier left. Our town had defeated them. The townspeople could hold their own. For now.

Iris flipped her thumb at me. "You've got this. Go get your man," she added with a smile, though it was tight and seemed forced.

Ronin was unusually quiet, and he kept throwing hateful glances at the portal. Hell, if I were to guess, he hated that thing more than me.

I turned back and faced the portal. "I'll see you when I get back." I hated how weak my voice sounded, betraying my outer, hard shell. I was terrified. I wasn't going to lie.

"I have more healing tonics for you when you do," called Ruth. She'd given me—*forced* me—to drink another three before we came here, after leaving my mother's place.

"Okay. Thanks." Not sure what else I was going to say.

"You come back now, you hear me?" Dolores's voice cracked, and my eyes burned.

I swallowed hard, not turning back because I knew I'd break down if I did. I needed my wits about me. I needed to be strong because I had no idea what waited for me on the other side of that hateful, shimmering circle.

I had to do this. I *needed* to do this.

With my mind made up, I stepped forward. I knew I'd chicken out if I didn't do this right now. I wasn't an idiot. I didn't want to die.

I felt the pulsing of the portal rubbing against my face like static electricity.

I kept walking. Only three more steps.

I gripped the strap of my bag, the weight filling me with hope. Ruth had supplied me with another mushroom poison hex that I was to use on the core of the world along with banishing balls, spider eyes—another type of detonating sphere—and something called blistering melon. No idea what that was. I didn't know if my magic would have some effect there, if any, so I'd armed myself with potions, something tangible, just in case.

One more step.

I braced myself, knowing if it felt anything like the times I'd traveled with Jack, the Soul Collector demon, it was going to hurt, and I was going to hate it.

I kept my eyes open as I stepped into the glowing disc. The first thing I noticed was that I couldn't hear the distant sounds of my world, like the humming of cars or my aunts' and friends' voices. My ears felt like they were stuffed with cotton, like I was floating underwater. My world shifted around me, and I was surrounded by golden light.

My vision turned into a curtain of golden agony that centered around my core. I felt a spinning sensation, and I was suddenly caught in a tempest, a twister that carried me forward, deeper into the portal. My feet slid across the floor of the shed. I jerked back with a cry, tapping into my magic, but it did nothing.

Next, I felt my feet leave solid ground as my body was hauled forward. I wondered if this was how Marcus felt. And then I realized with utter shock that I was being sucked into the other world.

I had a moment of panic, of regret, but it was too late. Fear hit, and I tried to scream. Tried to fight back. Tried to summon my magic. But it still didn't respond.

I was wrapped in this golden place. It was everywhere. It swallowed me and kept me for a long time as I drifted in silence, floating in nothing but endless gold.

The pain came next, a scorching kind of pain like my insides were liquifying, and every cell in my body was on fire. My body was being pulled in every direction at the same time. I was being torn apart.

And then it was all over.

The whirlwind lifted, and I stumbled forward into—a meadow.

I blinked into the bright light, covering my eyes at the glowing sphere that had to be a sun. Blinking, I waited for my eyes to adjust to the sudden light. When shapes were in focus, I spun around in a panic, expecting to see Dolores, Ruth, Iris, and Ronin, but all I saw were miles of greenery. Rolling hills of greens and specks of red, orange, and yellow spread out before me in all directions. Mature trees scattered the landscape, with red, orange, and yellow leaves rippling in a soft breeze. More leaves spread on the ground like a textured, colorful gown.

Energy rippled through the grasses, the flowers, the trees, and even in the air, pulsing around me and making my skin tingle. I couldn't see it, but I felt it course through me too. Magic. Or whatever magic this place held.

But it *was* beautiful, glorious, like an expert hand had painted this place in a perfect landscape. I'd never seen something this magnificent, and I could easily just lie down on the soft grass and soak in that wonderful sun, forgetting what I was here for.

Maybe this was part of some magical charm. This world wanted you to forget. Wanted to pull you in until you couldn't remember who you were. I could sense that tug now that Iris and Ronin had mentioned. Perhaps it was because I was here now, in this world, and its influence was more substantial. I had to be careful.

Once I stopped marveling at the landscape, I realized the air here was similar to ours. Marcus could breathe here.

"Where are you, Marcus?"

Okay, so this world was huge, or at least it appeared to be. Hundreds of miles in every direction. How the hell was I going to find him? It had been about two hours since I'd seen him get snatched up and dragged into the portal. And two hours was enough time to get into trouble or danger.

I turned on the spot. He could be anywhere.

I took a deep breath. The scent of roses, lilacs, and other flowers wafted in my nose. It looked and smelled equally amazing.

I looked at the ground, at the tall, swaying light-green grasses with pink tips, searching for tracks or a sign that a big wereape walked through here. But I didn't notice any bending or flattening of the grass. Who was I kidding? I wasn't a tracker. I wouldn't even know what to look for.

I thought of what my father had said. Someone had created this and, by the looks of it, took their time with all the attention to detail. A significant amount of effort was put into it. So, who did this? And why was I involved? Why take Marcus?

So many questions, and none of them made any sense.

A flash of white tipped the top of the grasses about fifty feet from me—a dash of bright red. I blinked. Then the white tips lifted through the grasses—white, furry ears.

I jogged a little closer. And then I saw it.

A bunny. Not just an ordinary bunny, but a bunny in a red suit jacket and gray pants ran toward me. He looked familiar. I realized this was the exact bunny I saw yesterday in the streets of Hollow Cove.

I waited until he was about five feet from me and jumped in his way. "Hi."

"*Ah!*" the bunny shrieked and stepped back. His ears flattened against his head, reminding me of Hildo when he was frightened or angry.

Since the Big Bad Wolf had understood English, I was betting this character did as well. And judging by his choice of clothing, I was guessing he was male, so I was going with it.

I didn't want to scare away this rabbit. He might be my only hope of finding Marcus. "Sorry I scared you. I mean you no harm." I raised my hands like an idiot, showing the rabbit that I didn't have any weapons on me. Well, in my hands at the moment.

The rabbit's ears straightened. "Well, you *did* scare me," he answered, confirming my suspicion that he understood me.

"What is this place? What do you call it?"

"This is Storybook. Why? Where are you from?"

I blinked. "Earth."

His pink eyes narrowed at me. Then they widened as though he'd forgotten something important. He reached inside his jacket pocket and retrieved a golden pocket watch. "Thundering typhoons! I must go. I'm late! I'm late!"

"What?" This was indeed a strange place. "Late for what?"

"I must go. Make haste. Make haste!" Before I could stop him, the bunny sprinted away, running fast.

"Hey! Wait!"

I ran to catch up. "Please stop. I need to ask you some questions," I panted. Damn, I did not want to chase this rabbit. I'd run enough, thank you very much. If I hadn't downed three of Ruth's healing tonics, I would have never been able to catch up.

"I don't have time for questions," said the rabbit. "She's going to kill me. Cut off my head if I'm late again."

"Who?" I figured if I showed interest in him, he might return the favor.

"The queen."

Great. They had a queen here. "Listen. I'm looking for my friend. His name is Marcus," I breathed in some air, running through the grasses, which was not as easy as I would have liked. "Big guy. Dark hair. Dark eyes. He had a chainsaw the last time I saw him. Maybe you saw him?"

The rabbit raced forward, never stopping. "No time for questions!" he called back. "I don't want to die. Dying is bad. Don't you understand?"

"Yes. I get it. You don't want your head cut off. But did you see him? He's really tall," I added and made a show of just how tall with my hand, but the rabbit was ahead of me. I lowered it. "Can you just stop for one minute!"

"No."

"Ten seconds?"

"No."

Okay. So I was going to have to use some of my aunt's spells on this sucker. Maybe this was a good time to test this blistering-melon thing. I thrust my hand into my bag while I ran, which made it nearly impossible to find anything while bouncing around.

"Stop!" I shouted as I slowed. "Stop, or I will hurt you. I'll use my *magic*."

The bunny halted in his tracks. He turned around, staring at me curiously. "You have magic too?"

I didn't know what he meant by that, but right now that wasn't important. "Have you seen my friend? He came through a portal, just like me. And I have to assume he came out the same way I did. Did you see him?"

The bunny watched me. "No. I'm afraid I did not see your friend—ah!" The rabbit froze like he'd been shot.

The sounds of many marching feet reached me. I stole a look over my shoulder and stiffened, just like my friend the rabbit here.

A dozen or so human cards—I didn't know what else to call them—appeared from the tall grasses and surrounded us. Human size, with arms and legs all sprouting from a center card that should have been a torso. They had heart-shaped heads and noses and small heart-shaped mouths. Red gloves were pulled over their arms, and floppy red shoes covered their feet. They carried red lances as weapons. Each lance was tipped with an upside-down heart. Each pointed in my face.

Swell.

"Intruder," said the card soldier with the ace of hearts on his front. "Penalty for trespassing in the queen's territory is death."

I held up my hands because that's what I thought I should do. "Sorry. I'm just looking— Ow." I jerked back. "You stabbed me," I said, mortified that the card soldier had jabbed me with his lance. But now I knew the pain in this world was the same as in mine. Was I bleeding? No idea.

"Move!" ordered the same card soldier, shoving his lance at me again.

"Wait a second," I said, not wanting to be caught by these nightmarish beings. First, I needed to find Marcus.

"Move!" The ace of hearts card soldier thrust his lance at me, scraping the front of my T-shirt, and a sting followed as it pierced my skin.

Now I was certain I was bleeding. I opened my mouth to tell him to stick his lance up his ass, but something at my knee level pulled my arm.

"This way, before they behead us both!" The bunny yanked on my hand and steered me with him.

Reluctantly, I let him, though I looked over my shoulder and gave the ace of hearts card soldier my best stink eye. He didn't react.

I yanked my hand from the bunny. "Where are they taking us?"

"To the kingdom of hearts. To the queen's castle."

Irritation and anger flared. "I don't have time to sightsee. I need to find my friend." I had to get away and find Marcus. I didn't have time for this shit.

"You'll need your head to find him," said the bunny. "Just do as you're told, and you might live to see tomorrow."

I trudged through the grass, staring at the card soldier on my left. I knew what this was, what they were. They were part of whoever had created this world, their imagination. Stories they wanted to come to life.

I looked down at the bunny. "What's your name?"

The bunny blinked and said, "White Rabbit."

Of course he was. "And I'm guessing the queen is the Queen of Hearts?"

The rabbit's mouth fell open. "How did you know?"

"Lucky guess." Not really. "Tessa in freaking Wonderland," I muttered, shaking my head. "Do you know where I can find the core of this place? This world?" I figured the bunny might have some use after all. He looked knowledge-able.

"No. I do not know what that is."

Guess not. "So you've never heard of it?"

The rabbit shook his head, sending his ears flopping. "Sorry. Maybe the queen will know. Though I wouldn't ask her."

"Why not?"

The bunny's ears twitched on his head like mini radar dishes. "She doesn't like questions. She'll most likely cut off your head."

"Excellent."

After a few minutes of walking, we crested a hill and finally came upon a castle. The castle, the queen's castle, I presumed, was situated on a picturesque lake and surrounded by fertile green hills of towering pine forests and chiseled mountain peaks. The black-and-red stone fortress appeared to be floating in the sky as it looked down over the surrounding wilderness. It had pointed turrets that shot into the air like a giant crown set with swords and was protected by a great stone wall.

The grassy trail quickly turned to cobblestones as we neared the castle. The closer we got to it, the angrier I became and the more frightened I felt, not for me but for Marcus. I didn't have time to get involved in this queen's politics of this place. I needed to find my man, find the core, destroy it, and get the hell out of this place.

My stomach knotted as I tried to control my nerves. As we crossed the drawbridge, I could smell the putrid fumes from the moat that surrounded the fortress. Next, we passed through a gatehouse and under a giant metal portcullis that looked like the mouth of a creature ready to devour us. Finally, we arrived inside a courtyard. I noticed there were no villagers and no one apart from the card soldiers, me, and White Rabbit.

The card soldiers shoved us through an arched entryway that led into a long hallway. I tried to get my bearings and remember the hallways and corridors of the castle in case I needed to make a quick exit. But I hardly had time to think as we strode down yet another hallway. Left, right, left, another left. After a few minutes, I was utterly lost. The halls all looked exactly the same.

Great.

We entered a vast chamber with gleaming rock columns that upheld the ceiling. The walls on either side were decorated with paintings, rich tapestries hung on the walls, and the fire sconces on the columns reflected yellow light off the gleaming black granite floor.

A woman with blonde hair piled high on top of her head, like a beehive, sat above a high dais, sprawled on her throne. A gold crown circled her head, and long gold earrings adorned her ears. Beautiful and voluptuous, she wore a revealing dress of exquisite black silk with red hearts embroidered on it. It crisscrossed at the front and left her midriff exposed. Her large breasts nearly spilled out from the top. She appeared to be bored and looked lazily at her fingernails.

I'd never seen a queen before, but that's not what had me frozen in place in utter shock.

It was because the Queen of Hearts was none other than my Aunt Beverly.

"Oh, hell."

CHAPTER
21

With all that had happened, I'd forgotten about my aunt. Dolores told me Beverly had stepped out to run some errands. It never occurred to me to wonder why she never came back.

Because she'd crossed over to Storybook.

Somehow, the portal called to her, and she'd listened.

Damn. This was the worst outcome. Not only was Marcus somewhere in this make-believe world for me to retrieve, but now I had Beverly to worry about.

I stared up at my aunt. "Beverly? What are you doing here?" I glanced at the two gorgeous, seminaked men, oiled up no less, cooling her with handheld fans. These men were human-looking and not like the card soldiers. I caught a glimpse of more of these half-naked manser-vants standing in the shadows of the dais. One walked forward, balancing a glass of red wine on a tray. The manservant, whose skin was the color of coffee, bent down and gave my aunt a lust-filled kiss on the lips as she smacked his ass.

Totally inappropriate.

The hot manservant gave my aunt a seduc-tive smile, the kind that said, *I'll smack you later*, handed her the wine, and walked off the dais.

Even an off-world version of Beverly had to have a few naked men surrounding her. It wouldn't have been Beverly without them.

"I'm sure Dolores would love that," I called out. "But seriously. Cut the crap, and let's go. We need to find Marcus. He's here too."

"What are you doing?" hissed the bunny, his tiny body shaking in fear. "Don't make her an-gry, you fool. She'll cut off our heads!"

I ignored the rabbit, though I didn't like him calling me a fool. "We don't have time for your games," I told my aunt. "We need to leave. So say bye-bye to your man-whores, and let's go."

At that, my aunt's eyes snapped to mine, and her face grimaced. Slowly, she tracked her eyes over me. "Who are you, and how *dare* you speak to me without permission?"

"Stop talking," whispered the rabbit. "Or we're both dead! I don't want to die."

I released a breath, reeling in my temper. "Very good, Beverly. Truly a fantastic performance. I almost believed you. I know you've always wanted to be an actress, and I know you have a penchant for costumes." I looked her over. "But this is a bit much, even for you. Listen, we *really* have to go. Your sisters don't even know where you are. We have to find Marcus and get out of this place."

Beverly's face twitched. In a flurry of black-and-red silk, she jumped to her feet. Her man-slaves hurried to keep fanning her. She thrust a finger at me, her face turning an ugly shade of red.

"You dare speak to me in my court!" Her voice thundered inside the chamber. It was deep, rich, and commanding. Her attention turned to the bunny. "You would sully my court with the presence of this female! This lower creature!"

The bunny bowed in submission. "Forgive me, your grace, your worshipness, your loveliness and holiness," he said, his forehead touching the hard marble floor.

This was so screwed up. The hair on the back of my neck rose. "What the hell is wrong with you?" I glared at my aunt, wanting to grab her crown and smack her in the face with it. "This isn't funny anymore. You've had your fun." I cast my gaze at the manservants, who were all staring at me like I was the most hated being in this world. "We need to go, like *now*. I don't have time for this." No. I needed to find my wereape, not participate in one of my aunt's twisted fantasies. Ew.

A smile lit up Beverly's face, making her eyes dance with vicious fires that caused me to draw in a sharp breath. She flicked a finger at me and cried, "Off with her head!"

Yup. She was pointing at me, not my friend, the rabbit.

"Excuse me?" I put my hands on my hips. Now I was pissed. "Have you lost your damn mind? What's the matter with you?" Something was off with my aunt. The way she looked at me was as though she'd never seen me before, like when you first meet a stranger, and they're sizing you up. It was as though she didn't recognize her own niece. Like she didn't know me at all.

Dread pierced my gut. And for the first time since I'd stepped into this world, I felt my hope slip. If she didn't recognize me, did she truly believe she was the Queen of Hearts?

Beverly snarled, actually snarled. The black kohl around her green eyes made her look more severe and evil. "And bring it back to me. I'll decorate my hall with her insolent head. She has a pretty face."

Before I could react, two card soldiers grabbed me by the arms. I tried to pull away, but their stupid lanky arms were too strong.

"Wait a second. Beverly! Don't you know who I am?"

She sighed dramatically and leaned forward, revealing more of her ample bosom. "An insolent female whose head will look marvelous on my wall," she answered with a knowing smile.

Yeah. I don't think so. "It's me. Tessa. Your niece. Don't you recognize me?"

My aunt's face held no traces of recognition, just a deep loathing for me. She turned to the rabbit and shook a finger at him as though scolding a child. "You know better than to lie to your queen, White Rabbit. Tell me who she is and where she came from. I want answers now. Or I will have *your* head as well. Your fur would make marvelous slippers."

The rabbit bowed even lower, and when he spoke, his lips smeared the floor. "I don't know, my queen," answered the rabbit. "It's the honest truth, your ladyship. I swear on my head. I would never lie to your worshipness. She appeared in the meadow. Just like the others. She followed me."

The others? Did he mean Marcus? And the other paranormals who had disappeared?

The chamber erupted with noise, mostly hisses and scoffs although a few of the card soldiers watched in silence. After a few moments, the chamber stilled until all I heard was the beating of my heart and the rapid breaths from the rabbit, still bowed.

A cunning smile played on Beverly's red lips. "We do require more slaves in the mines. Perhaps I will keep you alive for now. And when I've had enough, I will cut off your head." She drew a manicured red finger across her neck. "Take her to the dungeon!" The witch queen threw back her head and laughed without feeling. Seeing Beverly like this was creepy, like someone I didn't know, didn't recognize.

"Beverly! Wait!" I struggled between my captors. "What are you doing? You don't belong here! Wake up. Wake the hell up. Snap out of it. I need your help."

But my aunt had returned to her throne, her head back and giggling as her seminaked manservant fed her what looked like grapes while another stood behind her, massaging her shoulders. Such a cliché. And like soft porn.

I looked back at the bunny while being dragged. "White Rabbit? A little help here?"

The bunny lifted his head and looked at me. "Sorry, but you did this to yourself. I did warn you. I told you not to make her angry, and you made her angry."

I kicked out and screamed. I even spat, but the card soldiers hung on to me, dragging my ass through the chamber.

"Let go of me, you freaks!" I shouted, bucking like a wild horse. But those damn soldiers were strong, albeit they were partly made of paper.

Yeah, this was not going as well as I'd thought. Could it be worse? Of course it could.

They hauled me out of the chamber, and all the while, I kicked and screamed at the top of my lungs. I might have peed. Who knew?

I was mad, at myself, for following that stupid rabbit. If I could kick my own ass, I would. But then I would have never discovered Beverly. I would have dropped the mushroom virus on the core, grabbed Marcus, and left this place, leaving Beverly trapped here forever. Would she even survive here? I knew my aunt. I knew she wouldn't want to stay here. She'd want to return to her life, dates, and men.

I had to figure out a way to help my aunt remember and get the hell out.

But first, I had the minor issue of being a prisoner.

The soldiers took a left turn, dragging me with them. The smell of smoke from braziers, mildew, and wet stone greeted us. The air had shifted and become much cooler than the rest of the castle, as though a window or door had been left open to the outside. But the air wasn't fresh. It was stale and cold. Then I smelled rot, piss, the coppery tang of blood, and unwashed bodies. It hit me like a slap in the face. Even if this place was technically make-believe, the smells were real enough.

The card soldiers, or guards, led me down another narrow, dim corridor until we arrived at a larger chamber. It was still dimly lit, but at least it was spacious. The floor was filthy and covered in maroon stains. I could see manacles mounted on the walls and long tables with a collection of sharp tools and weapons. In the middle of the room was a tremendous circular stump of wood, an ax edged in it. No doubt the one used to behead us heathens.

"Am I late for a little Iron Maiden? The Rack?" I laughed. They didn't. "This is a mistake. Listen to me. I'm not from this world, and neither is your queen. I don't belong here."

One of the card soldiers shoved me forcefully toward the wall with the manacles. I tripped, not having anticipated that, and crashed to the floor. The hard stone floor cut into my hip, and I hissed at the pain. But I was on my feet again, boiling with anger.

"What are you waiting for? Come on, you spineless pricks. Let's see you try that again. Go ahead. Come and take me, you card bastards."

"Trespassers belong in the dungeon," said the card soldier who'd thrown me to the ground. His heart-shaped mouth smiled at my distress. "By order of the Queen of Hearts, you will be kept here until you are required to work the mines."

"I'm only required to kick your ass," I said proudly, tapping into my well of wonderous magic.

Only, I felt a whole lot of nada. Nothing. Zilch.

"Okay. So my magic is useless here. Fantastic."

One of the card soldiers snatched my bag and pulled it over my head.

"Hey! That's mine!" I lunged to grab it, but two other card soldiers intervened. They blocked me, grabbed my arms again, and hauled me against the stone wall, my head hitting it. Pain throbbed at the back of my skull.

Cold metal nipped at my wrists as the card soldiers secured the iron manacles. With my arms spread out, I was pinned to the wall. I was trapped. And they had my bag.

This was *not* going so well.

"Where're you going with that? Hey! That's mine." I pulled on my restraints, but I didn't have superstrength to break these or magic. I had nothing.

"Okay, now I really screwed up."

Terror and anger, both competing emotions, rattled me as I watched the last of the card soldiers disappear down the long, dark hallway.

I shook with rage. I was alone in a different world and tied to a freaking wall.

How did I get into this mess? And how was I going to get out?

A flash of gold and green zoomed into the dungeon and hovered in front of my cell. The tiny flash was holding my bag in her miniature human hands.

Tinker Bell.

CHAPTER
22

"Hey, what are you doing here? Did you follow me?" I asked the tiny flying being.

The fairy zoomed toward me and dropped my bag. "I followed you."

My brows lifted past my forehead. "I can understand you." Her voice was still high-pitched, and it still had the echoes of bells, but I could definitely understand her.

The fairy shrugged, still hovering at my eye level. "Of course you can. You're in Storybook now."

I frowned. "But then, how is it that Ruth could understand you?"

Tinker Bell smiled. "Those sensitive to all living creatures possess the gift of speech. I think you earthlings call it whisperers."

"Like dog and horse whisperers. Got it." I had to admit. I was a little bit jealous of Ruth. I'd love to have that talent, thinking of my aunt. "Do you think you can get me out of these chains?" I lifted my wrists as though she hadn't already seen my manacles.

"Easy peasy." The fairy fluttered over to my left wrist. She pulled out a wand from a… pocket? No idea. But it was made of wood with delicate, intricate symbols etched into it. She tapped the iron manacles once. A sprinkle of golden dust shot from the tip of the wand.

With a sudden clicking sound, the manacle snapped open.

My arm slumped down. "Wow. Look at you!" I was impressed.

Tinker Bell laughed, moved over to my right wrist, and did the same with her wand. The manacle popped open.

With both my arms free, I stepped forward, glad to have the use of my limbs back. I hadn't been suspended long enough for my arms to start aching, thank the cauldron. I reached down and grabbed my bag. I rummaged through it, thinking that the soldiers had discovered the mushroom poison hex I was to use on the core. My fingers wrapped around a glass vial, and I yanked it out. "Still here," I said, relieved. Thank the goddess. "How did you get my bag?" The last thing I knew, one of the card soldiers had taken it.

Tinker Bell tucked her wand under the belt around her waist. "I hit them with one of my sleeping spells."

"Nice. Thank you. Thank you for helping me."

The fairy's face split into a genuine smile. "My pleasure."

I wrapped the strap of my bag around my neck and secured it around my shoulder. "My Aunt Beverly. She's... she thinks she's the Queen of Hearts."

Tinker Bell lost some of her smile. "I know. She's under Storybook's spell." She flew over to me and landed on my shoulder. Tiny gusts of wind from her wings touched my cheek.

"What do you mean?"

"It's the lure of this place," answered the fairy. "When humans cross over, they lose their minds to it. They become under a spell, Story-book's spell, taking on a character from a story or fairy tale that calls to them. They become that person in every aspect. The longer they stay, the deeper the persuasion until nothing's left of who they were before. I've seen it happen."

"You mean, this isn't the first time people have crossed over?"

The flutter of her wings stopped. "It's not. But it only happened twice before."

Something occurred to me. "But I'm not affected. Well, at least, not yet." *And hopefully, I won't be.*

"I know." From the corner of my eye, I saw Tinker Bell lean forward to get a better view of my face. "You're different. There's something about you that this place can't corrupt. Why is that?"

"I thought you would know." I thought about it. "It's my demon heritage. My demon blood. It's the only thing I have that's different." Not to mention very rare.

"Cool." Tinker Bell leaped from my shoulder and spun around to face me, her wings flapping as she floated. She was super cute, and I got why Ruth had formed an attachment. Given the fact that she'd just rescued me, I considered her a friend.

"Tinker Bell," I said. "What do you know about this place? Do you know who created it?" I knew that was a long shot. The inhabitants of Storybook might not know anything apart from what they were designed to know.

"He created it," answered the tiny fairy. "He made a world of his favorite stories. Sometimes he adds new characters... and sometimes, he removes them. That's what happened to Robin Hood and Little John. One day they were just... gone."

That sounded ominous. But at least we were getting somewhere. "Who's *he*? Does he have a name?"

Tinker Bell shrugged, hovering before my eyes. "We call him the Creator."

"Have you ever seen him?"

"No. But sometimes, we can feel his presence."

I had no idea what she meant by that. "Listen. I need to get to Beverly. I need to get her out of this place. But I'm going to need your help to do that."

A frown squished the fairy's features. "Hmm. My magic can only do so much. There're too many of them. We won't get through the card soldiers. But with Marcus's help, I think we have a good chance. He's very… strong." Her cheeks flushed as though she had a crush on him or something.

My heart swelled at the mention of the chief. "You know where he is? He's okay? He's alive?" That was indeed some good news.

A smile spread her lips. "Yes. It's not that far from here."

That had me ask another question. "Do you know where the core of this place is?"

A cute frown wrinkled the fairy's forehead. "The core? I'm not sure what that is."

"Like the hub, the center of this world." God, I was hoping it was close.

Tinker Bell's mouth formed a little O shape. "Do you mean Storybook's heart?"

"Yeah." That sounded about right. "That's it. Do you know where that is?"

Tinker Bell nodded, her sweet, angelic face set in determination. "Yes. I can take you there after we get Marcus."

I let out a long sigh. "Great. Lead the way."

Tinker Bell zoomed down the hallway, leaving a trail of golden dust in her wake. I rushed after her, not thrilled to be running again. I was thirsty, and I realized I'd forgotten to pack any water or anything to drink.

Bundles appeared down the hall, and when I got closer, I realized it was two of the card soldiers. I couldn't tell if they were sleeping or dead, but I didn't care.

I followed the fairy for a few more minutes down dingy hallways, going left, right, and left until I was completely disoriented. I would have never been able to get out without her help.

Finally, Tinker Bell hovered before a large wooden door. "This way," she instructed. "This door leads to the back of the castle, to the east gardens. It will take us to Marcus."

Using my shoulder, I hurled my weight against it, and it finally gave way.

I blinked at the bright light. Once my eyes were adjusted, I looked around. I stepped into what appeared to be another meadow covered in swaying, tall grasses and wildflowers. A single path cut through the field.

At the end of the path stood another castle.

It was close enough to see all the details, the dark stone, the turrets, even the entrance. It had the same look as the castle we'd just left, only this one was darker, more sinister.

"He's in there?"

"Yup." The fairy flew ahead of me. "Hurry. As soon as the queen's—your aunt's—guards find you missing, they'll be onto us."

And then I was running again. Swell. I really needed to get fit. I'd been lazy using the ley lines as my number-one means of transport, and now I was paying for it.

Thankfully, the other castle was ridiculously close—like a two-minute jog.

"This place is so weird," I panted as I passed the iron front gates and made it to the entrance without meeting anyone. "And apparently deserted."

"It is. This way."

I ran after the fairy, across a large courtyard and through an arched entryway. My thighs burned as I ran—more like an awkward speed-walk—into a long hallway, and Tinker Bell stopped at the most enormous double doors I'd ever seen.

I craned my neck to try and see the top of them. Maybe twenty feet high? Maybe more?

"He's in here." She pointed at the doors, waiting for me to open them.

Catching my breath, I pushed on the first door. It was heavy as hell, but I managed to get it open. It squealed as it revolved around its hinges, and I pushed it far enough to slip through. Tinker Bell zipped past me.

We entered a vast, oval-shaped chamber with gleaming golden tile floors and floor-to-ceiling windows that let in all the natural light. Tall drapes lined the windows with the same gold as in the tiles. It had a distinctive gold vibe.

"It's a ballroom?" I realized, taking in all the pretty details of the marble columns that supported a forty-foot ceiling.

"It is," answered the fairy.

I didn't have to look hard to find Marcus. My heart slammed in my chest.

Sweet.

Mother.

Of.

Zeus.

Marcus stood by one of the windows, staring outside. His wide shoulders were draped with a blue Victorian jacket. Tight black dress pants showed off his muscular thighs. He wasn't wearing a shirt. Nope. His muscular, tan, and delectable chest peered from under his jacket.

He was spectacular. Magnificent. Even more gorgeous than I'd remembered. But how could that be? It was as though this place increased his sex appeal and his looks a hundredfold. Was he glowing? Hell yeah. He was freaking glowing!

He hadn't turned around at our approach. With his keen wereape hearing, he should have heard us come in.

"What's the matter with him?" I stepped forward, my eyes tracking the wereape, looking for signs of injuries.

Tinker Bell sighed, staring dreamily at Marcus, and said, "He thinks he's Beast."

CHAPTER

23

My lips parted, and I halted. "You mean…
Beast from *Beauty and the Beast*?"

Holy fairy farts.

Marcus, the chief of Hollow Cove, was Beast.

"Yup." Tinker Bell fanned herself. "He's the
most beautiful man I've ever seen."

That he was. She wasn't wrong.

"If only there was such a man for me." She
continued to fan herself. I wanted to ask her if
there were male fairies here, but I needed to
keep my focus on Marcus, or rather, Beast.

It fit him. And I could understand why this
place, or he, chose this persona. Or did he

become it? It was as though this part was made for him or vice versa.

I looked around the room. "Where are all the pots and candles? His staff?" I asked, remembering the animated Disney version of *Beauty and the Beast*. "Where're his people?"

Tinker Bell shrugged. "No idea. This is *his* version. In his world, maybe they don't exist."

It made me wonder what else was in this place. What else did Marcus create or not create? This was so messed up.

"What now?" I stared at the hovering fairy whose eyes were on Marcus, or Beast. "Do I kiss him, and he wakes up?" I asked. It was lame. But this was new territory for me. If he was in the same state of delusion as Beverly, I had a serious problem on my hands. How did I get him to snap out of it?

"No, silly. That only works for Sleeping Beauty."

"Right." I waited for her to elaborate, but she didn't. "What about your fairy magic? Can you use it on him to wake him up?"

Tinker Bell stuffed her hand in the pocket I couldn't see in her dress. "I don't know. I've never tried it before. But I will. I'll try and see if I can shake him out of it. Though..." Her eyes flitted across the ballroom. "He does look amazing. Doesn't he?"

A flame of jealousy ignited in my belly, but I squished it down. Look at me. Jealous of a tiny fairy. What if she could grow to human size? She was absolutely gorgeous. No. Tinky, as Ruth called her, had saved me. I shook the thoughts away. I needed my head screwed on straight if I wanted to get Marcus out of here.

I let out a nervous breath and walked over to him. "Marcus?" I called carefully, not wanting to upset the beast because, from what I remembered, Beast had a temper.

Marcus turned around, his face cast into a frown. But his features brightened at the sight of me, and he gave me one of those panty-melting smiles that I never got tired of.

"Belle," said Marcus, walking over to meet me, the muscles of his bare chest gleaming in the light. "I knew you would come."

"Uh-oh," whispered Tinker Bell, flying next to me. "He's full-on delusional."

Uh-oh, she was right. My chest tightened with nerves. "It's me. Tessa. Your fiancée."

Marcus, or rather Beast, came right up to me, grabbed my face between his big hands, and kissed me deeply. The kind of kiss that had my eyes rolling in the back of my head.

I pulled away. Seeing his desire in his eyes had my lady bits pounding in hooray! I swallowed hard, trying to ignore how my body reacted to this large man. "Marcus? Do you know where you are?"

A soft growl rumbled in Beast's throat. "I've been waiting for you."

"You have?"

"You're so beautiful, Belle," he said as he dipped his head and came in for another round of panty-melting kisses.

I jerked my head back. "My name is Tessa. I'm not Belle. Don't you recognize me? This is all wrong."

Something like recognition flashed in his gray eyes. "Yes. You're right. Something is wrong." He snapped his fingers.

I jerked as energy wrapped around me, tight like invisible ropes. Just as I started to panic, the force released, and I felt a tingling all over my skin, like the gentle caress of rain. I could feel that the air was alive with the gentle hum of magic.

I heard a squeak and snapped my head around. Tinker Bell had a hand over her mouth and was pointing *at* me.

I looked down at myself and cursed. Instead of my usual T-shirt and jeans, a golden-yellow, voluminous, off-the-shoulder, tiered ball gown clung to my body. I pressed my hands—my gloved hands—over it. Then I reached the top of my head. My hair was in a half-up style. And I had earrings. I never wore earrings.

The dress didn't bother me all that much. It was the fact that my bag was gone.

"There, my lovely Belle. Much better." Beast grabbed my hand, and as he did, classical music started playing. I was suddenly aware of a band of musicians who had mysteriously appeared, just like my dress, at the far side of the ballroom.

Beast steered me to the middle of the ballroom. When he found his spot, he turned, holding on to my hand, and put his other hand on my waist to nudge me closer. The heat from his touch soaked through my dress's fabric as I draped my left hand on his shoulder.

"You have magic?" I was still in shock that the wereape could manipulate magic. But this wasn't our world, and this wasn't Marcus. It was Beast.

Beast pulled me tighter against him until my breasts were pinned against his broad, bare chest. "I've always had magic. I can give you whatever you wish, Belle." His scent of musk and perspiration was intoxicating, and I tried not to drool. "I have plans for you tonight," he continued, pulling me around. I had no idea how to dance, so I just let him lead. "After dinner, we'll make love, and I'll give you all the orgasms you desire."

I swallowed. Blinked. Trying hard not to let his closeness and his sex talk distract me. It wasn't working.

"I want you, Belle. I want you now. Can't you feel it?" Beast grabbed my ass and yanked me against him, and when I say *him,* I mean the hard, ready-to-go mini-Beast.

Oh dear.

Trying to ignore my nether regions, which wanted nothing more than to join mini-Beast in a sex feast, I looked into his eyes, searching for a glimpse of recognition that the Marcus I knew was somewhere in there. But I found nothing.

Beast let out a purring sound and licked my neck, sending a volley of delicious thrills through my body. Holy crap. It lit my body on fire.

I was aware that Tinker Bell was a witness to all this foreplay, but I was stuck at the moment. I couldn't really do anything about that.

At that moment, there was just me and Beast and this magnificent ballroom and how he made me feel. The world around me shifted, and my head started to spin. Or was it the ballroom? It was as though the ground had moved beneath me. I blinked the heaviness from my head. The floor appeared to shift, and I struggled to keep it together. Why was I here again? I couldn't remember.

My hands sought his skin, and I rubbed them over his hard pectoral muscles. I tugged at his clothes impatiently, wanting to rip off that jacket. Where my hands touched, his skin sent delicious slivers of heat through my gloves.

Beast bit my neck, not hard, but enough to weaken my knees. He growled, primitive and beastly, and it nearly sent me over the edge.

I moaned as one rough, manly hand grabbed my ass while the other traced my back. Ripples of desire pulsed from his touch, and my skin flared up in goose bumps.

"I want you, Belle." Fire burned in his eyes, and another wave of desire washed over me. I wanted nothing more than to tear off his clothes and feel his hot skin against mine. To rip off this stupid dress and get busy on the floor.

I was ready for it. It was on!

"Ow." Something like a mosquito stung my neck with the *largest* stinger ever.

"Snap out of it." Tinker Bell glared at me from my left side. She had a small blade in her hand. The tip was red. Blood. My blood. She shook her head. "I'm going to have nightmares for weeks now."

My thoughts slowly became focused again. My brain fog cleared, probably because she'd just stabbed me. Oh crap. She was right. Marcus, or Beast, was pulling me under the spell of this place.

Beast snarled as he tried to swipe Tinker Bell like she was an annoying mosquito. I reached out and grabbed his hands, pulling him to me.

"Now, Tinker. Do it."

While Beast smiled seductively, thinking that pulling him against me must mean I wanted to have sex—I still kind of did—the fairy swooped down and tapped the top of Beast's head with her wand.

Showers of fairy dust fluttered down, covering his face, shoulders, and chest, and of course, now he was sparkling *and* glowing. Could he be even sexier?

I stared at him, waiting for him to wake up from this spell. "Marcus?" I tried. "Are you back?"

"It's time to mate," said Beast. And then, the next thing I knew, he grabbed my waist and hurled me over his shoulder like a caveman. He slapped my butt. "I'm going to make you scream, Belle. I'm going to give you the best sex of your life."

I didn't doubt it. The chief was a master-or-gasm-giver in the bedroom. I just didn't want it at the moment. At the moment, I had bigger problems.

Tinker Bell's magic didn't work.

Marcus was lost.

CHAPTER
24

Being hauled away on your man's shoulder to have some mind-boggling sex in a castle was a pretty fantastic fantasy.

But that's just what it was—a *fantasy*. One that consumed all. One that was dangerous. I wanted my Marcus back. And I was failing miserably at doing just that.

Now I was in serious trouble.

I kicked out my legs. "Tinker Bell. Do something!"

The fairy flew into my line of sight, upside-down. Wait! *I* was upside-down.

She shook her head, looking worried. "My magic didn't work."

"No shit." The floor bounced, making my head spin as Beast marched across the ballroom, taking me to some bedroom.

"If you let him… you know… do the deed… you'll never recover," said the fairy.

"Because he'll destroy my vajayjay?" I laughed. Totally not appropriate.

The fairy's face screwed up like she had no idea what I was saying. "Uh. Once you mate, you won't remember who you are. You'll become Belle, just as he's becoming Beast."

"Well, that's not good." I closed my eyes and tried to call up my magic, the magic of the elements, even my demon mojo.

The well of magic was as obsolete as Marcus's memory. I had nothing.

I had to figure out how to make him return to me without magic. If only I knew.

"Hang on," I said, staring at the fairy from upside-down. The blood rushing to my head was making me dizzy. "You need to stab him," I whispered, hoping Beast didn't hear me.

The fairy made a face. "What?" she whispered back, though I was pretty sure she'd heard me.

"Stab him. Like you did to me. I think… I think it'll work." I wasn't sure, but it was the only thing I had. It worked for me, so I was hoping it would work for him. "Do it. And do it *hard*."

The fairy looked positively horrified at stabbing the man she was crushing on. But then her face changed, taking on a determined expression. The tiny dagger reappeared in her hand, and then she flew up to the level of Beast's shoulder and drove her blade into the soft flesh of his neck.

"Arrgh," Beast growled, a hand on his neck where the fairy had stabbed him. He shook his head like he was trying to rid something from his mind. He faltered. And the next thing I knew, I sailed across the slippery marble floors.

Pain stung my right hip and my wrists as I attempted to cushion my fall. But I was up again.

Beast was on his knees, a frown on his face. Confusion was the winning expression. His body swayed like he was inebriated. I could see blood trickling down his neck where Tinker Bell had cut him.

I grabbed fistfuls of my dress, hiked it up, and hurried over to Beast. "Marcus?"

Beast frowned like he wasn't sure what I was saying. He cocked his head slightly to the side as though he were trying to hear something.

The cut had worked somewhat. But it wasn't enough. He wasn't waking up. I needed pain. *He* needed to feel pain. It was the only thing that seemed to work.

So I gave him more.

Crack!

My hand shot out and smacked him across the face as hard as I could.

Beast's head snapped to the side. His dark locks fell over his eyes, his jaw.

Oh shit. I braced myself for what would come next. It could be one of two possibilities. One, I'd have my Marcus returned to me. Or two, he'd still be Beast and would most likely rip my head off.

Beast's head slowly turned my way as his gray eyes fixed on mine. "Tessa?"

I fell to my knees. "Oh, thank the cauldron, even with Beverly in it." Long red fingers marked his cheek where I'd struck him. Oops. I really did smack him hard.

Marcus looked around the ballroom. "Where am I?"

"Storybook," I answered. "Look, we don't have much time. You were under the spell of this world. And if we don't get out soon, you might get pulled back under."

Marcus seemed to be remembering. "The portal. It grabbed me."

"I know."

I felt the hum of magic slip in and around me. There was a sudden flash of light, and Marcus's leather jacket, shirt, and jeans appeared on him—the same clothes I'd seen him wearing when he disappeared through the portal.

I looked down at myself and felt a whoosh of relief as my own clothes reappeared. My bag rested on the floor next to me.

Grabbing it, I stood up. "We need to find the core of Storybook. I have a potion, a virus. It'll shut down the portal for good."

Marcus rose to his feet. He rubbed a hand where Tinker Bell had stung him.

I didn't know what possessed me, but I reached out, grabbed his face between my hands, and kissed him. "Glad you're back."

The chief grinned. "Glad to be back."

I laughed and glanced at the fairy, who said, "He's still hot."

I smiled. "How far is it to the core?"

"Not far," answered the fairy. "About a minute to fly for me. So, I'm guessing a five-minute walk for you. Three, if you run."

Great. More running. But the fact that the core was so close was a good thing. It seemed this world wasn't as big as I thought. "We go to the core, and then we rescue Beverly."

"Beverly's here too?" asked Marcus, worry back on his face.

"She is. She's in that castle in front of yours."

"What is she doing there?" asked Marcus.

"She thinks she's the Queen of Hearts. She put me in chains. Long story. She's just as lost as you were in this place. First, we find the core, and then we get my aunt." I looked at the fairy. "Lead the way, Tinky."

The three of us rushed out of Beast's castle through the same way we'd entered. Tinker Bell took us around and behind the structure. Mountains soared up and away from the edge of a lake of sparkling waters. We crossed the grounds and moved toward a meadow of tall swaying grasses, orange lilies, and buttercups. Showers of blossoms fell over us from the crabapple trees and covered the grass in a carpet of reds and pinks. The air smelled like an expensive perfume.

"I was going to mate with you," said Marcus as he jogged alongside me. He laughed, sounding both a little embarrassed and pleased at the same time. Weird.

I nodded. "I know." I was trying not to talk. Talking would require more energy, and already just me running was taking all of it. I was already feeling a double cramp. Could people suffer double cramps? Well, this witch was.

Marcus was sprinting easily, beside me, like it was next to nothing and required as little effort as breathing. And Tinker Bell flying ahead of us left me irritated and looking like an old woman suffering from arthritis.

"I really believed I was him... Beast."

"Mmhhmm."

"I remember it all. I remember that I was waiting for you."

"Belle."

Marcus glanced at me through his long lashes. "The name doesn't change that I was waiting for my true love, my mate."

A hot flash soared at his words, and I nearly tripped. "You looked good as Beast."

Marcus laughed a deep rumble that I loved so much. "I am a beast." He cast me a sly smile that had my heart pumping harder.

That he was. And he was *mine*.

We hit another clearing on the top of a grassy mound. Rolling, golden hills of tall swaying grasses surrounded us. I could see a wall of forest behind me to the west. A magnificent white horse was grazing in a meadow with a herd of smaller but still glorious beasts. The horse's long, flowing mane and tail fluttered in a breeze. And upon its forehead was a single, spiraled horn.

I blinked. The horse had a horn?

I stumbled and nearly fell, embarrassed because it seemed I was the only one who couldn't train her appendages to function properly. "Is that… is that a *unicorn*?"

Tinker Bell eyed the spot I was glancing at. "Yup. Very private animals. They don't like you watching them. But they are splendid. Such graceful beasts."

Wow. Unicorns were real? But this was an imaginary world. Whoever this Creator was, it was obvious he liked them. Who wouldn't? They were amazing to look at. Ruth would love this. Hell, she would have gone up right to the unicorn. And knowing Ruth, the creature would have let her touch it.

The thought of my aunt made me realize how much I loved my life and didn't want to be stuck in this world. I wanted to go home, back to my life.

Tearing my eyes from the mystical beast, I kept jogging, tripping until we arrived at the largest tree I'd ever seen. Not only was it massive, but it was red.

The leaves and the trunk were the color of an exquisite red wine. Every leaf and branch were perfect, without a tear or an insect bite. The tree was immaculate. Magical. When I got closer, I could feel the rhythmic pulsing, like the beating of a heart.

"The core," I said, stepping even closer.

We'd found it.

CHAPTER
25

Tinker Bell pressed her hands on her hips. "We call it the heart of Storybook."

Ignoring the cramps in my sides, I reached into my bag and pulled out the vial containing the mushroom poison hex.

"What is that?" Marcus leaned over and stared at the vial.

I peered at the lime-green substance, remembering it bubbling in Ruth's cauldron. "A virus," I answered. "My magic doesn't work here, so this is the next best thing." When I noticed Tinker Bell eyeing the vial in my hand as though she regretted helping me, I quickly added, "It won't hurt the tree. It's just going to give it a

307

cold, which won't last long but will close the portal." Hopefully. This was all guesswork. The truth was, I didn't know if any of this would help. And if the virus ended up killing the tree, the heart of this place, cauldron help us all.

"Once I pour this, we'll only have about twenty minutes or less to get Beverly." Nerves twisted my gut. It wasn't much time. Hell, it sounded insane. I started to doubt myself and my plan. Maybe I should have grabbed Beverly first. Too late now. We were at the core.

"I'll take care of Beverly." Marcus grabbed my arm and gave it a squeeze like he was trying to comfort me. "Just do what you gotta do."

"She has an army with her."

"Just concentrate on your virus. I've got an idea."

Okay then. "Here goes nothing." Heart pounding, I walked up slowly to the immense tree, and using my thumb, I unstoppered the vial and poured the contents over the exposed roots. I waited for the lime-green substance, that reminded me of pea soup, to penetrate the roots, and stepped back.

"What's supposed to happen now?" asked Tinker Bell.

I shook my head. "Not sure. Wait. Look." I pointed to the closest leaf. "It's working. The leaves are changing color." They weren't really changing color, but more like a stain appeared on them, a dark navy stain. I glanced around, seeing the grass tips and flowers stained with navy about twenty feet from the tree's roots.

It was spreading. And spreading *fast*.

I let out a breath. At least that part of the plan seemed to work. "Now. We double back and get Beverly."

"This way!" Tinker Bell zoomed past us.

I waved at her, bending from the waist. "Just a second. I need to catch my breath." This was not good at all. Even with all the tonics Ruth had supplied, I wasn't made of steel, and my body was telling me to slow down. The running around didn't help.

I looked up at Marcus. "I don't think I can run."

"You need to hurry," said Tinker Bell. "Your virus has already reached the top of the hill where you saw the unicorn."

Shit. My father had told me we had about twenty minutes. Maybe he'd been wrong?

"I've got you." Marcus took two steps toward me, slipped one arm under my legs and the other around my shoulders, and scooped me up like a groom carries his bride.

I squealed like a little girl, loving the feel of his strong arms wrapped around me, and I took a moment to take it in. "But you can't possibly run with me in your arms? I'm not Tinker Bell. I'm huge." And I'd packed on the pounds lately with all that late-night wine and cheesecake.

"Watch me."

With a mischievous grin, the wereape, Marcus, Beast, sprinted.

"Eeeeee!" I shrieked, loving every second of being held so tightly.

I knew Marcus was strong, but I didn't realize how strong he was in his human form until now. I mean, who can sprint at that speed with a human female dangling in his arms?

Marcus could.

It was exhilarating. Fun. And incredibly comfortable, like I was pressed against a warm duvet cover. I was barely bouncing, just a light up and down like I was floating in water.

Tinker Bell flew next to us. She smirked and gave me a thumbs-up. I was going to miss that fairy.

In no time at all, we'd cleared Beast's castle, and following Tinker Bell, we soon found ourselves facing the same back door we'd used to escape from Beverly's castle, aka the Queen of Hearts.

Marcus gently set me down. He hadn't even broken a sweat.

I narrowed my eyes. "You're not even breathing hard. How is that possible?"

The chief shrugged. "I don't know. I feel great. I feel *strong*." He'd added that last bit with a hint of a growl. A strange smile spread over his handsome face.

"It's the magic of Storybook," said the fairy, seeing my uncertainty. "It's still heavy inside him. Like a steroid boost. Probably gave him that burst of strength and stamina."

Damn. Imagine what *that* would have been like in the bedroom with him... guess I'd never know.

Shaking my hormones away, I followed Marcus through the door. We came across the same hallway as before, and again, we met no one. We still found no guards as we slipped through another hallway and made it to the chamber where I'd first seen Beverly.

And once we stepped through, I understood why we didn't meet any card soldiers or guards. They were all in here.

Just as we passed the threshold, the army of card soldiers turned our way.

"Well, there goes our element of surprise." Did we even have one?

Beverly, or the Queen of Hearts, jumped to her feet from her throne where she'd been whispering something to one of her half-naked male servants. Her face flushed as she rounded her eyes on us. "Off with their heads!" she bellowed, tossing her wineglass.

I sighed. "I'm really tired of hearing her say that."

The twenty or so card soldiers rushed us.

I turned to Marcus. "Now what? You said you had a plan?"

A gleam shone in his eyes. "Yeah. You get Beverly." He cracked his knuckles and rolled

311

his shoulders like he was getting ready for a brawl. "I've got these."

Before I could stop him, Marcus, with a smirk on his face that said he was delighted to be in a fight, crossed the room with the sleek grace of a black panther. And then he threw himself at the soldiers.

"He *is* dreamy," said Tinker Bell.

I laughed. "And maybe just a little high still from this place."

I watched, mesmerized, as the chief took a few steps forward, his stride smooth, gliding effortlessly on fluid joints. He moved with the grace of a predator, a killer. Strong, supple, and deadly. It was hot.

The ace-of-hearts soldier thrust his lance at Marcus, but the chief was too quick and dodged it easily. He spun, grabbed the lance, and pivoted so it pointed toward the card soldier. Then he shoved it into his gut, or whatever was there. He was partly made of cardboard.

The ace of hearts soldier cried out, but no blood was coming from where his lance had perforated him. He rocked and then fell but did not get up again.

Three more card soldiers rushed Marcus. Metal clanged as he parried a blow with one of their lances. He hurled himself into more card soldiers. He lunged, thrusting the lance deep into the closest soldier's chest. The soldier howled, hissing as he tried to swat at him with his lance. Marcus jabbed and stabbed, twisting on his feet with the poise of a dancer. With a final thrust into the soldier's chest, his body went slack, and Marcus tossed him to the floor.

The chief was moving with the skill and style of an assassin. He laughed a few times. Yeah, he was enjoying this *way* too much.

Seeing that he held his own, I ran toward the dais. Attempting to be cool, I raised my leg using the same momentum over the platform's edge to easily glide over the rim. But unfortunately, my leg got stuck halfway, and I stumbled back.

"Need to lose some of my wine gut." Ignoring Tinker Bell's laugh, I tried again, this time using the steps to the left. I rushed to the platform and met one of the male servants, who'd put himself between my aunt and me. "Out of my way, dicks." They kind of were.

The manservant's eyebrows shot up. "You insolent female. I should cut out your tongue."

"Nah, I need it. Got big plans for it later." Without my magic, I was basically left with only my physical strength. Which meant, let's face it, I had nothing. So, I did what any intelligent witch would do under the circumstances.

I raised my leg and kneed him in the meat clackers.

He let out a tiny moan and collapsed to the floor, cupping his junk.

I grinned. "Guess that trick works in both worlds."

I jumped over the man-whore. Two more of those manservants lay on the platform, looking as though they were unconscious. My eyes found Tinker Bell hovering above them.

"They were sleepy," she said with a smirk.

Good. That only left my aunt.

I hurried over. At my approach, she jerked back, her eyes wide with fear and fury. "Beverly. It's me, Tessa."

"I shall have your head for this," she seethed. "I will decorate my hall with it."

"Right. You said that already. Get some new material. This is getting old."

"You will not get my crown!" she raged.

"You can keep it."

The queen grabbed a handful of grapes from a silver tray and threw them at me. They hit my face.

"Thanks." I glanced at the floating fairy. "Can you sting her? She's getting on my nerves."

Tinker Bell did some kind of salute, yanked out her tiny dagger, and before Beverly or the Queen of Hearts could react, stabbed her in the neck, just like when she did Marcus.

"What devilry is this?" The queen clasped her neck where the fairy jabbed her with the knife, and blood trickled between her fingers.

I moved closer and inspected her face, her eyes, looking for a sign of recognition. "Beverly? It's me. It's Tessa."

My aunt's lips quivered in a snarl. Her green eyes shone with fury. "You dare assault a queen! A queen! One as beautiful as me. You have soiled the flesh made by the Creator himself. How dare you touch skin made from *him*!"

Yeah. Even in another world, she was still Beverly.

"Your sting didn't work," I told the fairy.

"Your head will roll for this!" howled the queen. "I will have your h—"

Crack.

I smacked her across the face.

The queen stumbled back, a hand cupping where I'd slapped her. Her eyes narrowed to slits. "I will enjoy seeing you die."

Crap. "That didn't work either." I looked at the fairy again.

Tinker Bell eyed my aunt. "It worked for Marcus. But she's been here longer. Might explain why."

It did. "Maybe all she needs is *a lot* more pain." For some reason, pain seemed to wake them up from this stupor. It didn't make sense, but I didn't care.

So, I grabbed the closest thing I had, the silver tray.

"I will have your head on a spike for this!" cried the queen, my aunt.

315

"You do that." And then I whacked her across the side of the head.

The queen's eyes rolled in the back of her head. She staggered for a moment and then crashed to the floor.

Whoops. "Oh, crap. I think I hit her too hard."

"Ya think?" Tinker Bell was struggling not to laugh.

Panic rolled in my mind as I hit the floor, next to her. I touched her neck with my fingers. "I feel a pulse," I said with a sigh of relief. "I didn't mean to hit her that hard."

"It's fine," said Tinker Bell, floating around my aunt's body. "At least you shut her up."

"Yeah, but now she can't walk." I grabbed her shoulders and shook her. "Beverly? Wake up. We need to go."

"What happened to your aunt?" Marcus was on the platform next to me. I'd never even heard him walk up. I cast my gaze across the chamber. Bodies of card soldiers lay scattered, either dead or unconscious.

"She knocked her out," said Tinker Bell, hooking a thumb at me.

I shrugged. "By accident." But was it? "Now she can't walk. And we really need to leave." I figured we'd lost about ten, maybe fifteen minutes so far. But without a watch, I had no clue. Why didn't I bring a watch?

"I've got her." I moved over as Marcus knelt next to my aunt, slid his hands under her, and

316

flipped her body over his shoulder. He rose easily. "She's not heavy. Barely weighs anything." He looked at me, and I could tell he wanted to say that she weighed less than me, but he was a smart man and kept his mouth shut.

Still, if he could run with me in his arms like an Olympic four-hundred-meter-sprint champion, and I was much larger than my aunt, I had no doubt carrying Beverly wouldn't be a problem.

"Okay then. Let's go."

Tinker Bell zoomed past us and out of the chamber. We quickly followed, me winding my way around the soldier card bodies, careful not to touch any.

We arrived at the entrance and rushed through the courtyard. If Marcus hadn't carried me before, there's no way I could keep up now.

We ran under the metal portcullis, crossed the drawbridge, and hit the path that led up and back through the meadows and fields.

Once we crested the hill, I stopped and looked around. I recognized this meadow. It was the same one I'd been in when I first met White Rabbit. But something was missing.

"Where's the portal?" I scanned my eyes over the field, searching for that familiar glowing golden disc and seeing only more of the grasses and flowers. No disc.

Marcus halted and turned around with Beverly swinging over his shoulder. Her crown had fallen off along the way, and her blonde hair was tangled around her face so I couldn't see it. "You can't find it?" asked Marcus, and for the first time, since I got here, he looked nervous.

I shook my head, feeling a new sort of deep panic erupting inside me. "Um. It should be around here. I swear this is the spot where I came out. So, where is it?" My heart throbbed in my chest, feeling like it was about to implode as I searched the meadow. I'd assumed it would be in the exact same place.

But if the portal wasn't here anymore... did that mean...

Oh fuck.

The portal was closed. We were too late.

CHAPTER
26

Being trapped in another world for the rest of my witch life was *not* the future I had intended for myself.

Hell, I had a wedding to plan and a relationship that needed healing with my mother. Not that seeing Marcus as Beast again wasn't appealing. It was crazy, lady-bits-pounding appealing, but it wasn't real. It was a fantasy. *I* wanted *real*.

But now, it looked like my father had been wrong or maybe my aunts' virus was more effective than they first thought. It spread faster than we'd anticipated.

We'd run out of time.

I pushed the panic from my mind and focused. I rubbed my temples, trying to jump-start my brain to think of a plan. It didn't work.

Could I be in the wrong spot? "Maybe this isn't the same spot." I looked at Tinker Bell. "Can you tell where it is? You know, since you're from here?"

The fairy shook her head. "No. The times that I went through were like you. I could see it. Now I can't."

"Why did you go through?" I asked the fairy. I'd been meaning to ask her, curious as to why she'd risk her life going through a portal to an unknown world.

The fairy shrugged. "Fairies are curious creatures. I saw the portal, and then… I just had to go through it. I figured the Creator had made it, so it wouldn't hurt me."

I wasn't sure about that. I had a feeling this Creator was a no-good bastard. However, the unicorn was a nice touch.

I glanced at Beverly hanging over Marcus's shoulder like a bag of rice. My heart stung at how hard I'd hit her. Hopefully, she wouldn't remember. But I still needed to get her back to our world so Ruth could take a look at her. And soon, before the queen bitch in her materialized again.

We had to get home. And we needed to figure out a way, fast.

"Wait a second." I flicked my gaze around the meadow, grabbed a handful of grass, and inspected it.

"Looking for bugs?" asked the fairy. "We do have some pretty amazing butterflies. But I prefer moths. They're adorable and cuddly."

I could see why she and Ruth had paired up. "No. Look." I held the grass for her and Marcus to see. "There's no infection here. The virus hasn't reached us yet."

"Then, where's the portal?" asked Marcus.

Good question. "It's possible that it's hidden or a little bit affected, and that's why we can't see it?" I let go of the grass and pointed. "See. Those over there are infected. So maybe it's still here... just not visible." Yeah, it was a long shot, but I was grasping here.

Or maybe this Creator had hidden the portal on *purpose*.

I felt my mouth flap open as what my father had told me came to my mind again. The portal had taken Marcus on purpose, so *I* would go in after him. *He* wanted me here.

"The Creator did this," I said, the words spilling out and making a lot of sense now that I thought about it. It was a trap. A good one. One he knew I'd venture through because of Marcus. No matter what, I would have crossed the portal to find my wereape.

"The Creator?" asked Marcus, his gray eyes sliding over my face.

"The guy or god who created this place. He closed it or hid it."

"Why would he do that? That doesn't make sense?" Tinker Bell's face was screwed up.

"It makes perfect sense." Now that I figured it out. "He doesn't want me to leave. He wants me trapped here for whatever reason. For reasons unknown." I still needed to figure that out, but one issue at a time. "Marcus was taken here by force. He didn't cross like you and me. The Creator wanted to make sure I followed. And I did. He knew I'd come after you. He probably closed it as soon as I came through," I added, now realizing that I hadn't taken notice of the portal once I came out. I'd been too preoccupied with finding Marcus to think about glancing back at the damn thing and store it to memory.

"Oh. Sorry," said the fairy, looking sad as though this was her fault. It wasn't.

"Son of a bitch," cursed Marcus. "Tell me where he is, so I can kick his ass."

I looked up at that moment to find Marcus staring at me, his jaw clenched and looking like he was about to beast out into his alter ego, King Kong. Could he even change to his animal form here? If I couldn't access my magic, maybe Marcus couldn't shift either.

I smiled at my wereape. "Ease down, Beast," I teased. "He *is* a *god*." Yet Marcus had shown some incredible strength in this world. Maybe, just maybe, enough to kick a god's ass?

Marcus let out an irritated breath through his nose. "I'm sorry, Tessa. This is all my fault. I shouldn't have gotten so close to the portal. I thought I could reach the doors to the shed without getting too close. I was wrong."

"You couldn't have known it was going to reach out and grab you." The memory of that giant hand wrapping around Marcus still haunted me, and unease rippled through my body. "This is nobody's fault but that damn Creator guy."

"God," interjected Tinker Bell. "Just saying."

"Right." But I was on Marcus's side. If I could kick this god's ass, I would too. Not only did he want to trap me here, but he'd also let out that pirate ship that devastated Hollow Cove. I wouldn't forget that.

Still, a god who had it in for me? Why? What the hell did I ever do to the gods? Nothing. Come to think of it, they had turned my life upside-down with Lucifer taking away my magic, and Lilith turning up whenever she wanted, and her obsession with Marcus.

Maybe this was Lucifer. Perhaps he was pissed that I got my magic back? That didn't make sense. The last I checked, or saw, rather, he and Lilith seemed very much enamored. Lucifer had gotten his wife back. I didn't believe he'd be pissed at me. But if not Lucifer, who was this god who wanted to trap me here?

It didn't matter who he was. What mattered was getting out of here.

I had an idea.

My pulse throbbed with excitement because if I was right, it meant we still had a chance to go home if the portal was here, in this very spot, only hidden.

So, how did we find it?

I was magicless. So, there was that. My only connection to this world was Tinker Bell.

"Tinky," I said, looking over at her. "You said you can't see the portal. But can you *feel* it, maybe? I think it's still here."

The tiny fairy settled on the top of a white-and-yellow daisy. "Uh…" She cast her gaze around the swaying fields. After a moment, she said, "Nope. Sorry."

Damn. There went that idea.

But I wouldn't let it go. Looking at the virus creeping slowly toward us, I had to believe the portal was still open. The Creator didn't account for the fact that maybe we could find it some-how, so he didn't bother to close it.

That's what I was going for.

"Maybe we just start running in lines and hope for the best." I laughed. Yeah, that wasn't going to work.

"Huh… guys." Tinker Bell leaped into the air. "Trouble," she said as she pointed behind us.

I spun around. "Oh, well, that's unexpected."

A group of maybe thirty or more card soldiers were running in our direction.

"I thought you took care of these."

Marcus narrowed his eyes. "These are new or they healed quickly."

Either way, they were going to catch up to us in a minute or so.

"To the queen!" bellowed a voice.

"Kill the trespassers!" came another.

I tried to devise a plan, but usually, under duress, I suffered tremendous amounts of brain fog. Just like at this moment.

"Maybe you should hide?" Tinker Bell smiled at me.

"There's no time for that," I said. "We need to find the portal before it closes for good." I was still hoping I was right.

A sliver of fear tried to rise, but I quashed it. I had to find the source of the portal. Either we found it soon, or we'd be skewered by the card soldiers' lances.

"Belle? What are we doing out here?" Marcus looked at me with that same dreamy expression as he had in the ballroom.

"Oh, hell, no." I stared at the wereape, wishing I had that silver platter to smack him with.

Tinker Bell fluttered over to Marcus's face. "He's falling back under Storybook's spell."

Great. That's all I needed right now.

Marcus, or Beast, shook his head, blinking like he was trying to remember how he got here.

He looked at the woman still draped over his shoulder. "Who's this?"

"My aunt."

"Oh. I didn't know you had an aunt. Don't worry, Belle. I'll take good care of her."

Damnit.

Dread galvanized me. My heart jumped into my throat. I didn't want to be stuck here. I wanted to go home to my friends and family, to my life.

An idea crystalized in my brain.

As the card soldiers got closer and closer, trembling with a mix of fear and rage, I drew up my will—and called to the ley lines.

It was a hunch, but if I was right, the ley lines were a series of networks through which magic energy flowed throughout the world and Hollow Cove. If there was a hole, a gap in *this* world somewhere, I'd feel the power from the ley lines from *our* world reaching out, and that would lead me to the portal.

A slight tremor answered back. It felt shaky and uncertain, like drips of water coming from a broken pipe, but I *felt* it.

The ley lines!

"The ley lines, I can feel them," I said, shocked at my brainy self.

"The what lines?" asked the fairy.

"They're like invisible conduits of magical power that flow through our world," I said quickly, no time to elaborate.

Focusing, I tapped into the ley line again. A thrum of magic pounded through me, energy pooling in my center. Then, turning on the spot, letting the ley line's thrum guide me, I saw it.

Not the portal, the ley line, a translucent, rushing waterway that surged through a spot about ten feet from where we were standing. Now that I'd tapped into the ley line, I could make out blurred circular edges of the portal.

"Save the queen! Kill them all!"

I glanced over my shoulder. In about thirty seconds, the card soldiers would kill us.

"We gotta go, Beast," I told Marcus.

"Where to, my love?" said Marcus-Beast.

"Home." Before he could object and want to return to his castle, I grabbed Marcus- Beast's muscular arm. "Thanks, Tinky," I told the fairy, my heart swelling at the tears in her eyes. "Thank you for saving me."

Tinker Bell wiped her eyes. "Tell Ruth I'll miss her."

My eyes burned. "I will. Take care, little fairy."

"Take care, big human."

Laughing, I hauled Marcus-Beast with me, and at a run, we hit the portal and jumped the ley line.

CHAPTER
27

Candles sat in holders on the wall and over the Davenport House kitchen counters. Golden light and the scent of candle flames and hot wax filled the room.

"Sit still. I'm almost finished," ordered Ruth, shadows dancing around her face graced by candlelight. "Stop being such a baby."

Beverly let out a breath. "This is taking too long." She sat on one of the kitchen island stools while Ruth applied a pink substance that had the consistency of toothpaste over a large welt on the right side of her head. "Hurry up. I have a date tonight."

I propped my fists on my waist. "You're not serious? You can't go anywhere tonight. Look at you!"

Beverly glowered at me, her green eyes fierce. "And whose fault is that?" Her usual perfectly styled hair was a mess with a significant knot at the back like she hadn't brushed her hair in months and a squirrel had taken up residence. Mascara had smeared below her eyes and a streak of red lipstick pulled from the corner of her mouth across her left cheek.

Ouch. "I told you I was sorry I hit you so hard. In my defense, you did want to kill me."

Beverly shrugged. "You can't blame me for that. I wasn't myself."

I had the strange feeling that part of the real Beverly had been in there, in the queen. "What do you remember?" Marcus had remembered some of his actions as Beast—merely the one where Beast wanted us to mate. I was still wondering if I'd missed out on a spectacular love-making experience.

A tiny smile pulled Beverly's mouth. "Well, I do remember that I looked positively gorgeous as a queen. I was the most desirable, sensual woman in the land. And I had men worshiping me. Throwing their naked, sweaty bodies at me."

Ruth rolled her eyes. "We'll never hear the end of that one."

Ronin, sitting at the dining room table next to me, snorted. "Damn. Looks like I missed a hell of an adventure."

I looked at the half-vampire, seeing his smile. "We almost didn't make it back."

"Thank the cauldron you did," said Iris. She was holding on to Dana, her album, across her chest like a cushion, for comfort.

I turned my attention back to my aunt and raised a brow. "You remember all that, but you don't remember wanting to cut off my head and decorate your hall with it?"

Beverly pursed her lips like she was thinking about it. "No." She winced and slapped Ruth's hand away from her scalp. "Are you trying to kill me? That hurt."

Ruth clamped her jaw. "Well, if you'd stopped moving, it wouldn't. So stop moving so I can finish."

Beverly looked like she was about to protest, but instead, she sat straighter and let her sister continue applying that thick, pink paste to her scalp.

A smile touched my lips as I took in my aunts. My heart squeezed as a rush of emotions fluttered through my body. I was glad to be home. We'd come close to being stuck in Storybook for the rest of our lives. Beverly as the Queen of Hearts, Marcus as Beast, and I guess me as Belle? It was insane just thinking about it.

As soon as we'd stepped into the alley back in Hollow Cove, I'd turned around, seeing the portal become transparent. Then it folded on itself, getting smaller and smaller until nothing was left of it, as though it had never existed.

Dolores, Ruth, Iris, and Ronin were all still there, waiting for us.

"What happened to her?" Dolores had asked as she rushed over to Beverly, dangling from Marcus's shoulder.

"I had to knock her out," I told them. "She wanted to behead me. She thought she was the Queen of Hearts." And then, on the way back to Davenport House, I gave them an account of what transpired in Storybook.

"I'm going to miss that fairy." Ruth sniffed, and I could see tears forming in her eyes. "She was a good friend. She was sweet and good."

"She was." I took a sip of my glass of red wine to calm my nerves. "She saved me. When *Beverly* had ordered to have me *chained*, Tinker Bell found me, and she unchained me."

Ruth met my eyes. "Why didn't you bring her with you? You left her all alone."

My stomach clenched at the hurt on my aunt's face. "She's not alone." I had no idea if that was true. "I couldn't bring her back, Ruth. She didn't belong here. She belonged in that world this Creator made." Come to think of it, maybe not. Maybe Tinker Bell could have crossed over to our world. But she didn't.

Perhaps she knew she couldn't. That maybe, living in our world would eventually kill her.

Ruth turned from me without another word. I didn't know if she was angry at me for not bringing back the fairy.

"I'm glad she's gone," meowed Hildo on my lap. "This wasn't her world."

He was right, of course, but I knew he'd been jealous and hurt at how quickly Ruth had formed an attachment to the fairy. He'd felt replaced. But now? Now he was purring loudly, and I found it soothed my emotions, washing away my stress.

I slid my fingers through his silky black fur over his back. "I know," I whispered to him.

"What about this Creator character?" Iris watched me with the concern of a true friend. "What do you know of him? And why did he want to trap you there?"

I shook my head. "No idea. But my father was right. Whoever or whatever took Marcus through the portal meant for me to go after him. To trap me. I just don't know why." It reminded me that I needed to have words with Lilith.

"Won't he know that you escaped?" asked Ronin.

I had thought of that. "Yeah. Eventually. Hopefully, he won't notice for a while." While I tried to figure out who the hell he was and why he'd wanted me trapped in Storybook.

There was the sudden bang of the front door closing and then the sounds of voices chatting in the hallway.

Dolores appeared in the kitchen. She held a man by the throat. His gray hair was cut short, exposing some of his scalp. Dolores yanked him, and his black, glistening shoes slipped forward. His face and eyes had that lost, dreamy look I remember seeing on Marcus as Beast. Strings of drool ran from his mouth to his chin. Yeah, the guy was spelled.

Beverly sprang to her feet, reminding me of the Queen of Hearts at that moment. "What are you doing with Gregg?"

"You know him?" I asked Beverly.

Beverly looked from me to the spelled man. "Yes. He was supposed to be my date tonight."

"Doesn't look like he's capable of being anyone's date," said Ronin with a smile.

"Gregg, here," said Dolores, hauling him again by the throat, "thought it was okay to cheat on his pregnant wife."

Beverly's face fell. "He's married?" Clamping her jaw, she stepped over to Gregg and held up a finger in his face. She gave him a murderous look. "Why, you two-timing bastard. You never told me you were married. Cheating is bad enough. Cheating on your pregnant wife? There's a special place reserved in hell for people like you."

"Amen, sister," said Ronin, holding up his beer in salute.

Iris leaned over and whispered, "You cheat on me… and I'll burn your balls."

"Duly noted," said the half-vampire as he placed a hand protectively on his crotch.

"And he's here because?" I had a feeling I knew why the cheating bastard was here. I just wanted to hear it from Dolores.

"He's here to see the basement," informed Dolores. "Gregg here," she said, squeezing his throat, "is a carpenter. So I invited him to take a look and see what we can improve. Isn't that right, Gregg?"

Gregg nodded and said in a faint voice, "Yes. Here to see the basement."

"Good man, Gregg. Well, no need to keep you waiting." Dolores tugged the man forward while her other hand opened the basement door.

Beverly walked over to Gregg. Smiling brightly, she said, "See about the plumbing while you're in there, Greggy."

And with that, Dolores flung the man through the threshold and slammed the door shut.

I didn't hear a scream or a moan, just the thud of someone falling down the stairs.

Suddenly, the walls and floor of the kitchen shook. The lights blinked on and off as a loud sound spewed from the basement like House had let out a belch.

And then the house settled.

I knew I should be concerned about the dude called Gregg who was just... what... lobotomized? But I wasn't. I leaned forward in my chair. "Does that mean we have power now?"

As if on cue, we heard a loud buzzing sound, and then the house filled with light. There was a click from the refrigerator as it powered back on, and the sound of a TV came blaring from one of the upstairs bedrooms.

Dolores wiped her hands on her skirt, like touching Gregg had left filth on her skin. "Power's back, ladies."

If the power was back here, that meant we had power at the cottage. "I'm going to see if Marcus needs anything," I said, standing up and setting a half-asleep Hildo on my chair. I chucked the rest of my wine.

"We all know *what* he needs." Beverly smirked. "A beast will always be a beast in bed."

My face flamed. "See you later." Not wanting to have *that* conversation right now, I popped out the back kitchen door and headed for the cottage. I smiled as I saw the yellow light spilling from the windows. We had power. Yay!

I rushed to the front door and pushed in. "We have power!" I realized he probably was aware that we did, seeing all the lights, but I didn't care. "Marcus? Power's back. Dolores found House a new victim," I added, taking off my shoes at the entrance and padding in barefoot. I glanced in the living room and the kitchen. He wasn't there. Maybe he wasn't back from the office. I knew he had some paperwork to finish. And he'd wanted to check on the families who'd been affected by that damn pirate ship.

I moved to the kitchen and turned on the tap. Water spilled from the faucet. "Hello, pretty water," I told it. Yeah, I sounded insane, but we'd been out of power for a while now. I didn't realize how we took everything for granted.

"I've been waiting for you."

I looked up at the sound of the voice, and my breath caught.

Marcus came out from our bedroom. A blue Victorian jacket adored his broad shoulders, and tight black dress pants hugged his muscular legs. He wasn't wearing a shirt. Nope. His ample chest was on display, for my eyes only.

He looked... he looked *exactly* like Beast.

My heart pounded at the sight of him. My mouth flapped like an idiot. "I-I don't understand?"

Marcus joined me in the kitchen. "I asked Martha if she had a costume like this. She's in charge of Hollow Cove's Center of Performing Arts, and she just so happened to have one. She added a few spells to make it fit just right."

Sweet mother of all that was holy, did it fit right. My mouth seemed to be experiencing a malfunction. I couldn't speak, couldn't form co-herent words or thoughts. It was like my fantasy come true.

Beast was in my kitchen.

Yay me!

"Does this mean..." I swallowed, my mouth suddenly dry.

Marcus-Beast came around the counter and slipped a hand around the small of my back. "It means we have some *unfinished* business, you and I," he purred, his deep voice sending thrills down there and slapping my lady V to wake the hell up.

Oh yeah. It was happening.

I was smiling like a fool, taking him all in, the splendor of his face, body, and the scrumptious outfit. Well, that was the icing on the orgasmic cake.

He grinned a crazy predatory smile and yanked me closer. I slid my arms around his waist, crushing my body to his.

"I'm sorry I didn't have anything planned for your birthday," I said lamely.

Marcus set his smoldering gaze on my face. "Having one's mate risk her life to save his is the best gift there is. I'll require nothing, ever, after that."

Emotions rushed in, making me dizzy. I had nothing to say to that. Yeah, I'd risked my life for him. But he would have done the same without a second thought.

"You were sexy as hell as Belle," purred Marcus-Beast. "That yellow dress… mmmm..."

I grinned. "I know. I rocked that dress."

"I haven't been able to get it out of my head."

"How could you? I looked awesome."

In a flash, Marcus-Beast lifted me and tossed me over his shoulder. He slapped my ass, replaying what had transpired in the ballroom in Storybook.

I squealed and kicked out in glee as Marcus-Beast headed to our bedroom. I was dizzy from the lust and the blood gushing to my head.

And now, my fantasy was about to get on.

CHAPTER
28

I wrapped the foil paper around the glass baking dish to keep the lasagna from falling out. Some of the sauce had spilled, and I flicked it along the edge and licked it. I moaned. The sauce was divine. I couldn't take credit for it. It was all Marcus. He'd even cooked the pasta from scratch.

"I'm ready," called Marcus from the foyer. Two bottles of red wine hung in one hand while he clutched the fresh mixed-green-salad bowl. All from Ruth's garden. That, at least, I did.

"Coming." Giving the baking dish a last check, I scooped it up and joined him. "I know she loves lasagna. I don't know about my father, though. But I have a feeling he's not picky."

The following afternoon, after the night of X-rated Disney fantasies, I'd called my mother, told her we were all safe and sound, and that I needed to speak to her and my father around six in the evening. I'd hung up before spoiling the surprise.

The thing was, she'd prepared a nice dinner for Marcus and me the other night, the night when I didn't want to go and where Marcus made me realize how selfish I was. She would never win Mother of the Year awards, but she was my mother. My only mother. And I wanted to show her that I did appreciate her and the dinner she had planned, which had been ruined because of Captain Hook's pirate ship, though she had been clueless at the time.

I closed the door behind me and joined Marcus across the yard. "Thanks for helping me."

"Of course," he said as we took the sidewalk and headed down Stardust Drive. "What kind of husband would I be if I can't help out in the kitchen?"

My stomach did some flip-flops at the use of the word *husband*. "Well, thanks. I can honestly say that I'm not afraid they won't like it because I know they will. Coming from you."

As we walked, we spotted the area where the pirate ship had blasted some of the homes on Crystal Row. It was nearly six in the evening, and some paranormal males were still working on the site, hauling out the last of the rubble.

I felt a tightness in my chest that mimicked the one I saw on Marcus as we walked by. I never wanted to see that again. Ever.

Unfortunately, though, I didn't see her. Scarlett, Marcus's deputy was lost somewhere in Storybook. Well, that's what we concluded. She'd disappeared while guarding the portal. There was just one logical explanation for that. She'd gone through.

Hopefully, she'd become Mulan or some other cool, kick-ass character, but I was still sad she was gone.

"Glad the portal is closed," said the chief. "We had the shed destroyed. Just in case."

I didn't want to mention that I didn't think destroying the shed would make a difference if this Creator decided to put up another portal. He was a god. The thing with gods or goddesses was they were petty, cruel, unfeeling, and were only concerned with themselves. They did whatever they wanted and had the means to do so.

I didn't want to talk about that. I wanted to enjoy this evening as a couple. As a soon-to-be-married one.

We hit Moon Way, and my mother's house came into view. I walked up to the front porch, made a fist as I held it to the door.

The front door swung open.

"What's the matter? What is it? Are you pregnant!" My mother stood on the threshold with eyes wild and looking a little mad—not the frown mad, the crazy mad.

Shocked, I just stared. "Uh. No. Not pregnant."

She clamped her mouth shut and glared at me. She threw up her hands. "Then why, did you make me stress all day? What was *so* important that you had me ask your father to join us?"

"Hi, Tessa. Marcus," came my father's voice from inside.

My mother was a spaz. "We made you dinner." I lifted the lasagna. "Thought we could have a nice dinner. And you could ask all the wedding questions you've been dying to ask."

My mother's face darkened a few shades. She just stared at me, then Marcus, then me again, her eyes swimming in tears. She held her arms out like she was waiting for a parcel to fall from the sky. I placed the baking dish, with the lasagna, in her hands. A tiny whimper sounded from her throat, and then she spun around and disappeared down the hall to the kitchen.

Damn it. Now my own eyes were burning.

At least I knew I'd been right to do this. I knew it would mean a lot. And hopefully, she'd forgive me for the last time.

I cleared my throat. "After you." I gestured for Marcus to go inside, my voice betraying my emotions.

I shut the door as my father came over. "That is a very nice thing you did for your mom," he said, pulling me into a hug. I guess we were huggers now. I hugged him back.

My father, dressed in a spectacular olive-green suit, held his hand out to Marcus. "Marcus," he said with a smile.

Marcus flashed a grin and shook his hand. "Obiryn."

From inside his jacket, my father pulled out two cigars. "For later," he said, eyebrows high.

I had no idea if Marcus smoked cigars, and he surprised me when he said, "Montecristo? Nice."

"Well..." My father stood back and took us all in. Loud sniffles came from the kitchen, and I saw a flash of emotions cross my father's face. "I better go help your mother. She's a little fragile today." He looked at me and said, "We thought you were pregnant."

"I'm not," I told him as he walked away. I wasn't sure if he sounded disappointed or not.

The sound of dishes clattering pulled my attention to the kitchen. My father's voice was low, and I caught him rubbing my mother's back as she wiped her eyes and grabbed some plates from a cabinet drawer.

"I'll see if I can help," said Marcus as he headed for the kitchen. My mother looked up at his approach, her face beaming and gleaming with streaks of tears. Seeing her happy made me so damn happy too. Who knew?

I sighed. Yeah. Marcus was such a keeper. I felt blessed. Felt that I'd been lucky in my life. Lucky in love, work, and family. Though I never thought I'd hear myself say that.

Okay, so it wasn't perfect, but it was *my* family. And I wouldn't change a thing.

I jerked as a knock on the front door sounded behind me.

"Who's that?" I thought it was maybe one of my aunts or someone from Marcus's office looking for him.

But I didn't recognize the man who stood on the porch once I'd opened the door.

He was tall, taller than Marcus but slimmer. His blond hair was slicked back, making his sharp features stand out.

He wore dark clothes under a black cape of some material so light and sheer that it seemed almost unreal, and it drifted around him, catching the light in an opalescent sheen that trapped little rainbows and set them dancing against his pale skin. Red leather shoes poked from under his black trousers. Though his skin was as pale as new snow, his eyes were as dark as night. He was strikingly handsome, in a creepy sort of way. But something was off about him. Something that oozed danger.

My entire body seized up, as if Dolores had cursed me with one of her stone hexes. I stared at the stranger, not wanting to get too close. "Yes?" Who the hell was this guy?

He pulsed with power. A *lot* of power. A colossal amount.

But the way he was staring at me gave me the creeps, as though he loathed the very earth I walked on.

The stranger's face shifted into a forced smile. "Tessa Davenport."

"You know my name, and you are…" A creepy-ass dude.

The pale stranger looked around my mother's house like it was the ugliest thing he'd ever seen. I hated him immediately.

"I created Storybook," he said, pulling his dark gaze back on mine. "It was me. I created that portal."

Oh. Shit.

That's when buckets of panic hit. I was staring at *the* Creator. He was here, here in Hollow Cove. And standing right in front of me.

I should have peed myself, but instead, I had to ask. "But why?"

"But you escaped before I could reach you," answered the god.

"And why did you want to do that?"

"It's simple." He smiled coldly. "I'm here to kill you."

Well, *that* was unexpected.

Don't miss the next book in The Witches of
Hollow Cove series!

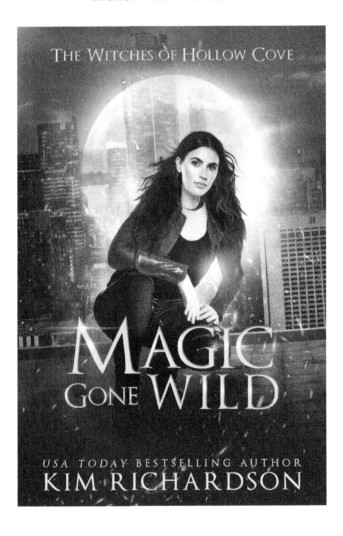

ABOUT THE AUTHOR

Kim Richardson is a USA Today bestselling and award-winning author of urban fantasy, fantasy, and young adult books. She lives in the eastern part of Canada with her husband, two dogs and a very old cat. Kim's books are available in print editions, and translations are available in over 7 languages.

To learn more about the author, please visit:

www.kimrichardsonbooks.com

Printed in Great Britain
by Amazon

18741411R00205